A FLOWER SHOP M

DIRTY ROTTEN TENDRILS

KATE COLLINS

KENNEBEC LARGE PRINT

A part of Gale, Cengage Learning

GALE
CENGAGE Learning

Detroit • New York • San Francisco • New Haven, Conn • Waterville, Maine • London

GALE
CENGAGE Learning™

LIBRARY OF CONGRESS CATALOGING-IN-PUBLICATION DATA

Collins, Kate, 1951–
    Dirty rotten tendrils : a flower shop mystery / by Kate
Collins.
        p. cm. — (Kennebec large print superior collection)
    ISBN-13: 978-1-4104-3339-8 (pbk.)
    ISBN-10: 1-4104-3339-0 (pbk.)
    1. Knight, Abby (Fictitious character)—Fiction. 2.
Florists—Fiction. 3. Large type books. I. Title.
PS3603.O4543D57 2011
813'.6—dc22   2010048695

Published in 2011 by arrangement with NAL Signet, a member of
Penguin Group (USA) Inc.

Printed in the United States of America
    1 2 3 4 5   15 14 13 12 11
ED045

"Courage is being scared to death — but saddling up anyway."

— John Wayne

Staring at that first blank page and knowing you have more than three hundred to fill with intrigue and humor is a formidable responsibility. This book is dedicated to the people in my life who give me the courage to saddle up: Jim, Jason, Julie, Nancy, Barb, Tasha, Mary, my Cozy Chick buddies; my incredible editor, Ellen Edwards; and my agent, Karen Solem.

CHAPTER ONE

Monday

My destination that morning was Bloomers, my cozy flower shop located across the street from the New Chapel, Indiana, stately limestone courthouse. I was taking a circuitous route to get there, however, because strangely enough the public lot where I usually parked was full. So I'd left my refurbished and much-beloved 1960 yellow Corvette under a shady maple tree across from the YMCA and started off for a leisurely stroll around the square, soaking up the sunshine of the brilliant early-spring day.

I love my small town. In New Chapel, unlike big cities, you won't experience heavy traffic snarls, clouds of toxic exhaust fumes, or frustrated drivers honking horns at every tiny irritation. What's more, you can park in a public lot for about two dollars a day or, as in my case today, along any side street for free. Try to do that in downtown Chicago.

I sniffed the air to catch a whiff of the crocuses blooming in the old cement planters that rimmed the courthouse lawn. They'd be followed by daffodils and tulips, and then by Knock Out Roses, all of which would suffer benign neglect by the parks-department employees until the winter snows blanketed them once again.

Up ahead I saw Jingles, the ancient window washer, wielding his squeegee with extreme precision against a boutique's display glass. "How's it going, Jingles?" I called.

"It's a different kind of morning, Miss Abby," he said solemnly, then pulled the wet squeegee from the top of the pane to the bottom and dried it with his yellow rag.

Jingles wasn't normally given to deep thought, and for him, that comment qualified. "It'll be fine, Jingles," I called. "We've got solid citizens in New Chapel. They're not going to go crazy because a local boy who took first place on a reality TV show is coming back to town."

Jingles just kept wiping the glass. On the other side of the window, the shop's owner was setting out an array of tropic-bright purses and stylish spring jackets. She waved and smiled.

Another benefit of small-town life is the friendliness of the townsfolk. Also, the easy pace. You can amble down any sidewalk and not be bothered by rushing commuters, jostling crowds, jackhammer drilling, or vendors shouting —

"Hey! Look out!"

A man in a cherry picker gestured frantically toward an old wooden sign dangling by one nail over the gift shop's doorway. With a gasp, I jumped back seconds before the sign broke from its tether and crashed onto the sidewalk in front of me, kicking up a cloud of dust and debris.

The shop owner, Mr. Hanley, who was about 140 years old, called from the recessed doorway, "Sorry, Abby. Gotta get my new signage up today, you know."

His *signage?* He pointed to a shiny new sign leaning against the side of the store. Instead of HANLEY'S GIFTS, it said YE OLDE GIFT SHOPPE.

"No harm done, Mr. Hanley." I shook detritus from my hair, brushed off my navy peacoat, took a deep breath, and continued up Lincoln Avenue toward Franklin Street.

At that moment a white pickup truck sporting the town logo pulled up alongside me with a shriek of dry brakes and a backfire of thick gray smoke. A man in tan overalls jumped out and began placing orange cones around a cracked square of the cement sidewalk. Another man followed with a jackhammer, which he immediately fired up.

Plugging my ears with my fingertips and trying not to inhale the fumes, I scurried toward the corner. As I waited for the light to change, I was joined by at least ten people, with a dozen more on the sidewalk across the street. On the green light, we surged forward en masse and narrowly missed being run down by two cops on motorcycles followed closely by a white stretch limousine. The limo driver laid on his horn, glaring at us as he sped past. Two black limousines followed. They honked, too, just for the practice, I suspected.

Behind them came a line of vans with satellite dishes on top and markings on the side for the four national television stations, ABC, CBS, NBC, and Fox, and our local cable channel, WNCN. They were followed by several more vehicles with men hanging out the windows armed with huge cameras with telescopic lenses. Three police cars trailed the parade, their sirens and lights fully engaged as they approached the court-house, as though to impress upon the citizens the importance of the limousines' occupants.

"That was him in the white car!" someone behind me screamed, and at once I was swept along with a tide of people in their stampede to follow the convoy, now creating a snarl of horn-honking traffic on the far side of the square. I managed to break free at the curb and make a frantic dash to safer shores.

As I stood with my back pressed against the door of the Down the Hatch Bar and Grill, people began to descend onto the courthouse lawn in droves, some carrying signs that said, WE LOVE YOU, CODY!, others waving banners, caught up in the kind of frenzy that only a celebrity could create.

And then, as though someone had cried "Action!", all along the streets surrounding the courthouse, workers emerged, some carrying paint cans and ladders, and others erecting scaffolding, pushing wheelbarrows stacked with bricks, and toting brightly colored awnings. The parks department had even sent men to spruce up the cement planters.

I stared around the square in astonishment. Then I noticed Jingles watching me with a look that said, *I told you so.*

The door behind me opened suddenly, and I had to grab the frame to keep from falling in. "Morning, Buttercup," said my boyfriend, bar owner and ex–Army Ranger Marco Salvare. He kissed the top of my head. "Come on inside and brighten my day."

I turned to face him, trying to form my distress into coherent words. Marco's forehead wrinkled as he studied me. "Are you okay?"

"I want my small town back!" I wailed, and flung myself into his arms.

Seated across from Marco in the first booth at Down the Hatch, which wouldn't open until eleven o'clock, I propped my chin on my hand and sighed grumpily. "If this is a sign of what's to come, I'm leaving until it's over."

"Come on, Abby. It's not that bad. When was the last time a celebrity came to New Chapel?"

"Cody Verse is hardly a celebrity. Two months ago only a handful of people had even heard of him. All he did was win a contest."

"You say that like it was the local spelling bee," Marco said. "*America's Next Hit Single* is a national television event. Cody had to outperform thousands of people just to get on the show."

"I get that, Marco, but come on! He didn't win the Nobel Prize. He sang a song that he cowrote with his friend and then took all the credit for."

"Or so his friend claims," Marco reminded me. "A friend who stands to gain a lot of money if he wins his lawsuit. Don't scowl at me. I hear what you're saying. Cody Verse's sudden fame has been blown all out of proportion."

"It doesn't hurt that he's dating Lila Redmond, either." Lila was the new It Girl, the hottest starlet since, well, whoever the last It Girl was.

Marco leaned back to stretch, lacing his fingers behind his dark, wavy hair, putting his hard-muscled torso on display. Today he was wearing jeans and a formfitting navy T-shirt with the white lettering DOWN THE HATCH running the length of one sleeve. He was a yummy-hot male and all mine.

"I need coffee," he said, and got up to go to the coffee machine behind the bar. "I didn't get home last night until two in the morning." He held up the pot. "Want some?"

I shook my head. Not to hurt Marco's feelings or anything, but his bar was not known for its coffee. Or its decor, for that matter. The last time Down the Hatch had

13

been decorated must have been in the seventies, when burnt orange, avocado green, and dark walnut paneling were all the rage and a blue plastic carp passed for wall sculpture.

I heard cheering in the distance and got up to look out the big plate glass window at the front of the bar. "You should see the crowds now. Little kids, too. Did they call off school today? Maybe the mayor declared a holiday . . . Cody Verse Day."

"The lawsuit should be settled in a day or two," Marco said, coming to stand beside me with a coffee mug in his hand. "Then everything will return to normal."

"With Ken 'the Lip' Lipinski as Cody's attorney? No way. When I clerked for Dave Hammond, I sat in on a few trials and saw Lipinski in action. The Lip is the kind of lawyer all those nasty jokes are about. He lies, stalls, grandstands, and cheats, and somehow he manages to get away with it because he wins huge settlements for his clients. Trust me, Marco. Lipinski will do everything in his power to turn this lawsuit into a major media event."

"And Dave will do everything in his power to keep that from happening," Marco countered. He had done private investigative work for Dave and, like me and many others, came to know Dave for the hardworking, honest, decent man he was.

"I'm afraid he'll be fighting a losing battle, Marco. Dave usually refuses to take a case when Lipinski is on the other side, but this time he was hired before he knew who the opposing counsel was. Now he's stuck."

Marco took a swallow of coffee. "Why doesn't he withdraw his appearance?"

"Because the Chappers have been with him for a long time, and he wouldn't do that to loyal clients. Have you noticed that Dave hasn't been himself lately, like something's weighing on his mind? Maybe it's his caseload. Being a public defender is never an easy job, and with the crime rate rising, he's busier than ever. Or maybe he's having some kind of midlife crisis. Whatever it is, having to deal with the Lip in a big, splashy civil case isn't going to help him any."

"I thought Dave's client was a young guy — Cody Verse's high school buddy," Marco said, heading for the bar. "Sure I can't get you some coffee?"

"No coffee, thanks. And technically, yes, Dave's client is Andrew Chapper, one half of the former Chapper and Verse duo. Andrew's grandparents have been with Dave since he first hung out his shingle.

They're the ones who brought Andrew to see Dave. Apparently, they raised Andrew after his parents died in a car accident."

Marco rejoined me at the window carrying a full coffee mug. He put his arm around me, and I leaned my head on his shoulder. Dave had helped me many times during my struggle to stay afloat in law school and often since then. I would do whatever I could to pay him back.

"I wish I could help Dave somehow," I said with a sigh. "Proving that Andrew cowrote the winning song is going to be tough. And who knows? It might not even get that far. If the judge rules in Lipinski's favor on his motion to dismiss, it's all over. Case closed. Andrew loses."

Marco nuzzled my ear. "It's not all bad news today, Sunshine. We've got something to celebrate, remember? Your engagement ring should be resized and ready to wear."

Oh, right. About that . . .

With the corners of his mouth curving in that sexy way of his, he lifted my left hand to his lips to kiss my fingers. "What do you say I pick it up and give it to you at dinner tonight?"

"Marco, we need to talk."

CHAPTER TWO

Seeing the flicker of dismay in Marco's gaze, I paused. Obviously I hadn't phrased that right. Still, considering all we'd been through together, he couldn't possibly doubt my commitment to him, could he?

Yet I had to keep in mind that being a fiancé was new territory for Marco, whereas I was familiar with the topography. I was engaged to Pryce Osborne II, the elder son of a preeminent New Chapel family, while attending my first and only year of law school. When the law school gave me the boot, so did my fiancé. The Osbornes didn't want the stain of my failure on their name.

Naturally, an experience like that could cause me to have a few scary thoughts about the forthcoming nuptials. But as I had to impress upon Marco, I wasn't doubting my decision to marry him, only the wisdom of spreading the news at this particular time. I just had to convince Marco that keeping the news to ourselves was in his best inter-est, too.

It wouldn't be easy. We'd picked out a beautiful half-carat diamond, and he was justifiably proud of it. And in truth, keeping our secret wasn't what I would have pre-ferred, either. I couldn't wait to wear the ring and announce to the world that we were engaged.

Just not yet. Not until I'd righted a wrong that I'd set in motion. The tricky part would be trying to avoid calling attention to that little factoid. I'd alienated a future mother-in-law once. I didn't want a rerun.

I wrapped my arms around Marco's ribs, pressed my ear against his solid chest, and hugged him hard. "I love you, Marco, and I can't wait to put that ring on my finger. It's just that considering what else is going on, I think we should keep our engagement a secret a while longer."

"The *what else* being Rafe's ad hoc wed-ding plans?"

"What else?"

"I don't get it. Why should we let his foolishness affect our plans?"

"You know what a stir your brother's surprise announcement caused. Your mom didn't come right out and say so, but I could tell by the shocked look on her face

18

that she believes Rafe is making a huge mistake in marrying Cinnamon and she would love nothing better than to talk him out of it. Not that I blame her.

"I mean, how could Rafe possibly know Cinnamon is the right person for him? How insane is it to meet a waitress during his first week as a bartender at Hooters, and date her twice before asking her to marry him? Rafe even admitted he knows little about Cinnamon's background. I'm sure he knows even less about her as a person, except what he sees on her exterior. So what can he possibly be thinking?"

"Probably about what he sees on her exterior." Marco sipped his coffee.

No doubt he was right. Cinnamon was one sultry babe — and by *babe,* I meant not yet of legal age — and Rafe was a virile twenty-one-year-old guy whose maturity level hovered somewhere in the vicinity of a fourteen-year-old's.

I hugged Marco again. "Thank goodness you're not like Rafe. You see what's below the surface, not just what's on top."

Marco's eyes darkened the way they always did when he had romance in mind. "What do you say we go back to my office and explore that concept?"

I ran my hands up the front of his shirt. "I

like the way you think, Salvare."

His mouth curved up devilishly. And then suddenly he was ushering me through the bar toward his office in the back. "We've got thirty minutes until my staff starts arriving."

"So you agree that we should postpone our announcement?"

"Mmm."

Translation: *My brain has shut down. Check back in thirty minutes.*

I came to a stop. Not that I wanted to spoil the mood, but it was important that we were on the same page before he picked up that engagement ring. "Was that a yes?"

"To what?"

"To *what?*"

He rolled his eyes as I perched on the last barstool and prepared to explain. "Here's the situation. Your mom has a lot on her plate right now. Not only is she having to deal with Rafe's hasty decision, but she's been uprooted from her home in Ohio and is living at your sister's house to help care for your nephew as Gina prepares for the birth of her second child. The last thing your mom needs is for us to toss our engagement onto the pile."

"Sunshine, the thing my mom wants most in the world is for me to get married. I don't think she'd mind us tossing that onto the pile. I think she'd carry it to the top." He glanced at his watch. "Twenty-five minutes."

Rats. He still wasn't seeing the light.

"So you believe it would be wrong for us to keep our news a secret because of how much joy it would bring your mom?"

"Yes. Let's go."

"I suppose you're right. Imagine the pleasure she — and my mom, too — will derive from planning the wedding, making up their guest lists, and selecting the reception hall, menu, and caterer, not to mention throwing the rehearsal dinner and all those bridal showers. Because you realize there is no way on earth they will turn over those duties to us. Once the two of them learn we're officially engaged and they put their heads together, we'll be lucky to choose the date."

"Bridal *showers?*"

"Sure. There will be a personal shower for close friends and the bridal party, another shower for extended family and close neighbors, and a gigantic shower for everyone from the first two showers plus all those to whom our mothers owe social obligations. You'll have to be there, of course. But don't worry. Food will be plentiful — lots of little finger sandwiches, petit fours, and strawberry punch. And just imagine the mountains of gifts we'll be unwrapping and admiring — and sending thank-you notes for. We'll probably need to set aside a whole day for that. And then —"

"Hold it." Marco sat down on the next stool and rubbed his jaw, pondering the situation. "So," he said, "if we make our announcement now, we'll take the focus away from Rafe's wedding, and he'll feel cheated."

"Naturally."

"Plus, if Rafe sees us going ahead with our plans, he'll get more excited about his own plans, and then there'd be no way for my mom to talk him out of it."

"You've got that right."

"And we'll be at the mercy of our mothers."

"Absolutely."

"So you're saying we should wait a while before making our announcement?"

"It would be for the best, Marco. Don't you think so?"

"I'm beginning to see your side of it. If we opted for a private, intimate ceremony —"

"And they found out? They wouldn't hear of it. We'd be better off figuring out when, where, and how we're going to do this and then sending out the invitations. If it's a done deal, what are they going to do? Shoot us?"

Marco slapped his knee. "You're right. We need to keep this under wraps at all costs. No one can know, not even your assistants."

"I'll have to tell Nikki. I can't live with her and keep all those secrets. But she won't say a word until I give her the green light."

"I'm cool with that."

Good thing, since I'd already told her. Nikki was my roommate and best friend since third grade. We shared everything, even colds. There was no way I could've kept news of our engagement from her. "I'm so glad we can have these discussions."

"Me, too, so let's have another."

"About what?"

"The real reason you want Rafe to be talked out of marrying Cinnamon. I know it's too soon for them to make that commitment, but a romantic would say it was love at first sight, and you're a romantic. So let's have it."

I checked Marco's watch. "Wow. Only twenty minutes left. Let's talk about this over dinner tonight, okay?" I hopped down from the stool.

"Abby."

"Now? Really?"

Marco folded his arms over his chest and

23

gave me his no-nonsense Army Ranger gaze. "Now. Really."

"It might spoil the mood."

"You've already taken care of that."

I sighed. "Okay, fine. Here it is. I don't think Rafe had any intentions of getting married until I sort of . . . fostered his engagement."

"How?"

I climbed back onto the stool. It wasn't going to be a quick explanation. "After Rafe got the job at Hooters, we were commiserating on how hard it is to be held to the standards of more successful siblings and —"

"You're speaking about your brothers now?"

"My brothers the successful surgeons. In Rafe's case, he feels compared to you, so he asked for my advice on how to cope with negative self-esteem issues. I suggested one way to handle it was to do something different so there wouldn't be any way to be compared."

"Rafe used the word *surprise*."

"What?"

"You told him to surprise us."

"Okay, I may have used that word, but he took it out of — wait. What? You already knew what I told him?"

Marco lifted an eyebrow. He did half of his communicating with his eyebrows, like a semaphore system. In this case he meant *Of course I knew.*

"Does your mom know?" I asked.

"No."

Whew! Close one. "When I told Rafe to do something different and, okay, *surprise* the family, I was referring to how I became a florist instead of a doctor or lawyer. How was I to know Rafe would take my advice to the extreme? Anyway, I swear to you that I've learned my lesson. I will never again give advice to immature males — after I advise Rafe to drop Cinnamon."

Marco threaded his fingers through mine. "Look, Sunshine, if you're serious about wanting to talk Rafe out of this marriage, get my mom to help you. The two of you working together would be an unstoppable machine."

"While that sounds like a good idea in theory," I said tactfully, "the problem is that she'd want to know why I was getting so involved, and I'd rather she not find out about my role in Rafe's engagement."

"Because you think she'll hold it against you?"

I nodded.

Marco studied me, his clear gaze seeing

deep down inside me to the scars I kept hidden from the world. He leaned across the space between our stools and kissed me tenderly, his lips lingering on mine, before saying softly, "My mom likes you, Abby. She wouldn't hold it against you." He kissed me again, then leaned back. "But I respect your feelings. If you feel better not enlisting her help, it's okay with me."

That was why I loved Marco. Sure, he was a gorgeous hunk of male; sure, he was smart and capable and sexy; but what made him stand out was that he listened. He didn't always understand, but he paid attention and didn't blow off my feelings.

I threw my arms around his neck and kissed him hard, then leaned back to gaze into his eyes. "Thank you. That means a lot to me."

Marco tapped his watch. "*And* we still have fifteen minutes."

He hopped off his stool and held out a hand to help me down. "What do you think I should do about my engagement ring?" I asked, taking his hand. "Have the jeweler hold it?"

"Wear it on a chain around your neck."

"And keep it tucked under my clothing! Perfect. That way it'll be close to my heart."

At that, Marco swept me into his arms

26

and gave me a kiss that started off sweet and gentle but quickly turned habanero-pepper hot. Quite understandable since we'd seen little of each other over the past week. Because of a difficult case he'd taken for his private investigation business, which he ran in addition to the bar, his long hours of undercover surveillance had kept us apart for too long.

When he turned to carry me to his office, there stood Gert, the scrawny, wrinkled, leather-faced waitress who'd worked at Down the Hatch for forty years. She was standing with her hands on her hips, shaking her head as though she thought we were silly.

"Don't tell me you never kissed anyone in this bar," Marco said to her.

"Honey," she replied in her scratchy voice, "I could tell you stories that'd make a sailor blush," then went straight into a coughing fit, caused by a lifetime of smoking.

"You're early, Gert," Marco said grumpily, putting me down.

"You told me to come in early, boss," she answered. "Eight thirty on the nose."

"Holy cow, it's eight thirty?" I exclaimed. "Lottie and Grace will be wondering what happened to me. I'm surprised they haven't phoned. Lottie always makes breakfast first thing on Monday mornings."

"Do you want me to take care of that errand we discussed earlier?" Marco asked, discreetly pointing to his ring finger.

"Thanks, but I'll handle it. Bye, Gert." I blew a kiss at Marco, then grabbed my purse and coat and headed for the door.

Bloomers is located two doors south of Down the Hatch Bar and Grill. The flower shop occupies the first floor of a three-story redbrick building built in the 1890s, and stretches from Franklin Street in front to the alley in back, with full use of the deep, dark basement below. The yellow frame door — yellow is my favorite color — with its beveled-glass center separates two big bay windows, one on the showroom side and the other on the coffee-and-tea-parlor side. At the back of the showroom is a curtained doorway leading to my private paradise: the workroom, where my creativity blossoms, so to speak.

My fears about missing breakfast appeared to be unfounded, thankfully. Lottie Dombowski, my chief assistant, was standing in front of Bloomers watching the activity across the street, which now included an impromptu brass band playing an extremely poor rendition of the theme song from

America's Next Hit Single.

"Hurry or you'll miss him!" Lottie called, waving to me over the tops of people's heads as I made my way up the crowded sidewalk. She pointed to the white limousine, which had been driven across the courthouse lawn to the rarely used side entrance. It was something I'd seen only once before in my lifetime, when a vice president had stopped by while in town to deliver a commencement speech at the New Chapel University School of Law.

While the white limousine idled there, and the brass band, now reassembled near the side entrance, played "Hooray for Hollywood," the black limos parked so as to form a protective vee behind it. Three big, stern-faced men in dark suits and sunglasses emerged, talking into their sleeves as they took positions around the vehicle's perimeter.

Maybe it *was* the vice president.

"Karl!" Lottie bellowed to one of her sons across the street. "Move up closer or you'll never get that photo of Lila and Cody. Stand on your brother's shoulders, for pity's sake!"

"Which brother?" Karl hollered back.

"Pick one." With a heavy sigh, Lottie said to me, "The last kid to come out has a tough row to hoe."

Lottie, a purebred Kentuckian, was a brassy-haired, vocal, generously built woman who brooked no nonsense from her sons. At the moment, seventeen-year-old quadruplets Jimmy, Joey, Johnny, and Karl were standing at the back of the crowd, whistling, hooting, pounding each other on the back, and generally showing off for the teenage girls who'd also come down to the square. That they were missing school for this nonevent surprised me. Lottie was a strict disciplinarian.

"Did the school declare a holiday?" I asked her.

"They should have," Lottie replied. "All the kids are down here. I'm sending the boys back as soon as they've seen Cody and Lila."

Lottie, a superb florist herself, had owned Bloomers before I did. In fact, I'd delivered flowers for her during summers home from college. Then Lottie was forced to sell Bloomers to pay her husband's hospital bills after he'd had major heart surgery, and I reentered the picture. A failure at love and law, with a yen to work with flowers, I used what was left of my grandpa's trust money to get a mortgage on Bloomers and hire Lottie to teach me everything she knew.

Now, as a bright orange helicopter buzzed the courthouse, I raised my voice to say, "Lottie, I'm heading inside."

"Okay, sweetie. Breakfast's waiting in the kitch— Lordy, would you look at that!"

I turned to see the copter landing in the street behind the courthouse, which had been blocked to traffic. In big fat black letters on the side of the copter it said AIR LIP.

"Air lip?" Lottie called in bafflement.

"Attorney Lipinski's ride," I replied, trying to make myself heard over the chopping of the blades. "Who else would be flamboyant and insulting at the same time?"

A moment later Lipinski emerged from the copter and ducked to run beneath the swinging blades, which wasn't too hard for a man of his short stature. He was instantly surrounded by reporters, cameramen, and photographers, who snapped away as the Lip made a show of removing his yellow jumpsuit to display a sharply tailored three-piece, dove gray suit with a white shirt and an orange-and-yellow-striped tie underneath. His dark hair was parted on one side and slicked back, making his large ears protrude, and when he smiled, he was all teeth.

Grinning like a monkey, he turned his back to the crowd, then tossed the jumpsuit over his shoulder as though he were a bride tossing her garter. The crowd went wild.

With the dark-suited security men encircling him, Lipinski hurried toward the white limo. The driver lowered his window to speak with him, then as one of the security detail opened a rear door, Lipinski walked around the limo and extended a hand to someone inside. There was a drum-roll from the brass ensemble as a small hand was placed in his. Then a woman's leopard-print high-heeled shoe and long, tanned leg emerged, followed by the other shoe and leg, then the immediately recognizable face of starlet Lila Redmond. She was clad in a copper-colored belted leather coat.

The roar of the crowd could have been heard in Chicago. I was surprised no one had rolled out a red carpet for her.

"I gotta make sure the boys get a picture of that," Lottie said, then charged across the street to direct Karl's photography efforts.

Lila Redmond tossed back her long black hair, causing it to ripple like liquid silk, then waved and smiled coyly as cameras flashed. Lipinski took her arm to escort her into the side entrance, and then the attention returned to the open limo door. Soon a chant of "Co-*dee,* Co-*dee,* Co-*dee*" built to a crescendo, turning into a huge shout of "Yay!" as a dark head appeared.

Cody Verse, tall, muscular, and good-looking, with jagged-cut coal black hair, exited the car, smiling and waving as though he were a returning war hero. He wore a full-length, silver-toned leather coat and was followed by a pudgy, middle-aged bald man in a brown wool suit — his agent, no doubt. Before the crowd could charge, the pair was rushed inside the courthouse and the side door was closed.

The defendant had arrived.

I glanced at my watch. In about fifteen minutes, Dave Hammond, the attorney for the plaintiff, would leave his law office on Lincoln Avenue and quietly make his way across the street to the courtroom on the fourth floor. No one would notice the somewhat stocky, nondescript man with thinning hair, wearing a plain brown suit and carrying a battered leather briefcase, nor would he want them to. Dave didn't want attention. He wanted results. But up against the Lip, he might get exactly the opposite.

CHAPTER THREE

I was dying to sit in the courtroom and watch Dave match wits with the Lip, as many people were doing, judging by the line at the rear of the courthouse, but the practical side of me, the side that needed to pay rent and buy groceries, decided to go to work.

After the hubbub outside, my flower shop was a haven of bliss. Closing the door behind me, I inhaled the sweet, heady aromas of fresh blossoms and glanced around in never-ending delight. Tables, shelves, and armoires spilled over with colorful floral arrangements and gift items. A glass-fronted cooler at the back of the shop displayed roses, daisies, gerberas, lilies, mums, and ready-made arrangements, while wreaths, vines, and decorative mirrors filled the walls.

The cashier counter was to my immediate left, and the doorway to the coffee-and-tea parlor to my right, where my other assistant, a sixtysomething Brit named Grace Bingham, was hard at work.

"Is that you, Abby?" she called.

"Hi, Grace," I replied, shedding my coat.

She was behind the coffee counter preparing for the customers who came in before work to have a cup of her gourmet coffee or one of her specialty teas and a homemade scone, the flavor depending on her whim that morning. I'd added the parlor as a way to draw in more customers, and luckily it had paid off. If it hadn't, I would have been in serious financial trouble.

Grace had been Dave Hammond's secretary when I clerked for him, but she had decided to retire about the time I bought Bloomers. Her retirement had lasted two weeks; then, bored to tears, she came to work for me. Running the parlor was a labor of love for Grace, which was fortunate, since I had little to offer in the form of pay.

"Good morning, love," she said, sailing in from the parlor. She was wearing a pleated gray skirt and a lilac sweater set, with silver earrings and a pendant, which set off her short, stylish gray hair. "How are we today? Did Lottie tell you your breakfast was waiting?"

"Yes, she did, and we are fine now that

we're safely inside, away from the insanity."

"I covered your plate to keep it warm, but without an oven, I'm afraid, your eggs are a bit chilled."

"No problem." I headed toward the purple curtain at the back of the shop. "Did you catch Lipinski's grand entrance in his orange chopper?"

"One could hardly avoid it," Grace said, following me. "The word *ostentatious* springs to mind. Are you aware that Mr. Lipinski owns the helicopters used by the hospital and the sheriff's department and makes a tidy profit from leasing them? It's quite true, you know. The odious fellow has his tendrils in everything. I was forced to contend with that man on several occasions when I worked for Dave, none of which I remember with pleasure. It's a pity our Dave must deal with such a tough case as well as so loathsome an opponent."

I hadn't been aware of Lipinski's other pursuits, but I didn't doubt Grace's word. She had great sources.

I parted the curtain and stepped into my pleasure zone, otherwise known as the workroom. Although windowless, the copious colorful blossoms and the heady fragrances made the area a tropical garden. Vases of all sizes and containers of dried flowers filled shelves above the counters along two walls. A long slate-covered work-table occupied the middle of the room; two big walk-in coolers took up one side, and a desk holding my computer equipment and telephone filled the other side.

Beyond the workroom was a tiny galley kitchen and an even tinier bathroom. At the very back was the exit onto the alley, guarded by a big, rusty iron door that needed to be replaced. I'd been waiting months for a permit to put in a bigger door as well as a ramp for deliveries, and had only just recently received word that the permit was on its way.

As Grace had promised, a foil-covered plate sat on the counter. I perched on a kitchen stool as Grace brought me a cup of coffee and a pitcher filled with half-and-half. I creamed my coffee, then took a sip and sighed with pleasure. "Yum. Delicious, as always. Do I taste a hint of chocolate?"

She gave me a secretive smile. Grace would never divulge her coffee recipes.

I tucked in to Lottie's skillet eggs, a dish made with olive oil, feta cheese, lemon pepper, basil, and bites of asparagus. Lottie liked to add leftover veggies from home. Whatever combination she used, it was always browned on the bottom, soft on top, and delicious inside.

"I wish Lottie made breakfast every day," I said with a satisfied sigh, rinsing my plate at the sink.

"But then Mondays wouldn't be special, would they?" Grace checked her watch. "It's nearly nine. I should get ready to open the store."

At once, there was a loud rapping on the front door. "Good heavens," Grace said. "Someone must need coffee badly."

While she went to open the door, I checked the spindle on my desk to see how many orders had come in overnight. Grace always printed them out and stacked them in the order they were needed. I counted eleven. Not great, but enough to keep me busy all morning.

Lottie came bustling in. "In all the excitement, I forgot to take my key."

"Did Karl get any good photos?"

"Mostly the backs of people's heads," she said. "A few shots of Lila. That's probably who he was after anyway. I'll turn on the radio so we can keep tabs on the hearing. There's no telling what will happen with the Lip involved."

Lottie had certainly called it. About eleven thirty, as I was finishing an arrangement for a twenty-fifth wedding anniversary, of red stargazer lilies, blue delphinium, lavender asters, alstroemeria, yellow solidago, and sprigs of senecio for greenery, the radio newscaster broke in to announce that Judge Hezekiah Duncan had declared a recess and ordered the courtroom cleared.

"Why would the judge need to clear the courtroom?" Lottie asked. She had come into the workroom for more flowers to restock the glass display case.

"Because, undoubtedly, Mr. Lipinski caused a dustup," Grace said as she slipped through the curtain. Somehow Grace always managed to be nearby when a discussion was taking place so she could offer one of her pithy sayings. She had an unlimited supply.

Right on cue, she struck her lecturing pose — chin up, hands clasping the edges of her cardigan as though they were lapels. "It brings to mind Oscar Wilde's description of a man of Mr. Lipinski's character. 'He would stab his best friend for the sake of writing an epigram on his tombstone.' "

Lottie and I clapped. Grace nodded in appreciation, then picked up the phone and punched in a number. When her call was answered, she said, "Martha, love, do you know what happened across the street?"

Martha was Dave's current secretary, whom Grace had come to know quite well. "I see," Grace said after listening for several moments. "Well, that's not good, is it? Keep us posted, dear, will you?"

She replaced the receiver. "Martha doesn't know why a recess was called. Dave hasn't checked in yet. However, the news did cause her to express her concern for Dave's well-being. She said he'd mentioned in passing that his blood pressure has been on the high side lately and he hasn't been sleeping well. Dave hates having a fuss made over him, so Martha wasn't able to press for details, but she fears the stress of his public defender workload is getting to him."

I knew from my stint as his law clerk that defending the accused was a thankless job, yet, as Dave always said, it was included in our Constitution for a reason. Our fore-fathers knew there was a mere thin line standing between freedom and authoritari-anism, and that line was our Bill of Rights.

But add Lipinski, not to mention a case that was becoming a major media event, to Dave's load and who knew what toll it would take on his health? I pondered the matter as I pulled clear wrap off the big roll. Maybe I could catch Dave before he left the courthouse and offer whatever assistance I could. Marco was still working evenings. I'd might as well do something useful, too.

I checked the gift tag on the anniversary arrangement. It was for Mrs. Denise Byrd, who lived within walking distance of my shop. Perfect.

As I slipped on my peacoat, I said to my assistants, "If you don't mind, I'll take the first lunch shift so I can deliver this arrangement."

Grace secured the gift card to the arrangement. "Do give Dave our best when you see him."

She knew me too well.

As I crossed Franklin Street and started across the grass heading toward the back of the courthouse, the side door opened and the security detail poured out, doing a visual sweep of the area around the limousines. They saw me hurrying toward the big building, my arms around a huge basket of flowers, and immediately one guard stepped forward. "No gifts! Get back!"

"This isn't for Cody, and I'm not even coming toward you." Giving him a glare, I detoured around the Green Zone and was approaching the entrance at the rear of the building when a gaggle of reporters burst out and raced straight toward me. I stepped back so my flowers wouldn't be crushed and watched as they ran around the corner to position themselves, since cameras weren't allowed in the courthouse.

As security guards hustled Lila Redmond from the side door to the white limo, reporters shouted at her, trying to get her attention. Lila paused to wave and smile, setting off a lightning storm of camera flashes. I started toward the entrance again, only to be swept aside by a flock of female court personnel who made a mad dash around the building to snap photos of Cody as he, too, was hustled out of the building. The women, all middle-aged, screamed when they saw him. Two fainted.

But it was the Lip who caused the biggest commotion. He strode out and motioned for the reporters to gather around, clearly gearing up for a press conference. I wasn't about to miss that, so I hurried around the corner and carefully edged my way along the border of the crowd so my flowers wouldn't be damaged.

"*Why* did Judge Duncan call a recess?" Lipinski said, repeating the reporter's question. "If you believe opposing counsel's story, part of his file is *mysteriously* missing." The Lip smirked, as though to say, *What a liar.* "If you ask me — and by the way, you did — I'd say it's a case of being ill-prepared and unable to proceed. In other words, ladies and gentlemen, a not-so-clever stall tactic."

A stall tactic? How dare he smear Dave's good name! No way was I going to let that pass. Elbowing my way to the front, still carrying my flowers, I yelled, "Excuse me. Have you *ever* known Attorney Hammond to be ill-prepared for a hearing?"

The Lip zeroed in on me with his beady eyes and condescending tone. "Maybe he's never had such a weak case before, Petal. Are those lovely blossoms for my client, sweetheart?"

The reporters chuckled. Many of them knew who I was and thus had their cameras and mics ready when I shot back, "You're not even half the attorney Dave Hammond is. He has more integrity in his little finger than you do in your entire body."

"I doubt anyone here is surprised that I'm not half the man Dave is," Lipinski said with a snicker. "I think it's no secret he's put on more than a few pounds this past year." The Lip mugged for the cameras, opening his suit coat to show his trim waist, garnering laughter among the men.

I was so angry, I was ready to pitch the basket at his head, but someone grabbed my arm and led me away. It was Connor McKay, a reporter I'd met when I got entangled in a murder case at the New Chapel law school. At the time Connor was working the crime beat for the *New Chapel News*, but because of cutbacks at the paper, he was now also working as a part-time roving reporter for the local cable TV channel.

He was a nice-looking guy, with silky brown hair that reached his shoulders, striking seafoam green eyes, and a wide, captivating smile. Unfortunately for anyone who thought to befriend him, Connor was way too into the whole reporter gig. He had tried to make me believe he had a thing for me when he was actually using me for information. It was a lesson I'd never forget. "Let go!" I said, yanking my arm loose.

"You won't win an argument with the Lip," Connor said. "He'll just keep egging you on until you bust a gut, and then he'll walk away the victor. I've seen it happen before and I'd hate to see it happen again, especially to my favorite florist."

I knew Connor was right, but it still took a minute for me to cool down. "That was such a cheap shot. Dave's a good lawyer — no, a great lawyer — and Lipinski knows it."

"Hey, no argument here. The Lip is slime.

44

Everyone knows that. Don't let it get to you."

I glanced over my shoulder and saw Lipinski duck into the limo with his clients. Then the crowd moved away as all three limousines backed up to the street and sped off.

I let out a deep breath and tried to shake off my fury. "Thanks for your advice, Connor. I can't stand silently by when I see someone like him pulling that kind of crap. I *hate* injustice."

"That's what makes you special." He winked, and I couldn't help but smile back. Connor was a cad, but a handsome one.

"Got time for coffee?" he asked.

"Sorry, no. I have errands to run."

"How about dinner, then? Or are you still seeing Mr. Down the Hatch?"

"Still seeing him. His name is Marco, in case you've forgotten."

Connor shrugged. "Can't blame a guy for trying."

His cell phone buzzed, so while he answered it, I took the opportunity to escape. I trotted up to the rear door of the courthouse and stepped cautiously inside, hoping I wouldn't get trampled by another mob. I was halted by a courthouse security guard with cookie crumbs in his shaggy moustache; he wanted to check my driver's license and have me scanned for weapons.

The guard and the scanner were new. No longer could I simply dash up the wide staircase or risk taking the ancient elevator to get to the floors above. Now I had to show ID and step through an X-ray machine before I could go anywhere in the building. Sad to say that even in a cozy little town like mine, fear prevailed.

"Nature of your business?" the guard asked stiffly as I pulled out my wallet.

"Delivery. Attorney Hammond." I separated the two to avoid a direct lie.

"Hammond's office is across the street," the guard said, pointing toward the back door.

"Actually, his office is on Lincoln" — I pointed toward the front — "which is that way."

He shone a light over my driver's license to make sure it wasn't a forgery, and suddenly he was all smiles and warmth. "Hey, you're Sergeant Knight's kid, aren't you? Knew you by your red hair and freckles. You sure take after your old man. Great guy, your dad. Everybody liked him here. Shame what happened to him."

The guard was speaking as though my dad had passed away, when actually he'd merely

46

retired. He'd *had* to retire because a drug dealer had shot him in the leg during a drug bust, and the surgery to remove the bullet caused a stroke, which, in turn, caused paralysis in his legs. In true Irish spirit, Dad was making the best of it, but I was still trying to deal with him being forever confined to a wheelchair while the drug dealer had been released after serving a short sentence.

Looking over the guard's shoulder, I saw Dave coming down the large central hall toward me. "Never mind," I said, and stepped aside so the next person in line could pass through.

Poor Dave had a grim look on his face, something I had rarely witnessed. I waved to catch his attention, but before he could reach me, a stocky, balding man in his sixties, clearly incensed about something, cut him off. The man was followed by a thin, pale, sad-eyed woman with salt-and-pepper hair curled into a tight flip, a look I'd seen only in photos from the sixties.

"Is Andrew's case being thrown out?" the man demanded, getting in Dave's face, his big hands clenched at his sides. "Is it?"

I glanced over at the security guard and saw him stop what he was doing to watch the proceedings.

"Calm down, Herb," Dave said quietly,

putting a hand on the man's arm. "The case hasn't been dismissed." The man had to be Andrew's grandfather, Herbert Chapper.

Dave's words seemed to incite him further. Throwing off Dave's hand, Mr. Chapper said through clenched teeth, "I didn't bring this case to you to defend so you could let that devil-in-disguise Lipinski outsmart you."

"Haven't I always done a good job for you?" Dave asked.

"That's not the point!" Mr. Chapper bellowed as his wife tugged on his arm.

"Herbert, you know Mr. Hammond's always done right by us," the woman said in a meek, beseeching voice, only to suffer a furious look from her husband.

"You have to trust me on this one, Herb," Dave said.

"Our grandson's future is at stake," Mr. Chapper cried. "It's all we can do for him, understand? You've got to win this suit." He gripped Dave's coat. "You can't let that fraud Cody Verse get away with his sneak offense. You can't let Lipinski win this battle."

"I understand, Herb," Dave said, loosening his hands. "Let's meet back at my office in fifteen minutes. I'll explain everything then."

Mrs. Chapper tugged her husband's arm and, in a pleading voice, said, "Herbert, Andrew is waiting for us in the car. Let's not cause him any more worry, okay?"

Mr. Chapper covered his face with his hands, seemingly on the verge of tears, and became docile as his wife led him toward the exit. People moved quickly aside to let them pass.

Dave sighed heavily, then saw me watching and motioned for me to follow. He didn't even comment on the huge floral arrangement in my arms as he held the door for me.

"Poor people," Dave said, shaking his head as we stepped outside. "They're desperate for Andrew to win this lawsuit. They want him to go to music school, and he refuses to go because they're both in ill health and don't have enough income to provide for themselves. Herb was a career army man but had to retire because of severe post-traumatic stress. He goes to the VA Hospital in Maraville for therapy, but I don't think something like that is easy to get over."

"Why did the judge clear the courtroom?"

"Because that bastard Lipinski took one of my exhibits," Dave said through clenched teeth.

The Lip had sure put a different spin on the story he was spreading, although I declined to tell Dave about it. He didn't need the extra aggravation. "How did he get into your file?"

"He didn't take it from my file," Dave said, as we walked around the other side of the building, away from the reporters, and headed toward Lincoln Avenue. "The court reporter asked us to bring all of our exhibits up to her before the start of the hearing so she could mark them for the record — Exhibit A, B, C, and so forth. Lipinski waited until I'd put mine on the desk in front of her, and then he put his down beside them.

"I didn't think anything of it until I was presenting my case and went to get my fourth exhibit, which should have been Exhibit D. I searched through my file and my briefcase, while the court reporter looked through everything on her desk, but that particular piece of paper was gone. And all the while Lipinski sat at the defense table looking like the cat that ate the canary."

"How important is the exhibit?"

"It's my most crucial piece of evidence, Abby. It's Andrew's handwritten memo to Cody Verse containing the lyrics he wrote for the winning song, with Cody's written

50

reply making some suggestions on them. Without that evidence, Judge Duncan may very likely rule in the defendant's favor and dismiss the case. Lipinski knew that. He should be disbarred for this."

"A photocopy of the memo won't work?"

"Copies can be altered." He glanced at his watch. "In fifteen minutes I have to meet with my clients and somehow soften the blow."

"The Chappers don't know about the exhibit?"

"No. As soon as I realized it was missing, I approached the bench to tell the judge, and he immediately cleared the courtroom. All my clients know is that there was a problem."

No wonder Dave looked grim. That loss could cost him the case. As we paused at Lincoln to wait for a break in the traffic, I asked, "How could Lipinski have palmed that exhibit in full view of the court?"

"It wouldn't be hard. The judge hadn't entered the courtroom yet, and people were still milling around. All Lipinski had to do was wait until the court reporter was busy, then slide my exhibit onto his pile, take everything back to his seat, and return it minutes later without that piece of paper."

"So what happens now?"

"Duncan called a recess until tomorrow morning to give me a chance to search for it, but I know it's gone."

"Shouldn't the judge have Lipinski's files searched?" I asked, as we hurried across the street.

"Ordering the opposing counsel's papers to be searched would be tantamount to accusing him of theft. Duncan's not about to do that."

In other words, Dave's client was screwed. "I'm sorry, Dave."

"Not as sorry as Lipinski's going to be." He opened the door to his office and went inside.

CHAPTER FOUR

Carrying the floral arrangement, which seemed to be getting heavier by the minute, I followed quietly behind Dave as he climbed the stairs to his office on the second floor. He opened the door and headed straight for his private office, snapping to Martha as he passed her desk, "Call Lipinski's office and set up a meeting for this afternoon. Then prepare a formal complaint against him. I want it filed with the local bar association before the end of the day. That SOB is not going to get away with stealing my exhibit."

Martha raised her eyebrows at me as she placed the call. I sat on a chair in the waiting area while she negotiated a time with the Lip's secretary. Martha hung up, then swiveled her chair so she was facing Dave's open doorway. "Attorney Lipinski will see you at four o'clock, Dave."

"He can bet his ass he'll see me," Dave

grumbled. "Abby, did you need something?"

I set the flowers on the next chair and went to the doorway. "Just wanted to offer my services. If there's anything I can help you with, I'd be happy to oblige. My evenings are free."

Dave leaned back in his old maroon leather chair, covered his eyes with his palms, and let out a long, weary sigh.

I moved inside his office and closed his door. "Dave, is everything okay? Healthwise, homewise . . . ?"

"Everything is fine." He sat up, turned his chair toward his monitor, and began to type, which meant he was not in the mood to talk.

"Okay, then. I'll be on my way. But if you do need my help, give me a call."

He didn't answer.

"See what I mean?" Martha whispered when I came out. "He's not himself."

As I walked the floral arrangement to the address on the envelope taped to the wrapping paper, I took out my cell phone and hit speed dial number two.

Marco picked up in one ring. "Hey, beautiful, what's up?"

"I'm concerned about Dave."

"I thought we had this conversation earlier."

"Marco, his most important piece of evidence is missing. Judge Duncan called a recess to give him time to search for it, but Dave is positive Lipinski took it. He's in the process of filing a formal complaint with the bar association, but meanwhile, the Lip is spreading it around that Dave's claiming the exhibit is missing because he's not prepared."

"You're kidding."

"No. I talked to Dave just now, and he looked really angry and tense and unhappy. He's got a meeting set up with Lipinski at four o'clock today, but I don't think he should go alone. Not in his current frame of mind."

"Abby, this is Dave we're talking about. Mild-mannered Dave. He's not going to shoot the man. He might be angry now, but he'll cool down by four."

"I've never seen him like this, Marco."

"It's okay for him to be angry. Wouldn't you be?"

"Angry doesn't begin to describe how I'd be. Wanting to choke Lipinski might be a better description. During his press conference, I nearly chucked a basket full of flowers at him."

"Dave would be the last person to choke anyone or chuck flowers at them. He's a trained mediator, for Pete's sake. He'll handle his anger."

"Maybe we should show up at Lipinski's office at four to give Dave moral support."

"Not a good idea. Dave might see it as a lack of confidence in him. Listen, babe, I've got a beer distributor waiting to talk to me. See you at six?"

"It's a date."

Unless Dave's meeting with the Lip lasted more than two hours, in which case I'd be late.

Mrs. Byrd lived down the street from the YMCA in an old-fashioned bungalow with a huge front porch equipped with a wide swing and a stack of empty flowerpots that were just waiting for spring planting season. I knocked on the door, then, when she opened it, smelled a deliciously spicy aroma that made my stomach growl — not surprising since it was past noon.

"Mrs. Byrd?" I asked the gray-haired woman in sneakers and a plum-colored jogging suit.

She smiled in delight as she opened the door. "Is that for me?"

This was the best part of my job. I couldn't begin to describe how delightful it was to experience the joy my flowers brought to people, to watch their eyes light up, see their bright smiles, and hear their exclamations of delight. It never failed to thrill me.

"Happy anniversary, Mrs. Byrd!" I sang out, handing her the basket.

Her smile turned to a scowl as she read the gift tag. "My anniversary is next month. The imbecile forgot the date again." Snatching the basket, she stepped back and slammed the door.

Okay, then.

As I headed toward the square, I remembered my Vette was parked on the cross street, so I detoured over to check on it. Yep, still there — with a huge glob of bird poop right in the middle of the windshield. Lovely. I got inside, started the engine, and hit the wipers. The washer liquid squirted over the top of the car, missing the glass completely, while the wipers smeared the wet poop across the entire windshield, creating a dirty white haze.

I searched the glove compartment for something with which to clean it, but save for a ragged-looking map of Indiana and some cherry lip balm that had lost its color, there was nothing. I'd have to remember to bring wet paper towels with me when I closed up shop.

I got out of the car, locked the door, and

started up Franklin toward the courthouse square, my stomach growling even louder than before. As soon as I picked up my engagement ring, I'd head for the Deli and get a sandwich.

Bindstrom's Jewelry Store, on the corner of Lincoln and Franklin, was full of customers, something I hadn't taken into account when I set out. I stepped inside, saw several women my mom knew, then ducked my head and scooted out the door. I'd have to figure out a better time to get my ring. Clearly, the lunch hour wasn't going to work.

Next stop, the Deli, which was among the shops on the square getting a face-lift. On one long side of the single-story building, workers sandblasted off layers of dingy white paint to reveal handsome multicolored brick underneath. In front, the big white signboard with magnetic letters had been replaced by a quaint wooden version that read YE OLDE DELI.

Ye Olde Gift Shoppe. Ye Olde Deli. I hoped this wasn't ye newe trend.

On the sidewalk in front of the Deli sat the four bistro table-and-chair sets usually put out in the summer. The black metal tables were placed in an area enclosed by portable white picket fences with flower boxes attached. The owners had planted pansies in them, but the poor blossoms had frozen overnight.

Surprisingly, in spite of the cool temperatures, two of the tables were occupied by middle-aged women dressed as though they were going to a summer tea party — wide-brimmed straw hats, sleeveless floral print dresses, and fleshy arms that had turned purple from the cold. Their chairs were facing the courthouse and their cameras were within arm's reach. If Cody appeared, they were ready. If they managed to get on TV, too — purple, but ready.

Inside, the place was jammed, the line stretching from the counter on the opposite end of the shop to the door. The line usually moved quickly, so I decided to wait, especially after inhaling the heady aromas of all the delicious meats and cheeses. But today, for some reason the line inched forward.

"What's the holdup?" I asked the man in front of me, who kept leaning out of line to see.

"Some idiot up there is talking on her cell phone instead of paying her bill."

"I hate it when that happens," I said, commiserating as I reached into my pocket to put my phone on vibrate.

Soon others in line began to grumble, too, and as the minutes ticked by on the big school clock on the wall, I finally stepped out to see who this rude person was.

Jillian Knight-Osborne. My cousin.

Before I could duck back in line, she waved to me and mouthed, "Hi, Abs." Then she said into her phone, "No, that's okay. Nobody important."

The people in line turned to glare at me, as if I was somehow responsible. "Sorry," I said. "She can't help it. She has a personality disorder."

It was called being self-absorbed.

Except for the signature Knight red hair, Jillian and I were nothing alike. At twenty-six, she was a year younger — unless you went by maturity, in which case she was twelve — had fewer freckles, was a head taller and a whole lot prettier — and had the svelte shape of a model. Somehow she'd graduated from Harvard, married well-to-do Claymore Osborne, the younger brother of the jerk who'd jilted me, and set up a business as a wardrobe consultant.

Although the disparities in our lifestyles were enormous, my one comfort was that even though I'd flunked out of law school, Jillian proved on a regular basis that I was still smarter than she was. I bypassed the

60

line and marched up to the counter, where she was waving her pen around while talking on her phone, as the harried clerk waited for her to sign her credit card slip. I yanked Jillian's phone from between her ear and shoulder, said, "She'll call you back" to the person on the other end, then shut it off and dropped it into the purse dangling from her wrist.

"That was a client!" she protested.

"Sign that slip!" I snapped back.

Jillian scribbled her name. I picked up the large brown bag on the counter, hooked my hand through her arm, and dragged her out of the store.

Outside, she jerked her arm out of my grasp. "Why did you do that? It was a business call."

"The mood was turning ugly in there, Jillian. People don't like it when you talk on the phone while you're ordering food."

"Why? It didn't stop me from paying."

"Yes, it did. People have time constraints, you know. Plus, you were rude to the cashier."

"Not true! I thanked him."

"No, you didn't."

"I did, too! I blinked *thank you* at him. Twice."

I sat down at one of the black tables and

opened the bag. Inside was a stack of containers filled with pastas and salads and meats, no doubt her dinner menu. On top was a paper-wrapped sandwich that smelled wonderful. Then again, I was so hungry, seaweed would have smelled wonderful. I unwrapped it, pulled it into two pieces, took one half, and handed her the other.

"Hey! That's my lunch!"

"That's what you get for making me lose my place in line to rescue you." I bit hungrily into the sandwich and chewed for a moment, then took apart the bread to see inside. "Is this seaweed?"

"Yes. With spinach, carrots, zucchini, and feta cheese." Jillian began to eat her half.

"You ordered a vegetarian sandwich?"

"Well, duh. I'm a vegetarian."

"Since when?" I took another bite. Any port in a storm.

"Since I heard that Lila Redmond is vegetarian. Isn't it too exciting to have her in our town? I mean, who does fashion better than Li'l Red? Want to know the best part? She's bound to want to shop while she's here, but she'll have no idea where to go! That's where I come in."

"*You're* going to take Lila Redmond shopping?"

"Once Li'l Red finds out that I'm a personal shopper for some big names in Chicago, of course she'll want me to take her shopping."

"Stop calling her Li'l Red. No one calls her that."

"Sor-*ry!* You're just jealous because that should be your nickname."

"Jillian, if you *ever* call me Li'l Red, I swear I'll —"

My cell phone vibrated against my hip, startling me. Giving my cousin a scowl, I wiped my fingers on a paper napkin, pulled out the phone, and glanced at the screen. It was Marco, no doubt wondering if I'd picked up the engagement ring, which I could not talk about in front of my blabbermouth cousin.

"Hi, Marco. I'm having lunch with Jillian right now, so how about if I call you back in a few minutes?"

I heard Jillian talking and glanced over at her. She was back on her phone.

"Never mind, Marco. I can talk."

"Where are you?"

"Freezing at a table outside the Deli. Excuse me — Ye Olde Deli."

"Then eat inside."

"Can't. There's an angry mob inside. More on that later."

"Did you pick up your ring?"

63

I swiveled so Jillian couldn't hear, then whispered into the phone, "I couldn't. Too many familiar faces in the store."

"Want me to get it?"

Like that wouldn't tip anyone off. "How about if Rafe picks it up? If someone should ask, he could say it was for Cinnamon."

"But then Rafe would know about our engagement."

"Oh, right."

"I've got an idea. Leave everything to me. We can meet here for dinner to celebrate."

"Awesome." I made a kissing sound into the phone and hit END, then turned to find Jillian watching me.

"I hope that was Marco you were air-kissing."

"Yep." I stuffed the last bite of sandwich in my mouth and stood up. "Thanks for lunch."

"What are you being so secretive about?"

"Was I being secretive?"

"You turned your back on me to talk."

"I can't concentrate when you're talking, too."

She pursed her lips, pondering my answer. "I heard you mention Rafe. Were you discussing what to do about his alarming choice in brides? I mean, seriously. Cinnamon? Is her mother a fan of the Spice Girls?

Is her last name Sugar? What is her last name anyway? Or is she pulling a Madonna?"

"I don't have any answers, Jillian." Before she could quiz me further, I slipped the strap of my purse over my shoulder and said, "Gotta run. Lots to do today."

"Would you like me to bring La Lila by Bloomers?"

Now it was La Lila. I sighed. "Yes, Jillian. You do that."

Jillian was delusional. Lila Redmond wouldn't give her the time of day.

CHAPTER FIVE

When I got back to the shop, Grace and Lottie were waiting to hear the news about Dave. I filled them in on what Lipinski had pulled and told them about the meeting set for later that afternoon. "And Martha was right about Dave being stressed," I added. "I've never seen him look so dispirited. I tried to get him to talk about it, but he brushed me off."

"I hope his health is all right," Grace said.

"And I hope that jackass Lipinski doesn't make mincemeat of Dave," Lottie said. "You know how vicious the Lip can be. I heard him at a restaurant once cussing out the entire waitstaff because he got snap peas instead of snow peas. He had two waitresses in tears. And he owns the restaurant!"

"Lipinski owns a restaurant here in town?" I asked.

"Sweetie, a quarter of the property in town is his. Let's just hope he doesn't provoke Dave into taking a swing at him. I can see the lawsuit now."

"Even more reason for me to show up at Lipinski's office in time for the meeting," I told them. "Maybe Dave will let me take notes for him. That way the Lip won't be able to claim Dave said or did anything he didn't. I'm sure Lipinski will have one of his many law clerks with him, or even his associate."

"I didn't know he had associates," Lottie said.

"One," I told her.

"Is it wise for you to simply show up?" Grace asked. "Perhaps you should run your plan by Dave first."

Like that would work. "It won't be a problem," I assured them. "I'll be tactful."

"Here," Lottie said, handing me a sticky note. "Be tactful about this."

The note read, *Your mom will be by after school.* "Did she say why?" I asked.

"It's Monday," Lottie replied. "She didn't need to say why."

"I suppose she didn't say what, either?" I asked.

Lottie shook her head. Or maybe she shuddered.

My mom, Maureen "Mad Mo" Knight, was a mild-mannered kindergarten teacher by day and an amateur artist by night, although what kind of artist was debatable because she changed mediums as often as most people changed shoes. She had started with clay, then moved into plaster, vinyl, feathers, beads, mirrored tiles, and — I'd forgotten the rest. On purpose.

The piece that had garnered her the most attention was her infamous Dancing Naked Monkey Table, a quartet of neon-hued baby chimps prancing in a circle while holding up a glass top, a description that didn't do it justice. Solitary confinement might have.

Mom made it her practice to complete a new piece each weekend, then bring it to my shop on Mondays after school so we could put it out with our other gift items. She truly believed she was helping us draw in customers, and in a way she was. The members of the Monday Afternoon Ladies' Poetry Society never missed a meeting in our parlor because they couldn't wait to see what Mom would dream up next.

"Okay, girls," Lottie said, "I'm off for a quick lunch at the Deli."

"Correction," I said. "Ye Olde Deli."

Lottie rolled her eyes as she headed out the yellow door.

Ten orders had come in for a funeral the

next day, with a viewing that evening. Lottie had finished three arrangements while I was out, so that afternoon, while Grace served tea and scones to the poetry club and Lottie waited on customers in the shop, I hurried to complete the remaining arrangements so I'd be done in time for Dave's meeting.

At three o'clock, we loaded the flowers into the back of our rented minivan; then Lottie headed off to the Happy Dreams Funeral Home to deliver them. With Grace still serving customers in the parlor, I manned the shop, taking orders, ringing up purchases — and glancing at the clock, wondering why Mom hadn't put in an appearance yet. Even the poets had given up and gone home. What could I do? Mom would be hurt if I left before she got there.

But as the hour hand moved closer to the four, I had no choice. As soon as Lottie returned, I headed for the workroom to retrieve my coat. Then I heard the bell over the door jingle, and my mom say, "Goodness, what a day this has been."

Fudge. Twenty minutes until the meeting with the Lip started and now Mom shows up. I couldn't sneak out the back way, either, because those rusty old door hinges would give me away. I'd just have to keep my eye on the time.

"Maureen," I heard Grace say, "how lovely of you to drop by. Did you bring something for us?"

I tiptoed to the curtain to peek out, watching as Mom began to take tissue-paper-wrapped items from a shopping bag and set them on a display table. They appeared to be the components of a cute ceramic tea set — a pot that resembled a giant strawberry, with four little berry cups, a sugar bowl, and a creamer to match. Great! She had returned to her pottery wheel. I could deliver a few honest compliments and be on my way.

"Hi, Mom," I said, striding through the curtain. "Let's see what you made. Oh, how pretty! You outdid yourself this time."

"Abby, dear," Grace said in a tone I should have recognized as a warning.

But I forged recklessly ahead, almost giddy with relief that at last Mom had made something completely normal. "I mean it, Mom. This has to be your best work yet. Your attention to detail is amazing. Look at this. The top of the pot is the stem and leaves of the strawberry. And look at these cute little berry cups. We should have no problem selling this set. I might even buy it for myself."

I suddenly caught sight of Lottie standing

70

to one side, gesturing for me to zip my lips. What had I said?

"I bought the tea set at Target," Mom said.

I blinked hard, trying to absorb the magnitude of my gaff. I glanced at Grace for help, but she had apparently decided to let me sink. She went to the door and held it open while Mom stepped outside and wheeled in what I could only describe as an enormous golf tee. I turned to see Lottie slipping through the purple curtain. Coward.

The giant wooden tee was about two and a half feet tall and finished with a coat of glossy ivory paint. It had a circular flat top less than two feet in diameter and a tapering stem that was planted in a circle of artificial turf edged with inch-high brass filigree. Brass casters on the bottom gave it mobility, and a wooden golf club attached to the base served as a handle of sorts.

"This," Mom said proudly, "is what I made."

But what was it made *for?* I glanced at Grace again, this time with a pleading look.

"What a lovely tea cart," Grace said.

A *tee* tea cart? "And an exceptionally ingenious one at that," I said, gushing a little too hard.

Mom ignored me. I knew I'd hurt her feel-

71

ings. She placed the pot and cups on top of the cart and stepped back. "I call my art *Tee Time.* It's designed with golfers in mind."

"Quite clever," Grace said.

"And so — practical!" I kissed her cheek, discreetly checking my watch. Quarter of four. "Unfortunately I have to go to a meeting now, Mom. Why don't you stay and try some of Grace's new coffee blend?"

"You don't like the cart, do you?" Mom asked bluntly.

"Why would you think that?" I asked, trying to look offended.

The bell jingled and my thirteen-year-old niece, Tara, bounced in. She was dressed like a half-pint rap artist in a hot pink satin baseball jacket and cap, balloonlike cargo pants that sported pockets on the legs big enough to accommodate baby kangaroos, and white sneakers that were barely visible beneath the voluminous pant legs.

"Hi, Grandma," she said, giving my mom a hug. "Awesome tea cart."

Brat.

"Thank you, Tara," Mom said, shooting me a look.

"Hi, Grace. Hey, Aunt Abby." Tara headed straight for the parlor, where I soon heard a chair being pulled out.

"Tara, what are you doing here?" Mom called. "I thought you had piano lessons at three thirty on Mondays."

"Just a minute," came the muttered reply.

"I hope Tara's not ditching," Mom said. "It's important to learn a musical instrument to get a well-rounded education." This from a woman who grew up on a farm where instruments were saw blades and empty jugs.

She said to Grace, "My boys took to the piano like ducks to water. They have those long surgeons' fingers, you know."

Probably why they became surgeons and not pianists.

"Abby, you enjoyed piano lessons, didn't you?" Mom asked.

Three years of torture enhanced by a piano teacher with green teeth whose breath smelled like sour tobacco. "Loved them. Listen, Mom, about your tea cart. I really, really —"

"I know. You like it. Now would you ask Tara why she isn't at her piano lessons? She'll tell *you*."

I was about to reply that *she* was the grandma and therefore the in loco parentis, with emphasis on the loco, but since I'd already offended Mom once that day, I thought better of it. I glanced at my watch.

It would be a ten-minute drive to Lipinski's office. How was I going to make that meeting now?

"Abby," Grace said, "shall I call and find out if the meeting has started? Perhaps they're running late."

I gave her a quick nod. Grace hurried toward the workroom, and I headed for the parlor. Tara had parked herself in a chair at one of the white ice cream tables in front of the bay window and was busy working her cell phone keys.

"What happened to your piano lesson?" I asked, walking up to the table.

"Codycation," Tara replied without looking up.

"What?"

"Cody. Cation." Her fingers flew over the tiny keypad.

I put my hand over the screen. "What's a *codycation?*"

"A day off because Cody's in town. Now can I finish my tweet?" She narrowed her eyes at me. It was like looking at a younger version of myself — same flame red hair, same freckles, same green eyes, and same feisty temperament.

"The piano teacher gave you a day off because of Cody Verse being in town?"

She shifted her gaze away. "Kind of."

74

Translation: She ditched.

"Can I please finish now? I'm the official Cody Tweeter, and your window is the perfect lookout."

I removed my hand from her phone. "You're too late. Cody left the square at noon."

"He's coming back."

"Not until the hearing resumes, and that won't be until tomorrow morning at the earliest."

"Wrong. Cody and Lila are coming to the square at six o'clock tonight to sign autographs. See their tent?" She pointed out the window.

I leaned over for a look. Sure enough, a big green-and-white-striped tent was being erected on the lawn in front of the courthouse, and a crowd had gathered to watch. The TV news vans were back, too. "We lock up the flower shop at five o'clock, Tara, and I have plans this evening."

Grace came through the doorway. "I'm sorry to report that the meeting has started."

Which meant I was out of luck, since I couldn't very well barge in. I sank down on another chair at the table, hoping Dave didn't do or say anything rash.

Tara's flying thumbs paused. "Please let me stay, Aunt Abby. I won't touch anything.

I'll just sit here tweeting."

"I'll stay with her," Mom said, pulling out a chair at the table.

"What about Grandpa?" Tara asked.

"Grandpa is perfectly capable of making himself a sandwich. Abigail, leave me a set of keys, and I'll lock up when Tara is done."

"Thanks, Grandma," Tara said, smiling at her. "You're awesome."

"And *you* have to make up your missed piano lesson," Mom said, wagging her index finger at Tara even while she beamed at the compliment.

"I'll put on some coffee for you before I leave, Maureen," Grace said cheerfully, heading for the counter at the back.

"Y'all have a good evening," Lottie called to us on her way out.

Terrific. Everyone was happy, if you didn't count me. I took myself back to the workroom to finish the orders on the spindle before my six o'clock dinner date with Marco. At least that was something to look forward to.

At five o'clock it started to rain. By five thirty the rain had turned into a full-blown thunderstorm, with wind gusts up to twenty-five miles an hour, eardrum-shattering claps of thunder, and jagged bolts

76

of lightning that had our electricity blinking.

I checked on Tara and Mom and found them packing up. "The signing was called off," Mom said. "Severe storm warnings are out. I'm going to take Tara home."

"I'll be back tomorrow after school," Tara promised.

"Can't wait," I said.

As I watched them dash to Mom's car, the phone rang. I locked the door, then hurried to answer it at the cashier counter. "Bloomers Flower Shop. How may I help you?"

"Abby," Martha said, "have you heard from Dave?"

"No, why?"

"He didn't come back to the office after his meeting with Attorney Lipinski, and he'd said he would. I thought maybe you'd spotted him around the square or he'd stopped by Bloomers to talk to you about the meeting, since you'd volunteered to help him with the case."

"I haven't seen him. Maybe he went straight home."

"I called his house, but Peg hasn't heard from him either. I phoned Lipinski's office and no one answered, but it's after five o'clock, so everyone's probably gone for the

77

day. I tried Dave's cell phone, too, but he isn't picking up. I don't know whether to be worried or not."

"He could have stopped at the grocery store on his way home," I said. "My cell phone cuts out in some stores. Maybe his does, too."

There was a pause and then Martha said, "You're right. I'm sure it's something as simple as that. Anyway, if you should hear from him, tell him I got the complaint filed and within an hour had a call from a reporter who somehow got wind of it. I wanted Dave to be prepared."

"Will do, Martha. And, likewise, if you hear from him, please let me know." As I hung up, I spotted Mom's tee cart in the middle of the showroom floor. I pushed it into the corner beside a tall dieffenbachia and hoped a golfer with a tea habit would come in to order flowers.

In the workroom I sat down at the computer to look up information about a new variety of rose I wanted to order. But I kept thinking about how upset Dave had been, and then I started to worry. What if he'd suffered a heart attack after meeting with the Lip? What if he'd blacked out while driving home and was lying in a ditch somewhere, unable to call for help?

78

I had fifteen minutes until I was supposed to meet Marco, time enough to make the drive from Lipinski's office to Dave's house. I put on my coat, took our spare umbrella from the workroom, locked the door, and got ready to race around the corner to the public parking lot.

Then I remembered my Vette was parked three blocks away.

I opened the door and a gust of wind tore the umbrella from my hand. I stepped back into the recessed doorway and watched it tumble wildly up the sidewalk. Damn!

I went back inside, tore off a big piece of clear wrap, covered my head with it, then stepped outside, locked the door, and hurried up the sidewalk to Down the Hatch. The wind snatched the wrap before I could dash inside.

The bar was full and the television was tuned to a sports channel, so no one heard me enter. I made my way through the people standing three-deep along the counter and discovered Marco mixing drinks behind the bar. He smiled when he saw me, then called over the noise, "Hey, there's my ray of sunshine. Wait for me in my office. I'll be done in a few minutes."

I motioned for him to come down to the open end of the bar.

"What's wrong?" he asked.

"Dave's been out of contact since his meeting with Lipinski. Martha's been trying to reach him, and his wife hasn't heard from him, either. Something's happened to him, Marco. I feel it in my gut."

"Give me five minutes and then we'll go look for him."

CHAPTER SIX

Marco's green Prius was parked in the alley behind the bar. We dashed out the back door in the rain and slid inside; then as we headed for the Lip's office, I filled Marco in on Martha's phone call. "It just isn't like Dave not to call his wife if he's going to be late," I said.

"Maybe Dave had such a bad day that he needed to cool off before he talked to her."

"Is that a male thing? Because the female thing is to talk to somebody in order to cool off."

"Male thing."

Silly males.

The Lipinski building was on the state highway just south of town, a short ten-minute drive. It was a two-story Federal-style redbrick building with high, narrow windows, black shutters, a white portico, and gigantic gold letters on a big sign in front that said LAW OFFICES OF LIPINSKI &

LIPINSKI, even though only one Lipinski was in residence.

There had been two Lipinskis at one time, but the Lip and his father had parted in a fight so bitter that the elder Lipinski had *de*parted soon after. The Lip's brother hadn't spoken to him since their father's passing, nor had the extended family. Lipinski had one child, Ken Junior, by a former mistress. Little Kenny was supposed to follow him into the practice, but instead ended up in prison. Then there was Darla Mae, the wife Lipinski had divorced five years earlier, after a yearlong battle over marital assets that included a Bentley, a million-dollar "cottage" overlooking Lake Michigan, and a Labradoodle named TuLip, all of which the Lip got.

The rain was letting up as Marco pulled into the deserted parking lot and circled the darkened building, but we saw no sign of Dave's car. We headed back toward New Chapel, taking a route Dave would likely follow to get home, then tried several variations, with no luck.

Out of ideas, we returned to Down the Hatch and sat in the last booth to discuss the situation over dinner. I didn't have much appetite until the Reuben sandwich arrived — two hearty slices of rye bread browned on the grill, with thin slices of hot, tender corned beef, sauerkraut, melted Swiss cheese, and brown mustard — and then suddenly I realized how hungry I was. Marco ordered two microbrewed beers for us, so before we started on our food, he clinked his bottle to mine and said, "To Dave's safe return." We drank to that, and then Marco picked up his hamburger.

"Don't we have something else to celebrate?" I asked.

Marco paused, his burger almost to his mouth. Then he put it down, sat back, and scratched his nose, as though slightly embarrassed. "There's been a slight delay, so let's celebrate tomorrow night instead."

"Okay. Tomorrow night." I took a bite of sandwich, chewed and swallowed. "So, what caused the delay?"

"I'll tell you tomorrow night. How was your day?"

He was evading my question, but I decided he must have a surprise up his sleeve, so I dropped the topic. Over dinner, I told him about my mom's tee cart, Tara's new career, and the Cody signing event that had been canceled.

As we were finishing our meal, Martha called on my cell phone. "Abby," she said, "Dave is home. I just spoke with Peg. Apparently he stopped to visit his mother in the nursing home and his cell phone doesn't always work there."

I gave Marco a thumbs-up. "Wonderful! Did he say how his meeting went?"

"I didn't speak with him," Martha said. "Peg said he walked in the door, told her he'd fill her in later, and went to take a shower."

"I'll call him at work tomorrow, then. Thanks for letting me know." I put my phone in my purse, feeling extremely relieved. Dave was fine. Nothing bad had happened.

A mosquito was buzzing around my head. I kept swatting it, but the pesky bug kept coming back. I finally felt it land and smacked my forehead to kill it. The pain woke me. I sat up and realized it wasn't a mosquito at all, but my cell phone vibrating on my dresser. Simon, Nikki's white cat, was perched behind it, tail curled around his lean body, watching the phone jiggle across the wood surface. He gave it a push with his paw, then watched as it fell to the carpet.

"Simon!"

He glanced at me in that innocent way all cats have, as though to say, *What? It was headed in that direction, anyway.*

As I scrambled for the phone, I glanced at my clock. Six thirty in the morning. Time for me to get up. I saw Marco's name on my caller ID, which surprised me, since he'd had another late night of surveillance work. I wasn't expecting to hear from him until ten o'clock or later. "Marco?"

"Hey, Sunshine." His voice sounded tired, but also tight. "I hope I didn't wake you."

"Not a problem. What's up?"

"Your gut feeling was right. Something happened last night."

My stomach knotted. My instincts were rarely wrong. "Is it Dave? Is he okay?"

"Dave's fine, but Ken Lipinski is dead."

"What!"

"The cause of death is unknown at this point. A secretary at his office discovered him first thing this morning slumped over his desk. She called an ambulance, but by then he'd been dead for several hours. The autopsy is scheduled for nine o'clock this morning. Then we'll know more."

Unbidden, my mind leaped to a horrible thought that Dave had gotten so angry he'd choked Lipinski. But no, that was impossible. Dave wasn't a violent person. I felt guilty for even thinking it. "Let me know what you hear, okay?"

"Will do." Marco yawned. "I'm going to try to get a few more hours of sleep. I'll talk to you later."

It wasn't the best way to start my day, and it didn't get any better when I found news crews parked all around the square, including in front of Bloomers, taking up valuable customer spaces. Reporters were interviewing passersby while they waited for a press conference that was scheduled for later that morning.

"Abby, wait up!" Connor McKay called.

I pulled my coat tighter against the brisk spring wind as he jogged toward me from the courthouse lawn. He had on a tan zip-front suede jacket, brown pants, and sneakers, and was pulling out a notebook as he arrived breathlessly before me.

"What do you hear about Lipinski?" he asked, his sea-foam green eyes searching mine.

"Who are you working for today, McKay? The *News* or WNCN-TV?"

"Does that matter?" He tried his Prince Charming smile on me, but I merely scowled back. Looking over Connor's shoulder, I spotted a photographer on the opposite side of the street, adjusting his lens, so I moved to let Connor block me from the camera's view.

"So what's the buzz?" he asked. "I'm sure you've been in touch with your former boss, or at least your buddy on the police force."

As if I'd tell Connor anything. But he would never believe I hadn't gotten the news somewhere. "Sorry. All I know is what I heard on the radio."

"Yeah, right." Connor gave me a wink. "Come on, Abby, strictly off the record — what's Dave Hammond's involvement?"

"Why would you think Dave is involved?"

"Rumors, kid. Rumors and innuendos. You know how the gossips are in this town."

"And just what are these rumormongers saying?"

"That the Cody Verse lawsuit could have made Dave a wealthy man, secured his retirement, but the Lip cut him off at the knees in court yesterday, so Dave cut him off for good last night. Personally, I understand how the Lip's actions could make a man snap —"

"Lipinski didn't cut Dave off at the knees, McKay, and Dave certainly didn't kill him. You're fishing now."

"So toss me a tuna, baby. Is it true Dave was incommunicado all evening? That he was the last to see Lipinski alive?"

The last? Dear God, please don't let that be true! "Not true at all."

"So you *have* spoken to him?"

"No! Look, all I know is that Dave Hammond went to see his mom at Whispering Willows after his meeting with Lipinski, then went straight home. So if anything is going to be cut off at the knees, how about those nasty rumors? Attorneys face each other in court every day. They don't kill each other afterward."

"If you say so, sweetheart, it's good enough for me. So what were *you* doing yesterday evening, Freckles, other than missing out on dinner with me?"

"Good-bye, McKay." I unlocked the yellow door and slipped inside, locking it behind me. The photographer appeared to be taking photos of Bloomers, so I stepped back out of sight.

"Was that the reporter who jerked you around last fall?" Lottie asked. She was standing in front of the big bay window where we displayed a continuous rotation of flower arrangements.

"Yes, but don't worry. I'm wise to him. He'll never get anything useful from me again."

"Some news about the Lip, wasn't it?" Lottie said, as I joined her at the window. "What will it do to Andrew's case?"

"Cody Verse will have to hire another

lawyer," I said, "and the judge will have to give the new counsel time to prepare. Dave could be in for weeks, even months, of this media circus."

"Poor Dave," Grace said, and we all sighed in sympathy for him.

We stood at the bay window like lost souls, gazing across the street at the people milling about on the courthouse lawn, waiting for something to happen.

"Time to get on with things, then," Grace said, and we all headed in different directions.

We were busy all morning, until suddenly around noon there was a buzz of activity on the courthouse steps as microphones were set up. The shop emptied out immediately as people rushed across the street to hear the latest news.

"Anyone want to see what's happening?" I asked Grace and Lottie.

"You go ahead, sweetie," Lottie said. "I'm not in any hurry to freeze my toes standing in that cold grass. Are you, Gracie?"

With their blessings, I grabbed my coat and jogged across the street just as Melvin Darnell, the chief prosecuting attorney — or DA, as the lawyers called him — stepped up to the row of microphones. "All's Well

Mel," as he had called himself during his campaign for office, was in his late fifties, well over six feet tall, with thinning blond hair and a wholesome country-farmer appearance that belied his relentless, single-minded nature. He'd tried to pin a murder on me once, an experience I never wanted to repeat.

Today the chief prosecutor had on a gray overcoat with his U.S. flag pin prominently displayed on one lapel. Mel was always looking for a way to keep himself in the public eye so he'd be a shoo-in come the next election. This presented the perfect opportunity for him.

"Thank you all for your patience," he began. "I understand there are a host of rumors and a great deal of speculation circulating about the cause of Mr. Lipinski's death. We pride ourselves on the thoroughness of our investigations, and this is no exception. The facts as we know them are these: Mr. Lipinski died between five and eight o'clock yesterday evening. The preliminary autopsy report suggests that the cause of death was a toxic mix of drugs and alcohol. It is not known whether they were administered by Mr. Lipinski's own hand or someone else's. An investigation is being conducted at this time. We will keep you informed of any further developments."

By Lipinski's own hand *or someone else's?*

At that, reporters began firing questions.

"Were the drugs prescription medications?"

"Is it true he had a weak heart?"

"Was Mr. Lipinski receiving death threats?"

"Do you have any suspects?"

"Is it true Attorney Hammond was the last person to see him alive?"

That question was asked by Connor McKay.

The chief prosecutor held up his hands. "That's all I have at this time, but if you will wait just a moment, Cody Verse's agent, Sam Rhodes, will read a prepared statement."

Darnell motioned for someone to come forward, at which point the bald man in the brown wool coat stepped up to the mics as cameras flashed.

"Cody Verse and Lila Redmond" — Rhodes paused as the crowd cheered — "send their deepest condolences to Mr. Lipinski's family and will do everything in their power to see that the legal proceedings are carried out as Mr. Lipinski intended. Normally, this could take months, but as my client has a new recording contract that must be fulfilled" — more applause — "he has asked the court to allow Mr. Lipinski's associate, Scott Hess, who is already familiar with the case, to take over."

Hands went up and some reporters shouted out questions, but Rhodes waved them down.

"Please wait until I've finished. My client has also asked the court to reconsider his motion to dismiss, and I understand that there will be a status hearing on Friday to determine what will happen next. I'm sure you can all appreciate how distraught my client is, so please respect his privacy in this difficult time. I'll take your questions now."

I listened to the question-answer session for a few minutes, but since there was no new information, I decided to head back to Bloomers. I turned to leave and saw Marco striding toward me. I also noticed more than a few women watching him cross the lawn. He was wearing his black leather jacket, slim blue jeans, and black boots; a strikingly good-looking male, he always turned heads. Amazingly, he didn't seem to notice. His focus was on me.

"Hey, Irish, how's my woman this morning?"

I was oddly pleased by the question, despite its caveman feel. "You just missed the DA telling us what a great job his office does. But all he said about the Lip was that he died between five and eight o'clock last night, and that the preliminary autopsy report suggested the cause of death was a toxic mix of drugs and alcohol. He didn't say what kind of drugs or whether they were legal, but he hinted that there might have been foul play. Have you heard anything?"

"Let's walk back to Bloomers." He put his arm around my shoulders and spoke in a low voice as we strolled. "I checked in with Reilly a few minutes ago," he said, referring to Sergeant Sean Reilly, our police buddy, who had worked with Marco during his stint on the force. "His information matches what you just told me. Reilly also said that the police have Dave down at the station for questioning."

"That's not a good sign, Marco."

"But no reason to panic, either. As far as Reilly knows, the detectives are talking to everyone Lipinski saw yesterday. And at such an early stage they won't rule anyone out, Dave included. This is all part of a routine investigation."

"So you're saying there's nothing to be alarmed about, even if Dave was the last one to see the Lip alive?"

"Where did you hear that?"

"Connor McKay. He stopped me this morning before work."

We checked for traffic, then started across the street. "You didn't tell McKay anything I said to you earlier, did you?" Marco asked.

"I know to be careful around him."

"Good, because I'd hate for reporters to start nosing around in Dave's private life. You know how they can slant a story to make even an innocent person look like a serial killer."

"At least Dave has a good alibi."

"Not really, Abby. His mom has Alzheimer's. She wouldn't be a reliable witness."

"But people at the nursing home could verify that Dave was there. In fact, why don't we drive over there right now and see how many we can find?"

"Not a good idea. Dave will let us know if he needs our help."

But what if Dave didn't know he needed it?

"Listen, babe, I've got to get back to the bar. If I hear anything new I'll call you."

"Okay." I raised up onto my toes to kiss him. "Are we still on for dinner tonight?"

"Yep. Let's make it six."

Perfect. That would give me a small window of time in which to drive to the nursing home and find a few witnesses. Just in case.

CHAPTER SEVEN

Tara showed up after school and immediately installed herself in the coffee-and-tea parlor at a table by the window. She came equipped with her cell phone, a bag of banana chips, a bottle of water, and a pair of her dad's binoculars.

"Anything happening?" I asked, stopping at her table to grab a chip.

"Not yet." She put the binocs down and tapped letters on her cell phone screen.

"If nothing's happening, what are you writing?"

"Nothing happening." She rolled her eyes, stuck a chip in her mouth, and peered through the binocs again.

"Do you expect anything to happen? I mean, given that Cody's attorney just died, I'd think Cody would wait a day or so to do any publicity events out of respect for the man."

"Nope. Cody is going to hold a memorial

signing at seven o'clock this evening."

"A memorial *signing?*"

"That's what I heard." She put down the binoculars and typed another message. I peered over her shoulder to see what she was writing. It said, *Stl nthng hppng.*

"Why is Cody even sticking around town? He won't have to appear at the status hearing, and he has to be bored after living the glam life in LA."

Tara sighed, as if she were the mom and I the dim-witted child. "Aunt Abby, have you noticed the TV cameras following him everywhere? Cody wouldn't get that kind of publicity in LA. Every other person is a star of some kind there. But in his hometown he's a superstar. He'll make the cover of all the teen mags, with headlines like AMERICA'S NEXT HIT SINGLE STAR GOES HOME, and weepy stuff like that."

"How come you know so much about publicity?"

"Reality shows." Tara glanced out the window, then typed in, *City trucks arrvd!!*

Wow. Big news. "Is Grandma coming to stay with you when I lock up this evening?"

"My mom's coming. She wants to go to the signing, too." Tara picked up the binocs and surveyed the activity. "Did you hear that Aunt Jillian is going to take Lila Redmond shopping?"

"It's wishful thinking, Tara."

Tara didn't answer. She was typing, *Tent going up!!*

I went back to my workroom. The excitement was too much for me.

Before locking up for the day, Grace, Lottie, and I said goodbye to Tara and my sister-in-law Kathy, who was working a sudoku puzzle while Tara tweeted, then headed our separate ways. I hurried up the sidewalk to Lincoln and then went two blocks east, past the Daily Grind coffee shop to an out-of-the-way public parking lot — the only place I could find to park that morning. I had forty-five minutes to find a few witnesses and get back to Down the Hatch, but I didn't foresee any difficulties with that.

Whispering Willows Retirement Village consisted of four long, tan brick, one-story buildings that made a large square. In the center was a small garden with benches and a fountain and a few picnic tables. One of the buildings was devoted strictly to Alzheimer's patients, and it was there I headed.

The sign on the door said visiting hours were from one o'clock in the afternoon until seven at night. Entering the lobby through wide glass doors that swooshed open as I approached, I saw a counter at the back of the large reception area where a woman seemed to be helping three people sort out some paperwork. Around the room were clusters of comfy chairs, areas where family members could congregate, plus a beverage table with a coffeemaker, paper cups, condiments, and two pitchers of water.

I stood behind the people at the counter for several minutes, then grew tired of waiting and headed up a long hallway to see if I could find someone else to help me. I passed several offices on the way, but the doors were closed. At the end of the hallway was a recreation center with two rows of reclining chairs facing a big-screen TV, four game tables, a wall of shelves filled with books, and two nurses working with patients. No one looked up to see who had entered. No one stopped me when I left.

I returned to the reception counter, but the same three people were still engaged in conversation with the receptionist. I finally stepped up beside them and said, "Excuse me?"

They all looked around, surprised to see a stranger there.

"I'm sorry to interrupt," I said, "but I just want to ask a couple of quick questions."

"Of course, honey," the receptionist said.

They all smiled at me. And waited.

"In private," I said to her, "if you don't mind."

She stepped around the long maple counter and we moved a short distance away to talk. The woman appeared to be in her early seventies, and was round and plump, with permed white hair, kind brown eyes, and a name tag that said *Nadine.* "How can I help you?"

"I'm doing some investigative work for Attorney David Hammond. I'm sure you know his mother, Mabel, a resident here."

Nadine gazed at me, apparently waiting for more.

"I'm looking for people who saw Dave here yesterday. Any chance you can help me out?"

"Well, let me think where I was yesterday. I work afternoons and evenings three days a week, that being Mondays, Tuesdays, and Wednesdays, and then I'm off on Thursdays — that's when I get my hair done. Thursdays at the beauty salon aren't as busy as other days, lucky for me. And then on Fridays, I attend a stretching class before —"

I didn't need her bio. "So you'll help?"

"Yes," she replied, as though shocked by the interruption.

"Do you remember Attorney Hammond coming in yesterday after five o'clock?"

Nadine blinked at me for several moments, until I started to fear she'd either gone deaf or had a stroke. "No, I can't say that I do."

"Could you check your visitor log? Maybe he came in while you were out of the room."

"We don't keep a visitor log."

"How do you keep track of visitors?"

"We don't. Funny thing, though. A reporter asked me the same question earlier." She pursed her lips. "Now what was his name? Connolly? Conrad? Oh, pickles, I almost had it."

"Connor?"

"That's it. Connor."

Darn that McKay. I wanted to pickle him!

"Connor said he was doing background information for an article on Alzheimer's patients. Now that I think about it, he seemed particularly interested in Mabel Hammond's case, asking how often her family visited and whether she was able to recognize them. As I told him, it's just her son and daughter now, because her husband passed away last year, although I hadn't seen either one of them in the past few days."

Pickles! Connor would be all over that.

101

Why had I let it slip where Dave had gone?

"I told him he could talk to Mabel's family if he wanted to know more," Nadine said. "My, but he had the most gorgeous eyes."

I glanced at my watch. Five twenty. That didn't leave enough time to search for more witnesses. "Thank you for your help, Nadine."

She pointed to my left hand. "I noticed there's no ring on your finger. You should make a play for that Connor. He's a handsome devil."

I agreed with the devil part. I just hoped there wasn't hell to pay for my slip of the tongue.

When I stepped into Down the Hatch, every eye in the place was glued to television sets mounted on the wall at either end of the bar. The local news was on, and given the photo of Lipinski being shown on the screen, I knew the topic.

"Earlier today," one of the news anchors reported, "police removed several bags of evidence from Mr. Lipinski's law office, but they say it will be days before they've had a chance to comb through everything. Meanwhile, at a press conference, Chief Prosecutor Melvin Darnell had this to say:"

The screen switched to a clip of an interview with the DA. "If there is a crime here," he said, striking the podium with his fist, "we will uncover it. If there is a murderer here, we will ferret him or her out. Justice will be served. I promise you that."

Blah, blah, blah. No answers, just more rhetoric.

Marco was behind the bar and didn't realize I'd come in until I tapped him on the shoulder. He turned and saw me. "Hey, Fireball. How's my girl?" Then, putting an arm around me, he went back to listening to the news report, where the anchor was now saying:

"Reporter Charity James caught up with Attorney Lipinksi's secretary, Joan Campbell, as she was leaving police headquarters this afternoon, to ask her about the possibility of foul play."

"No comment," Joan said stiffly, trying to dodge the mics shoved in her face.

"What was Mr. Lipinski doing when you left the office?" Charity asked.

"Having a meeting with Attorney Hammond."

"Do you know what that meeting was about?"

"They were discussing a case."

"Regarding Mr. Lipinski's client, Cody

Verse?" Charity asked, trying to keep up with her. "I would imagine that was quite a heated meeting, considering what happened in court."

"No comment."

"Is it true Mr. Hammond filed a complaint with the bar association against Mr. Lipinski over claims that your employer removed a piece of evidence from Attorney Hammond's file?"

"A complaint was filed, yes."

"Was anyone else in the building when you left for the day?"

"Just the two attorneys, as far as I know," Joan answered.

Charity James turned back to the camera and said dramatically, "A heated meeting. Two angry attorneys. One of them now dead. This is Charity James reporting from in front of the New Chapel police headquarters."

Talk about slanting a story. She'd just tipped it on its side.

Marco ushered me to the last booth and motioned for Gert to bring two beers.

"That was just wrong," I fumed. "Dave's complaint against Lipinski should have been kept quiet. It makes him look like a man with an ax to grind."

104

"Take it easy," Marco said, reaching across the table for my hand. "You know the media loves to pump up a story. The evidence will prove Dave's innocence."

"It better!" I sat back and folded my arms in front of me. What a way to ruin a dinner.

Gert brought our beers, then pulled out her tablet. "Can I get you kids anything to eat?"

"I'll have a turkey burger and sweet potato fries," I said.

"A bowl of chili," Marco said. "Thanks, Gert."

Marco took his bottle and touched it to mine. "To justice for Dave," he said, then took a drink. I let mine sit. I was too upset to swallow.

"I hope Dave will hire legal counsel to represent him," I said, "if there's a problem."

"The last time I spoke with him, he said he's an experienced defense lawyer and if the need arises he can handle it himself."

Yet, as Dave often said, a lawyer who represented himself had a fool for a client.

I finally took a sip of beer, trying to tune out the talking heads on the television, but then I heard the news anchor say, "Now, from Connor McKay, our man-on-the-street reporter, who caught up with local florist Abby Knight —"

What?

I glanced up at the television, saw my face in a box on the screen, and felt my stomach going south. Luckily, Marco was listening to a message on his cell phone.

"You'll never guess what Cody Verse has planned for tonight," I remarked when he shut his phone, hoping to distract him until Connor's piece was over. "A memorial signing. Nothing like taking advantage of a situation to do some self-promotion."

"Did I hear the reporter say your name a moment ago?" Marco asked.

"She's on TV now," Gert told him as she passed our table.

Marco twisted to see the TV, where Connor was saying, "Knight, Attorney David Hammond's former law clerk, stated that Hammond had visited his mother, a patient at Whispering Willows Retirement Village, after his meeting with Lipinski. Yet my investigation turned up no record of Hammond's visit, nor was he seen entering or leaving the building." Connor gazed into the camera, his eyes narrowing. "So where was Attorney Hammond? Connor McKay reporting for WNCN news."

Marco swiveled toward me, a look of disbelief on his face.

I still couldn't believe it myself. Hadn't I said to Lottie, *I'm wise to him. He'll never get anything useful from me again?* When I'm wrong, I'm really, really wrong.

"In other news," the anchor said, "Cody Verse will be holding a short memorial service at seven o'clock this evening on the courthouse lawn in honor of his former attorney."

"Oh, sure. Now Cody's calling it a memorial *service*," I said lamely, trying not to look at Marco.

"Abby, you told me you didn't give McKay any important information."

"I know, Marco. I goofed, and I'm sorrier than you can imagine. I didn't think Dave's visit would be an issue because I figured lots of people saw him there and that the facility would keep a log, too. But they don't. I stopped by this afternoon and talked to the receptionist who was on duty yesterday evening. She didn't remember Dave stopping by, but she didn't even notice when *I* walked in. I went all the way to the back of the building and came out again and had to practically get in her face before she saw me. I'm sure that's what happened to Dave."

Marco stared at me as though he didn't know what to say.

"Look, Marco, someone at the home must have seen Dave. I'll go over there as soon as visiting hours start tomorrow and find witnesses."

"That would be wise. The sooner we can clear up any questions about Dave's movements after his meeting with Lipinski, the better." Marco took out his cell phone and flipped it open. "I'd better let Dave know what happened — if he hasn't already heard."

"Really, Marco, how big a deal can this be? Who watches the local cable news when we can get all the Chicago stations? I never do. I've never seen you have it on here at the bar, either."

"We don't usually, but the staff wants it on so they can keep up with Cody happenings." Marco dialed Dave's number and listened, then shut his phone. "It went to voice mail."

My cell phone vibrated. I checked the screen and saw Grace's name. "Sorry to bother you, dear," she said, "but I thought you should know that you were on the telly just now."

Grace watched the local channel, too? "I saw it. I'll explain everything in the morning."

At that moment the front door opened,

bringing in a gust of chill air and the heavy scent of a sweet, flowery perfume. The same kind of perfume that Marco's mother wore.

"Ah! There you are!" a melodious voice called. "My bambinos. Hiding in the back."

Just what I needed to top off my day — Mama Salvare. I whispered into the phone, "Marco's mom is here, Grace. I have to go."

"*Bon chance,* love," Grace said, and hung up.

As I slipped my phone into my purse, Francesca Salvare swept up to our booth with a dramatic flourish, leaned over to give me a fierce hug, then scooted in beside Marco. She was dressed in a black silk blouse with a yellow, white, and black silk scarf at her neck, black slacks, and black flats, and she carried a black wool coat over her arm.

Francesca reminded me of a fifty-year-old Sophia Loren, all curves and gorgeous dark hair, big dark eyes and olive skin, a generous mouth and a wide smile. Her laugh was also generous, as were her gestures. She gave Marco a loud kiss on the cheek, then reached across to take both of my hands and give them gentle squeezes as she smiled at me. "*Bella,* Abby. It's always good to see you. Such lovely skin and clear eyes. Should you have little ones one day, they will be beautiful, eh, Marco? Even if they do inherit the red hair."

"What's up, *Mama?*" Marco said, putting an Italian accent on her moniker.

She patted his cheek. "Can't I drop in to see my favorite son?"

Marco regarded her steadily without saying a word. Her happy facade dissolved into a miserable sigh. "Your brother wants me to meet Cinnamon's parents."

"What's wrong with that?" Marco asked.

"At dinner."

"You love to cook for people," he said.

"At Cinnamon's parents' house," Francesca said, as though that explained it all.

"That's even better," I said. "You won't have to lift a finger."

Francesca tried to smile. "You're right, of course."

She was humoring me.

"You'll do fine, Mom," Marco said, taking a sip of beer. "It's just one evening."

"It's tomorrow evening, and you're invited, too, Marco." She said it as though it was just punishment for him not agreeing with her.

I was about to snicker when his mom said, "You, too, Abby."

"Why are you balking at their invitation?" Marco asked his mom. "It's your chance to

110

get to know Rafe's future in-laws."

Francesca shrugged dramatically and glanced away.

"Don't you want to meet them before the wedding?" Marco asked.

She muttered something under her breath that sounded very Italian. Marco, apparently, understood her.

"Then you need to tell Rafe your concerns about his decision to marry," he said.

"Marco, you know he doesn't listen to me. He's headstrong, just like his papa was. If he listened, would he be here now? No. He'd have gotten a degree back in Ohio and gone into business with your uncle Benny. All I can do now is hope Raphael comes to his senses before he puts a ring on that child's finger . . . unless you want to talk to your brother?"

"Leave me out of this," Marco said. "I've tried talking to Rafe about other matters, like his career, but he doesn't listen to me, either."

Francesca threw up her hands. "See? That's what I mean. Raphael never listens to anyone."

I noticed Marco trying to catch my eye. He nodded toward his mom and gave me a look that said, *Here's your chance to offer your help.*

I shook my head. Not now! I hadn't prepared how to explain my position to her. But Marco raised his eyebrows in a challenge: *Just do it. I dare you.*

Damn it! He knew I was unable to resist a challenge.

I took a deep breath, then plunged in. "Mrs. Salvare, perhaps I can talk to Rafe —"

CHAPTER EIGHT

Instead of waiting for me to finish, Marco's mom clapped her hands together as though she were about to pray. "Oh, yes, *cara mia!* Bless you! My Raphael thinks the world of you. I know he will listen when you say he shouldn't marry Cinnamon."

"Um, I'm not sure I can go that far, but perhaps I can suggest he get to know Cinnamon before he takes such a big step." And then, hopefully, Rafe would decide on his own that he wasn't ready for marriage.

Francesca's eyes narrowed skeptically. "What do you mean by 'get to know her'?"

"Not in the biblical sense of the word," I assured her. "I mean get to know her by dating her for a while to see if they are compatible. My grandma used to say you have to summer and winter with someone to get to know them."

Francesca thought it over, then nodded. "Your *grandmama* was a very wise woman. I think this is a smart plan." She caught my hands again. "Thank you, *bella,* for doing this for me."

Actually, it was more for me, but if it earned me points with my future mom-in-law, all the better. "No problem."

Gazing at me with gratitude, Francesca said, "Marco, you have chosen well."

Although I felt a bit like a puppy at the animal shelter, I knew this was high praise coming from her. I smiled at her and squeezed her hands. "Thank you, Mrs. Salvare."

I glanced at Marco. With a grin playing at one corner of his mouth, he lifted his bottle of beer in salute to me.

"So you will talk to Raphael before the dinner tomorrow night?" his mom asked.

One day to convince Rafe to drop Cinnamon like a sticky bun? "I can't promise anything, but I'll do my best."

"*Bella,* Abby. I thank you from the bottom of my heart." She fanned her face with her hand. "I feel so much better now. I should go back to Gina's and make a big plate of cannoli to take to the dinner tomorrow. Everyone loves my cannoli." Smiling, she slid out of the booth, blew kisses at us, and swept through the bar like a movie star.

Marco took a swallow of beer, watching

me. "What are you going to say to Rafe?"

"I have no idea."

"Here you go, kids," Gert said moments later, setting plates of food in front of us.

Before I could reach for my sandwich, my cell phone vibrated again. I checked the screen, saw Jillian's name, and switched it to mute. Let voice mail deal with her. I was ravenous. I took a bite of burger and a glob of mustard squeezed out the other end, dripping onto the fingers of my left hand. I put down the sandwich to wipe my fingers — and that reminded me.

"This may not be the best time to mention it, but I thought we were going to celebrate something." I held my hand up and wiggled my fingers.

Marco swallowed a bite. "Not tonight. So is Tara twittering from Bloomers again?"

That was clearly a diversionary tactic. "Yes, she is, and it's called tweeting. Listen, Marco, I'm really sorry about spilling that information to McKay. I hope you're not angry about it. I promise I won't talk to him again."

"I'm not angry. More like shell-shocked, but I know you didn't mean to do it."

"Great." I smiled, hoping he'd offer up a reason for not giving me the ring, but he

115

merely smiled back, then took a bite of his chili.

Hmm. What was the problem? "Did something happen to my ring?"

"No. It's fine," he said a tad too vigorously. "It's just not available yet."

"I don't understand. Yesterday, the jeweler told me it was ready."

"I know, but . . . tomorrow."

"That's what you said yesterday."

"Tomorrow. I promise."

Because we'd be attending Rafe's dinner the next night, Marco left right after our meal so he could put in extra hours on his PI case. He'd reached Dave and explained about my run-in with McKay, then said afterward that Dave hadn't sounded too concerned. He didn't think his alibi would be a problem. I was more determined than ever to make sure it wasn't.

I stayed to finish my beer, then checked my cell phone and saw I had four voice mail messages — one from my mom, one from Lottie, one from my roommate, Nikki, and one from Jillian — all asking if I'd seen myself on the news.

I wasn't in the mood to explain my blunder four times, so I sent one group text message that said, *Saw the news. Will fix. No wor-*

116

ries. I hit SEND, then noticed I had one missed call. *Number blocked,* it said. A salesman, no doubt. Anyone else would have left a message.

When I headed back to Bloomers at seven thirty, a tremendous number of people had gathered on the courthouse lawn in front of a wooden stage that had been erected within the last hour and a half. The television news crews were back, hanging out in their vans while workers set up loudspeakers and tall, powerful lights to illuminate the stage. A group of teenagers lined the curb, acting as lookouts for the limo bringing their fave pop star. Many had on navy sweatshirts with Cody's face stenciled in glow-in-the-dark white, with letters beneath that said: *Code Blue.* I wasn't sure what that signified. I made a mental note to ask Tara.

Speaking of Tara, I could see her face in the window on Bloomers' coffee parlor side, so I waved. Tara ducked down. Obviously waving wasn't cool. My sister-in-law Kathy motioned for me to come in. She met me at the door and opened it so I could step inside.

"Did you know you were on cable news?" Kathy asked.

"Does everyone in town watch that channel?"

"Someone from Whispering Willows must watch, because a woman called here just a few minutes ago asking for you."

"Did you get her name?"

Kathy shook her head. "She wouldn't leave it, but I checked caller ID afterward and the number listed was for Whispering Willows. I asked if she'd like to leave a message and she said no. Just for me to let you know that Dave was telling the truth."

"About visiting his mom?"

Kathy shrugged. "She hung up before I could ask. Maybe she'll call back in the morning."

I hoped so. That could be just the witness we were looking for. "How is our tweeter?"

"She's been tweeting nonstop. I don't know why her thumbs aren't numb."

"Mom!" I heard Tara call. "Cody's limo is driving up! OMG!"

I glanced through the glass door pane and saw the white stretch limousine follow two cops on motorcycles straight across the lawn to the side entrance. They were followed by two black limousines, squad cars, and a screaming mob. At once, security guards poured out of the black cars and joined the cops already stationed there to form a barricade.

Tara came tearing out of the parlor just as

118

three young girls ran up to Bloomers from the outside. They were all dressed in the same costume: hot pink satin baseball jacket and cap, voluminous pink cargo pants, and white sneakers. They squealed at each other and at Tara, and jumped up and down until Tara unlocked the door for them.

"Code Blue!" they cried, high-fiving each other.

"What does 'Code Blue' mean?" I asked.

"That's the title of Cody's hit song," one of the girls replied.

"Is the song about death?" I asked.

Tara gazed at me as though marbles had just rolled out of my ears. "It's about love. Duh."

"That was going to be my second guess."

Tara rolled her eyes for her friends' benefit.

"Excuse me," I said, "but I work long hours here, and when I get home the last thing on my mind is a reality TV show. And if you roll your eyes at me again —"

"We named our rap group after Cody's song," one of Tara's friend interjected, possibly trying to stop an argument. The girl unzipped her pink jacket to show me her white T-shirt with a bluebird painted on the front.

"You formed a rap group?" I glanced at

Kathy in surprise, but she merely shrugged.

"We're the Code Bluebirds," one of Tara's friends answered.

Original. "How long have you been a group?" I asked.

"Since we heard Cody was coming to New Chapel," Tara said.

Kathy added, "They've been rehearsing every spare moment."

"Want to hear us?" one of the girls asked, still bouncing with excitement.

"Not now, Krystal," Tara said. "Mom, can we go across the street now? Please?"

"Let me get my coat," Kathy said. "Want to keep me company, Ab?"

"As delightful as that sounds, Kathy, there's something I have to take care of first. But don't tell me you're a Cody fan, too."

"I like his hit song," Kathy admitted, "but his appeal is mainly to Tara's age group. So come join us when you're done. I could use some adult company."

After they'd gone, I put in a call to Rafe. When his phone went to voice mail, I left a message asking him to get in touch with me as soon as possible. Then I headed across the street to find out why Cody Verse was such a hit.

When Cody took the stage, the roar from

the crowd was deafening. Police stood shoulder to shoulder across the front to prevent fans from rushing him, but two teen girls managed to slip through anyway. They scrambled onstage and bared their midriffs for Cody to sign. I could see his mouth moving as he spoke into an almost invisible microphone that wrapped around the side of his face, but whatever he said was lost in all the screaming. He was wearing a sequined white satin baseball jacket, matching baseball cap, voluminous cobalt blue pants and white sneakers. I understood now where Tara had gotten the look.

Cody scribbled on the girls' stomachs, and then, as police led them offstage, he tried quieting the crowd by giving them the peace sign, then finally strummed a dissonant chord on his electric guitar that bounced off the buildings, boomeranging from one side of the square to the other. He held up his hands, asking for silence.

As the roar faded to a manageable buzz, Cody put his guitar aside and began to yell into his mic as he strutted around the stage. "Thank you, New Chapel! It's great to be home! You guys rock! Wooo-hooo! Yes! You rock!"

"We want Lila!" a male called from the crowd. He was joined by others, until finally

Cody held up his hands.

"I hear you, man. Who wouldn't want Lila?" He turned and motioned to someone.

As the audience clapped, Lila Redmond climbed up the steps at the back and glided across the stage toward him, her glossy black hair rippling in the spotlight. She wore a black furry vest over a colorful, long-sleeved print tunic, with a pair of black leggings and high-heeled gold gladiator sandals. She waved at the crowd and blew kisses, causing more than one male to shout, "I love you, Lila!"

As she stepped to his side, Cody put an arm around her and pulled her tightly against him. "Lila Redmond, everyone."

The audience cheered as Cody and Lila smiled at each other. But oddly, despite the show of teeth, the look that passed between them seemed hostile. In fact, Cody looked ready to bite.

He released her and turned toward his adoring fans. "Lila knows how happy I am to be back in this wonderful town — my hometown — New Chapel, Indiana!"

That brought on a swell of cheering and clapping and shouts of "New Chapel!"

Cody sure knew how to milk it.

"And tomorrow morning we'll appear on WNCN's morning talk show," Cody told the crowd, "so remember to tune in." He laughed at a remark about his relationship with Lila, then said, "Sorry. You'll have to wait for tomorrow to find out. Okay, so I guess we're ready to —"

Lila gave him a nudge. Cody glanced at her and then said, "Oh, right. I forgot to announce that Lila will be starring in a movie called *Beach Belles of Summer,* coming out in July."

Lila used a portable mic to say in her breathless voice, "I hope you'll come see me in it."

That started a new round of applause, along with some wolf whistles.

"Now, then — are you ready to call a code?" Cody shouted, as Lila backed away from the center of the stage and stood just beyond the reach of the lights.

The crowd went wild and began chanting, "Code Blue!" as he picked up his guitar and put the strap around his neck.

"Don't forget," Cody yelled above the racket. "Signed copies of my *Code Blue* CD will be on sale after the performance at the tables set up behind the stage."

He was about to launch into his song when he seemed to remember the whole purpose of the event. As though rushing to get through it, he said, "I'd like to dedicate this evening to the late Ken Lipinski and to the family and friends he left behind."

There was a smattering of applause as people in the crowd glanced at each other as though to say, *Is that why we're here?*

"Cody didn't even mention that Lipinski was his attorney," Kathy said to me.

Cody strummed a few opening bars to whet the audience's appetite. "Here it is — what you've been waiting for — my winning song!" As the crowd hooted and cheered, he began to sing, "My heart belongs only to you. If you leave me, just call a code blue." Then he hit a loud chord and took off in a wild frenzy, shattering the air with his electric guitar, leaping around the stage, setting off nearly every set of female lungs in the audience. He pumped up the volume even higher, until I could feel the vibrations through the soles of my shoes. And although my ears were ringing, I found myself dancing with the crowd, caught in the spirit of the music.

"Can you see why 'Code Blue' won the contest?" Kathy shouted in my ear.

Cody waited until the crowd quieted to introduce his second number, a song he had just written, he announced proudly. And although the girls still screamed as he performed it, and those decibels still stabbed my eardrums, the music was bland and the lyrics repetitive and uninspired. I wondered if the missing ingredient was Andrew.

Before Cody could begin his third number, a figure suddenly leaped onto the back of the stage and grabbed the mic from Lila's hand. Before the cops or guards realized what was happening, the young man yelled, "Cody Verse is a fraud! I wrote the words to 'Code Blue'!"

The cops had managed to scramble onto the stage after him and now grabbed his arms and forced him off the platform. It didn't prevent him from yelling, "You know what you did, Cody. You know you're guilty, man! You can stall the lawsuit all you want, but I won't let you get away with it!"

He struggled but finally gave up as the cops folded him into a squad car.

"Who was that nut?" Kathy asked, as the car took off, lights flashing.

"I'm guessing the nut is Cody Verse's former songwriting partner, Andrew Chapper."

After the interruption, or maybe because of it, Cody ended his performance, which didn't thrill Tara and her group or the other teen girls in the audience. Cody brought his agent onstage, who thanked him for the great performance, then introduced Cody's new attorney, Scott Hess, Ken Lipinski's only associate, who wanted to say a few words in tribute to his late boss.

Hess was a thirtyish, brown-skinned man of slight build and average height who seemed elated to be onstage with Cody. After repeatedly shaking his hand and then Lila's hand, Hess finally took the portable mic from her and proceeded to give an effusive tribute to his deceased employer, whom he credited for hiring him when no one else would.

After he spoke, the mayor took the mic, thanking Cody for generously giving of his time in memory of such an upstanding attorney, while in the background Cody and Lila ducked into their limo and were driven off. As soon as the fans saw them leave, they jumped up and raced for the tables to buy Cody's CD, leaving the mayor talking to rows of empty chairs.

My cell phone vibrated, so I said goodbye to my niece and sister-in-law and answered the call as I headed toward my car.

"Hey, Abby, it's Rafe. I just got your message."

"I can hardly hear you. Where are you?"

"Standing in line to buy a Cody Verse CD."

I turned around and glanced back toward the tables. "On the courthouse lawn?"

"Yeah."

"Can you meet me at my flower shop when you're done?"

"Tonight?"

"Hey, we're both downtown, so why not?"

"Well . . . I guess so. What's up?"

What was I supposed to say? *I have to talk you out of your wedding?* "Oops, got another call. See you in a few, Rafe."

I glanced at my watch. Eight o'clock. Still early. I let myself inside the shop, made a cup of honey-and-lemon tea to warm up, then sat at a table to stare out the window, planning what I was going to say. Rafe showed up fifteen minutes later — with his bride-to-be in tow.

Well, there went that plan. Now I'd have to find a way to speak to Rafe alone.

I let them in, then locked the door behind them. Cinnamon gave me a quick smile and a distracted "Hi," as she glanced around, twirling a lock of neon orange hair that had fallen over one eye. Rafe stood just inside the door, jingling the keys in his pocket as though on edge.

"Come on in," I said. "Anyone want tea?

127

We've got quite a few flavors, but no coffee, unfortunately. Grace is the only one who knows how to run the machine. It's one of those multitaskers that does everything except drink the coffee for you."

"Nothing for me, thanks," Rafe said, still jingling.

"I'll have a double espresso latte with cocoa," Cinnamon said, snapping her chewing gum.

Had she missed that whole bit about me not being able to work the machine? I looked at Rafe, but he was helping Cinnamon with her coat. Although the evening was chilly, she had on a red miniskirt with a short, quilted black coat, bare legs, black flip-flops, and, as her coat came off, a red striped tube top, no bra, was revealed. She eyed me from the right side of her face, as her hair hung like a curtain over the left side, then angled up sharply to the nape of her neck in back.

"No coffee tonight," I said. "Sorry."

She didn't look pleased. "Got any diet soda?"

"Nope. Tea or water."

She gave an unhappy shrug, then began to explore the room. "Water, I guess." She paused beside my mom's tee cart and scrunched up her face in distaste. "Is this, like, the biggest golf tee in the world?"

"Yes. Rafe?"

"Water is fine."

I led the way into the parlor and got two bottles of water from the minifridge under the back counter. Cinnamon was standing in front of the bay window watching the workers take down the stage, her palms flattened against the glass.

Rafe pulled out a chair for her; she parked herself on it, then sat back and crossed her legs, glancing around as though she didn't have a care in the world. Rafe took a seat beside her but sat on the edge, his knees bouncing nervously as he opened his bottle and took a long drink.

"What did you think of Cody's performance?" I asked.

"Totally awesome," Cinnamon said in a matter-of-fact voice.

"So what's up?" he asked me.

"I thought since we were all down here at the same time, we could sit and talk, warm up a while. It's brisk out there." I rubbed my arms and shivered, though I wasn't sure why I felt the need for body language.

Rafe ran his fingers through his wavy dark hair, looking very uncomfortable.

"Hey, Rafe, as long as you're here — a light went out in my workroom and I can't reach the bulb. Would you help me? It'll only take a minute."

"Can't you climb on a stool?" Rafe asked.

"I fall easily. I promise we won't leave your girlfriend alone long."

"Fiancée," she corrected. Popping her gum, she held up her left hand and pointed to it with her right. "Officially."

At first all I saw were her long fingernails decorated with shiny multicolored stars on a black background. Then I noticed the ring on her fourth finger, a small marquise-cut diamond in a gold band etched with tiny chevrons on either side.

She was wearing my engagement ring.

CHAPTER NINE

I grabbed Rafe's arm and practically pushed him ahead of me through the shop and the purple curtain and into the workroom, where I flipped on the overhead light. It simply wasn't possible that Cinnamon and I had the same taste in diamond rings, but I couldn't just accuse Rafe of pilfering my ring for his girlfriend. What if he had indeed picked out the exact same style for his intended? What if he and Marco shared a preference for more than pizza toppings? Was there such a thing as a jewelry gene?

"I don't see a burned-out bulb," Rafe said.

"In the bathroom." I grabbed a fresh bulb from a cabinet, shoved it at him, and pointed toward the rear of the building. I needed to buy some time.

While he was hunting for the dark bulb, I paced from one side of the workroom to the other, trying to figure out how to address the situation without revealing our engagement. As soon as he reappeared with the burned-out bulb, I said, "I hope you didn't put that ring on credit, Rafe, because it looks expensive, and the last thing you need is to start out in debt —"

"I didn't buy the ring." Rafe glanced at the curtain, then said quietly, "Cinnamon found it."

She *found* it? "Would you care to explain?" I asked as I disposed of the bulb.

He combed his fingers through his hair. "I really screwed up, Abby. I was just supposed to pick up a package at Bindstrom's Jewelry for Marco and drop it off at Down the Hatch —"

My ears started to buzz. Marco sent Rafe for *my* ring after telling *me* it was a bad idea?

"— but the clerks at Bindstrom's were busy, and I had to wait so long that I was going to be late for work, so as soon as I had the package, I went straight to Hooters instead of stopping at Marco's bar to drop it off. Then when I gave Cinnamon a ride home, she saw the bag in the glove compartment and assumed it was for her."

Ack! Cinnamon *was* wearing my diamond. Make that *flaunting* my diamond. Unclenching my teeth, I said, "Why would she assume a package in your glove compartment was for her?"

132

"It had Bindstrom's Jewelry written on the gift bag. I'd just asked her to marry me. Why wouldn't she assume it was for her, especially when she saw what was inside?"

He had a point. "Rafe, you had to know who that ring was intended for."

"Yeah, for you. But I figured you and Marco were keeping quiet about it; otherwise he would have told me. What am I going to do, Abby? Marco's waiting for that package."

"He doesn't know yet?"

"I made up some excuse about storing the package in the boss's office safe so it wouldn't get stolen, and then the boss leaving for the day, so I couldn't get back inside to pick it up. I've got to tell him soon, but he's going to kill me when he finds out what happened."

No sympathy there. Rafe wasn't even thinking about how I felt seeing my ring on Cinnamon's finger. At least now I understood why Marco was stalling, even if he didn't know the full extent of it. "So let me get this straight. You haven't told anyone how you got the ring?"

"No."

"And Marco doesn't know Cinnamon has it?"

"No. And I can't ask her to give it back.

She loves that ring. It would break her heart."

Cinnamon's heart was not at the top of my list of concerns. Getting my ring back was, but so was keeping my secret from our parents, which meant from the rest of New Chapel as well.

"I'm so going to pay for this," Rafe moaned, clapping his hands to his head in a gesture worthy of a child of Francesca Salvare's.

"Hush, Rafe. Go check on Cinnamon. She might be getting antsy."

When Rafe slipped through the curtain, I paced some more, and by the time he came back to report that Cinnamon was talking to a girlfriend on her phone, I'd made a decision.

"Okay, Rafe, if you want my help, you'll need to look me in the eye and swear that what I tell you next won't go any further than this room."

He slid onto a stool, then put his hand over his heart. "I swear."

"Fine. Here it is. Your brother and I decided not to tell anyone about our engagement until we made a decision about when, where, and how we're going to be married. I was going to keep the ring hidden for the time being. Neither of us wants to rush anything. Marriage is an important step in a person's life and rushing things wouldn't be smart. Do you understand what I'm saying?"

I knew by his expression my message had gone over his head.

"That's fine if you guys want to wait," Rafe said, "but what am I going to do? I can't even imagine what my mom will say when she sees Cinnamon wearing that ring tomorrow night. She knows I can't pay for it. I can't tell Cinnamon I made a mistake because I'd have to explain why, and I just promised you I wouldn't tell anyone. Besides, she'd want me to buy one just as nice, and, well" — he rested his chin on his hand, looking like a dejected little boy — "my credit card limit is five hundred dollars."

"So you're stuck with a diamond you can't afford, and I'm stuck watching your fiancée wear my ring." I sat down on the stool beside him and, with a sigh, rested my chin in my hand, too. After a moment, I said, "You're going to have to confess to Marco tomorrow."

"Can't you tell him? You can explain it better. If I tell him, he'll probably kick me out of his apartment and ship me back to Ohio with Mom."

Well, that would solve things, wouldn't it?

Maybe I'd be better off letting that scenario play out . . . except that Cinnamon would probably keep the ring as her consolation prize.

"Please, Abby. I'll do anything. Sweep your flower shop every night for a year. Shovel snow in the winter. Give your yellow door a fresh coat of paint. Anything you ask."

Anything? Hmm. Maybe there was a way out that would work for both of us.

I hopped off the stool and peered through the curtain to be sure Cinnamon wasn't in the vicinity. "Okay, Rafe, here's the deal. I'll tell your brother about the mixup — and I'll even make him promise not to send you back to Ohio — on two conditions."

"Okay," he said eagerly.

"First one is that you cannot get married for six months."

Rafe's mouth fell open. "Six months? Why?"

"It'll give you time to save up for a ring, and it'll also give you the opportunity to get to know Cinnamon. You don't really know her all that well, Rafe."

"We can get to know each other after we're married."

"Not a good plan. What if you discover you don't like her?"

"Abby, for Pete's sake, you saw her. What's not to like?"

"You're seeing what's on the surface, Rafe, not what's beneath. You may not like what you find under there. Have you ever lifted up a rock? Okay, maybe that isn't a good comparison. All I'm asking is for you to wait half a year. If you're really in love with her, it won't make a bit of difference. You'll still see her whenever you can and —"

"But she's already decided on a wedding dress. Her mom is busy planning the showers and reception, and her dad has a hall picked out."

Cinnamon was living my nightmare. "They'll hold, Rafe. Trust me."

Rafe shook his head. "I can't do it, Abby. What if she tells me it's now or never?"

"Then she definitely isn't the right girl for you. Come on, Rafe, you just said you'd do anything for me."

He looked miserable. "I wasn't expecting you to ask that."

"So you'd rather take your chances with Marco and your mom?"

Rafe stared at me for a long moment, a debate going on behind his eyes. I was starting to fear that he would decide to chuck everything and elope with Cinnamon when finally he sighed, his shoulders drooping.

137

"Fine. I'll wait six months."

"Good for you!" I clapped him on the shoulder. "You're doing the right thing, Rafe."

"But I'll need time to figure out how to tell Cinnamon."

"As long as it's within reason."

"What's the other condition?"

"Tell Cinnamon you have to return the ring because it's not the one you selected for her."

"But she likes that ring."

"Say she'll like the real one more, then take her to Bindstrom's and have her guess which one. She can pick out the design she likes, and then you can pay for it on the installment plan."

"What if she says she's fine with that one?"

"Then tell her it's a fake. A mock-up. A synthetic stone. And just a reminder here. As you pointed out, your mom will see Cinnamon wearing the ring tomorrow night unless you get it back beforehand. Now we'd better get out there before she comes looking for you."

I needn't have worried. Cinnamon was busy texting. She didn't even glance up when we sat down at the table. Rafe picked up his water bottle and took another drink. I merely stared at my ring sparkling on her finger.

As soon as I got to my apartment that night, I texted Marco: CALL WHEN U CAN.

He phoned half an hour later. "Is everything okay?"

"Fine. I just wanted to tell you what happened this evening."

He sighed. "Next time would you include that in your message? I thought something had happened to you."

"Sorry. Let's start over. Do you have a few minutes?"

"Go ahead. If I have to be on the move, I'll hang up and call you back later."

Those stakeouts could be tedious. I'd gone on a few with Marco and hadn't enjoyed them one bit. "I'll make this quick, then. Rafe's going to postpone his wedding."

"No kidding? That's unbelievable, Abby. How did you convince him?"

"I'll let you in on the secret right after you tell me when you were going to inform me that Rafe had my ring."

I could almost hear the sheepishness in his voice when he asked, "How did you find out?"

"A matter of deduction. I saw Cinnamon wearing it."

"Wearing *your* ring? Are you telling me that Rafe gave it to his *girlfriend?*"

"Make that his official fiancée . . . who discovered the box in Rafe's glove compartment and thought it was for her. She loves the ring, by the way."

Marco was muttering something under his breath that I wasn't even sure was in English.

"The important thing is," I said, "that Rafe agreed to postpone the wedding for six months and get my ring back. In exchange, you won't tell your mom about the ring mixup and you won't send Rafe back to Ohio."

There was a long moment of silence. Then Marco sighed. "I can't *believe* Rafe didn't tell me. I'm truly sorry about the ring, Sunshine. I had the jeweler put the ring box inside a bigger box and put it in a bag so Rafe wouldn't figure out what it was."

"Rafe didn't figure it out. Cinnamon did. But that's okay. You'll make it up to me."

His voice turned husky, making me feel warm and tingly all over. "I will definitely make it up to you. Tomorrow night, after the dinner, it'll be just you and me and two glasses of champagne. I'll get the ring from Rafe, and we'll take it from there."

Some paybacks were good things.

■ ■ ■ ■

On Thursday morning, I woke up early so I'd have time to catch Cody's interview on the local cable channel before work. By seven o'clock I'd already fed Simon half a can of tuna and had my breakfast of peanut butter and honey on whole wheat toast. I poured the last of the coffee into my mug, then turned on the TV, adjusting the volume so I wouldn't disturb Nikki. She worked the late shift at the hospital as an X-ray technician and got testy when awakened too early.

I curled up on the sofa, and Simon immediately jumped up beside me, standing on my knees and rubbing his nose against my chin.

"Phew, Simon. Fish breath." I moved him beside me, where he began to claw at the space between the cushions.

Since the morning show always began with local news and weather, I indulged Simon by digging out the plastic straw he'd lost and tossing it across the room. He chased it, batting it around the floor as though it was a mouse, then carried it back for another round.

Six rounds later, the morning show host, Guy Louden, a slender fiftysomething man dressed in a stylish suit, announced that his special guests that morning would be Cody Verse and Lila Redmond. For a small television station, landing two celebrities was a major coup. However, when Cody finally came onto the set, it was not with Lila. He was with his new attorney, Scott Hess, who wore a sophisticated three-piece, gray pinstriped suit, a pale purple shirt, and a purple tie.

Cody had chosen the casual route, wearing black leather pants so tight I was surprised he could move, and a hooded black vest over a cobalt blue T-shirt that showed off his enormous biceps, triceps, chest, and neck, making me suspect he had a personal trainer — or took steroids. His eyes were rimmed with black kohl liner, his fingernails sported shiny black polish, his wrists were wrapped in leather strips, and he had a two-day growth of beard, a look some women found sexy. I'd always preferred a hint of five-o'clock shadow on a clean, smooth face — coincidentally, that was Marco's look.

After welcoming Cody onto the show and shaking hands with Hess, Louden said to Cody, "How does it feel to return home a hero?"

"It feels awesome," Cody gushed. Then, in an effort to appear humble, he added,

"But I wouldn't call myself a hero, Guy."

"To your many fans here in New Chapel, you are," Louden said. "I know you gave a brief performance on the courthouse lawn, but do you have any plans for a local concert?"

Before Cody could reply, Scott Hess leaned over to whisper in his ear. Cody flattened his hair down over his forehead as he listened, then said to Louden, "Something is in the works, but I can't talk about it yet."

Louden, known for his pointed questions, said, "Lila Redmond was scheduled to be on the show with you, and obviously she isn't here. I can't help wondering, Cody, why you feel the need to have an attorney present instead."

Hess immediately jumped in. "As you know, Guy, my client is involved in a lawsuit, and because of the emotional and traumatic turn of events yesterday, I felt the need to protect him."

Protect him from what?

Louden said, "Do these emotional events have anything to do with Lila not being here? A rift in your relationship, perhaps?"

Cody sat forward, lacing and unlacing his fingers as he said earnestly, "No, man. Lila and me, we're doing great. Couldn't be better."

"So the reason she's not here is . . . ?" Louden waited for Cody to supply the rest, but it was Hess who jumped in.

"I felt it was in my client's best interests."

What was that supposed to mean? That it wasn't in Cody's best interests to share the spotlight with Lila?

"Let's discuss the reason you're in town," Louden said. "I think our viewers are aware of the lawsuit filed against you, but let me review the allegations. And just to make it easier, I'll refer to the plaintiff in the case by his name, Andrew Chapper. All right, here we go. First, Andrew Chapper is alleging that he cowrote the song 'Code Blue,' which won the contest on the TV show *America's Next Hit Single*. Second —"

"That's a total lie, by the way," Hess declared earnestly.

Louden paused, looking annoyed by the interruption. "Second, Andrew alleges he was not given credit for the song or allowed to share in the subsequent royalties. Third, and maybe most importantly, Andrew is seeking damages in the amount of five million dollars and punitive damages in the sum of fifty million dollars. That's a lot of money, Cody. Are you prepared to pay if the ruling goes against you?"

Before Cody could open his mouth, Hess

said, "It's simply not going to happen, Guy. As lead counsel, I have every confidence that we will prove the plaintiff's claim to be frivolous. My client won't have to pay a dime."

I could tell Louden was losing patience with Hess. He wanted Cody to talk. That was who the audience had tuned in to see. "Cody, I'm sure the death of your attorney, the late Kenneth Lipinski, came as quite a shock to you."

"Yeah, man. I'm still not over the shock," Cody said, trying, but not quite succeeding, to arrange his expression to look like he was suffering. He seemed jumpy, one of his knees bouncing up and down, as though he couldn't wait to stand up. He sure lacked the spark that I'd seen when he was onstage.

"Do you think Attorney Lipinski's death will impact this lawsuit in any way?" Louden asked him. "Are you worried about losing?"

Hess immediately answered, "It won't have any effect whatsoever. I'm prepared to mount a strong defense and win the suit. All this, Guy, is just one more case of someone being jealous of a star's fame and trying to capitalize on it."

"Are you claiming there's no merit to the allegations at all?" Louden asked Cody.

"None whatsoever," Hess answered for

145

him. "These types of suits are a dime a dozen."

"Let's allow Cody a chance to respond," Louden said pointedly. "Cody, you're claiming Andrew Chapper had no hand in composing the song that won the contest. Are you referring strictly to the melody or does that include the lyrics?"

At that moment Simon launched himself onto my lap, startling me. I grabbed the straw he'd left by my feet and tossed it, then leaned forward to hear Cody's answer.

"It's the whole song, Guy," he said, his knee bouncing faster. "Look, Andy and I were best friends in high school. Sure, we had jam sessions with our guitars and wrote a few tunes together, but 'Code Blue' is one hundred percent mine."

Louden glanced at his notes. "As I understand it, the two of you performed as Chapper and Verse for several years, up until the time you left to attend UCLA. That's more than just jam sessions — wouldn't you agree?"

Hess was practically shredding his lower lip in an effort not to jump in with answers. He finally unwrapped a stick of gum and stuck it in his mouth, chomping furiously on it.

Cody crossed one ankle over his other

knee and sat back, trying to give the impression of nonchalance, but his fingers tapped out a rapid staccato on the side of his shoe. "We had a few gigs, sure."

Louden let it ride. "What is your relationship with Andrew now? Have you seen him since you've been back in town? Spoken with him?"

Simon scratched my pant leg, trying to get my attention. I picked the straw up and tossed it again just as Cody answered. "No, man. I tried to talk to him, but Andy's not the same guy. He's changed. It's all about money with him now."

"I understand Andrew had to drop out of college to help care for his grandparents," Louden said. "Do you think that might have motivated him to file this lawsuit?"

"Sure. He needs money. He'll take it any way he can get it, even by making up ridiculous claims." Cody looked straight at the camera, which zoomed in close enough to catch the perspiration on his face. "Listen, buddy, just come see me, all right? I'll lend you money for school. You don't need to sue me, man. Maybe I can even find a job for you."

How magnanimous. I wished I could call Marco and tell him to watch the show, so we could dis Cody together, but if Marco

147

had worked late, he'd want to sleep in.

Louden said to Cody, "Just so you know, our producer has invited Andrew to appear on our show tomorrow morning to present his side. We're waiting to hear from his attorney as to whether that will happen."

Cody shrugged. "Hey, it's a free country. Andy can do what he wants. Give him his fifteen minutes of fame." He shrugged again, or maybe it was a nervous twitch.

Simon scratched my pant leg. I tossed the straw, but this time he ignored it and just stared up at me with big sad eyes. "What, Simon?"

He meowed a tiny kitten meow in an effort to seem pitiable.

"Just a minute," I said, and reached to scratch under his chin. He ducked my hand.

"I couldn't help but notice your security guards," Louden said as the camera switched to a shot of two behemoths standing off to the side. I recognized them as the men who'd tried to stop me as I crossed the courthouse lawn Monday morning. "Do you typically have bodyguards with you?"

"I do now, man," Cody said. "I mean, someone knocked off my lawyer. I could be next. I'm not taking any chances."

"Whoa," Louden said, sitting back as though stunned. "All we've been told is that the police are investigating Mr. Lipinski's death. Are you saying he was the victim of foul play?"

"Don't answer that," Hess said to Cody.

Ignoring his attorney's advice, Cody said, "That's what I'm telling you, man."

"Let me get this straight," Louden said, clearly realizing the potential for a major scoop. "You believe your former attorney was murdered, and now you fear for your own life?"

"Totally." Cody thought about it again, then nodded. "Yep, totally."

"Do you believe Mr. Lipinski's death is connected to your lawsuit?"

"Totally, man." Cody shrugged off Hess's hand on his arm.

"Then if you believe that Kenneth Lipinski's death came as a result of defending your lawsuit," Louden said, "and you also believe the killer might be after you, it sounds as though you're accusing Andrew Chapper of murder."

Scott Hess jumped to his feet and walked toward the camera, waving his hands to block the view. "That's it. This interview is over."

CHAPTER TEN

I muted the volume and sat back, trying to process what I'd just witnessed. Why was Cody so certain the Lip had been murdered? And why had he seemed to agree with Louden's outrageous suggestion about Andrew being the killer? If Andrew had been that incensed over the lawsuit, wouldn't he have gone after Cody rather than the Lip? Did Cody really fear for his life or had he said it merely to create more media buzz?

At that moment, NEWS BULLETIN flashed on the screen in giant letters, so I unmuted the volume as the local news anchor came on.

"We're interrupting *The Morning Show* to bring you this special bulletin. New Chapel police have just announced that attorney Kenneth Lipinski's death is now being deemed a homicide. The police spokesperson would not comment on potential suspects but said they are seeking witnesses who passed by the Lipinski law office building after five o'clock Monday evening and noticed a vehicle in the lot or a person or persons entering or leaving the building. Anyone with information should contact the New Chapel police at the number shown on your screen. To repeat, Attorney Kenneth Lipinski's death has been ruled a homicide —"

I turned off the TV. Cody must have known beforehand that Lipinski had been murdered. He wouldn't be stupid enough to make such bold declarations without some basis. His new attorney must have gotten word before they set foot on that stage.

Now newshounds from all over the country would descend on New Chapel, hungry for a juicy story of murder with a celebrity tie-in. The local reporters were probably already calling Dave and Andrew for comments.

Simon meowed again, then trotted toward the kitchen, pausing to wait for me to follow. He led me to his food dish, where he posed prettily, tail wrapped around his body, giving me his *I'm starving* gaze. He tried this ploy at least once a week, hoping I'd forget that I'd already fed him.

"Not going to happen, big boy," I told him.

Simon stalked off, white tail whipping back and forth to show his annoyance. My cell phone began to ring, so I grabbed it, checked the screen, and saw Dave's name.

"Abby, I hope I didn't wake you. I wanted to have a chat before I head to my office."

"You didn't wake me. I was just watching TV and saw the news bulletin about Lipinski. Have the reporters started calling you yet?"

"No, I'm still at home. What bulletin is that?"

"His death was officially ruled a homicide."

"Well, I'm sorry to hear that. I had my beefs with the man, but no one deserves to have his life taken away. At least now I see why I've been called for another interview."

"The detectives want to see you *again?*"

"Yes, ma'am, at nine o'clock this morning. Martha's going to have to reschedule all my appointments. I have no idea how long I'll be there."

"I'm so sorry about letting it slip to that weasel of a reporter that you went to see your mom. I had no idea he would seize that and run with it. I hope it's not my fault that you're being called back in."

"Forget it, Abby. The information was bound to come out — just maybe not so soon."

"Are you the only one the detectives are talking to?"

"I don't know. Darnell is running things, and he's being tight-lipped at this point. I suspect he's looking for a motive, and because of what happened in court with my exhibit, it would appear I have one."

"You can't be the only attorney who's ever had evidence stolen by Lipinski."

"Definitely not. His thievery is legendary."

"What happened at your meeting with Lipinski?"

"Not much. We sat down in his office, I confronted him about the exhibit, he refused to admit he took it, so I told him I wouldn't withdraw my complaint. Then I left. That was the extent of it. The secretary who had been at the desk outside his office was gone by that time, as was the receptionist in the lobby. I didn't see anyone in the parking lot."

"Just out of curiosity, did Lipinski drink anything during your meeting?"

"He had a drink on his desk, but he didn't touch it while I was there. The reason I called, Abby, is that Marco mentioned that you visited Whispering Willows yesterday.

Did I understand correctly that you spoke with Nadine and she didn't remember seeing me Monday evening?"

"Right. But I had to get in her face before she noticed me, so I'm not surprised that she didn't see you."

"Nadine can be oblivious."

"Not a good trait in a receptionist. I'm still shocked that there's no guest log."

"It would certainly help strengthen my alibi," Dave said. "Would you be able to go back to Whispering Willows to find witnesses who saw me there Monday evening?"

"Of course I will, and by the way, someone did see you. A woman from Whispering Willows called yesterday evening while I was out, but didn't leave her name. I'll find her and hopefully others who can testify on your behalf."

"Thanks. That'll be great. At this point I don't know if I'll need alibi witnesses, but I'll feel better knowing I have them. Martha will fax over a copy of a photo of me so you can show it around. Some of the residents know me by sight but may not connect the name. Visiting hours start at ten a.m."

"I'm really glad I can help, Dave. And by the way, prepare yourself for calls from reporters about some remarks Cody Verse made on the morning cable TV show."

"I'll alert Martha. What did Cody say?"

"He said someone knocked off his lawyer and might be coming after him next. He hinted that Andrew killed Lipinski."

"You've got to be kidding."

"Cody wouldn't elaborate, and when the host tried to get him to be more specific, his new attorney jumped in and ended the interview."

Dave sighed. "I'll have to give Andrew and his grandparents a call. I'm sure they'll be upset when they hear about it."

"This probably isn't important, but Cody also said he hired bodyguards to protect him from the killer, yet I happen to know he came into town with those guards. He couldn't have known in advance that he needed that kind of protection."

"Now you sound like a lawyer. Maybe you should have applied yourself more in law school."

I couldn't suppress my shudder. Nine horrendous months of struggle had left a permanent bad taste in my mouth. "It wasn't a good fit, Dave. Even if I had been able to pass the tests, you know how I feel about injustice. I wouldn't have been able to stand jerks like the Lip. I'd be arrested for contempt within an hour of setting foot in the courtroom."

"A good lawyer has to ignore the jerks, Abby, and stay focused on his client's needs, which is what I must do now. My focus is to make sure Cody's allegations don't hurt Andrew's chances of getting a fair judgment. I'd better call Andrew right now and remind him not to give any statements so he doesn't do anything to damage his case."

"Oh. Then you didn't hear about Andrew's stunt last night."

"Andrew's stunt?"

"He jumped onstage during Cody's performance and called him a fraud. The cops had to take him away. I'm amazed you didn't get a phone call."

"They must have released him. I'd better have a serious talk with that boy."

"You'll probably get a call from WNCN, too. They want Andrew to appear tomorrow for a rebuttal."

"Do you have any *good* news for me today?"

"I will after my trip to Whispering Willows. Good luck with your interview."

Mornings at Bloomers always start with cups of Grace's gourmet brew and a discussion of current events as we prepare for the day. So over several cups of coffee, we analyzed the report on Lipinski's death,

Cody's evening performance on the courthouse lawn, his dull performance on television, and my conversation with Dave and subsequent quest to find witnesses. Grace informed us that Lipinski's funeral had been scheduled for Friday evening, and Lottie reported that Cody had agreed to judge a local talent competition, which her sons planned to enter. I was betting Tara and her Code Bluebird girlfriends would, too.

Once we'd thoroughly dissected those topics, the ladies prepared to open the shop for the day while I headed to the workroom to start on the orders that had come in overnight. At nine thirty, Lottie breezed in to replenish our supply of flowers in the display case up front. She was followed by Grace, who carried a tray with a steaming pot of green tea.

"Isn't it odd that no orders have come in for Lipinski's funeral?" I asked, taking a cup of tea from her.

"Perhaps they'll come in later," Grace said. "The obituary was in the paper only this morning."

"Or maybe the Lip was such a jackass, no one wants to buy him flowers even as a send-off," Lottie cracked as she opened the door to one of our big walk-in coolers.

Grace cleared her throat loud enough to

bring us to a standstill. "I believe we should bear in mind the words of Henri Frederic Amiel," she began, "who said, 'Life is short and we have never too much time for gladdening the hearts of those who are traveling the dark journey with us. Oh, be swift to love; make haste to be kind.' "

At that moment, the bell over the door jingled, so, giving Lottie a pointed glance, Grace glided out of the workroom to see to the customer.

Lottie waited a beat, then said, "Was she scolding me?"

"I think so," I said.

"She must sit up at night memorizing those quotes." Lottie noticed what I was making and came closer for a look.

"Do you like it?" I asked. "It's a dinner arrangement for Donna, the owner of A Window on the Square. She wanted something contemporary. This vase is perfect, isn't it?"

I turned the arrangement so Lottie could see the clear glass vase we'd received in a shipment only the day before. It was ten inches tall, a foot long, and ultra narrow, reminding me of a fish that looked wide from the side, but was a mere sliver in the water from the front.

To fill the vase, I'd combined bold yellow

tulips with a variety of bright orange canna lily called Wyoming. I cut all the stems short so they'd stand just a few inches above the top of the vase, then added water. The result was a striking, modern arrangement in which the glass container was integral to the design.

"You've really developed an eye, sweetie," Lottie said. "That's a beauty."

Her praise gave me a warm glow, something I'd never experienced in law school. Before coming to Bloomers I'd felt like such a failure. How lucky I was to have found a place where I fit.

I wrapped the arrangement to protect it from the elements, set it carefully inside a box, and put sturdy pieces of foam padding around it to keep it from tipping. As I was tagging it, Marco called.

"Hey, you're awake!" I said. "I have lots of news for you."

"Hey, yourself, Fireball," he answered in a sleepy, sexy voice. "I just stepped out of the shower and wanted to tell you about the dream I had — about *you.*"

He spoke in a deep, caressing tone that caused tingles to heat up my body in all sorts of interesting places, making me forget all about my news. I lowered my voice so Lottie and Grace wouldn't hear me. "A good dream?"

"Wish I had you here to show you how good," he murmured, making my blood pulse with desire.

I sighed, imagining Marco with a towel around his torso, his hair still wet, his skin gleaming, his eyes beckoning . . . "Wish I had time to run over there."

"We have to make time."

"Tell me about it."

"I'd rather show you," he said huskily.

I had to sit down and fan my face. "That makes two of us."

"These late-night surveillances have put a crimp in our love life."

"What are you doing today at noon?"

There was a pause, and then he said softly, "Waiting for you."

Hearing that, I was ready to drop everything and make a dash for my car. But common sense prevailed. "Noon it is, Salvare. I'm heading over to Whispering Willows on a mission for Dave right now, but I'll be back in plenty of time."

At that, Marco was all business. "What kind of mission?"

"To find witnesses who saw Dave visiting his mom Monday." I didn't remind him that I'd wanted to do that from the beginning. No need to spoil the mood. "But let me

160

start at the beginning. First of all, this morning on live TV, Cody Verse insinuated that Andrew killed the Lip."

"Based on what evidence?"

"No evidence. That's just what Cody believes. He also thinks Andrew may come after him next. His appearance was followed by a news bulletin announcing that investigators have ruled Lipinski's death a homicide."

"I'm not surprised. A guy like Lipinski doesn't kill himself. But I wonder what led the detectives to that conclusion."

"Me, too, because Dave was called in for another interview."

"Damn," Marco muttered.

"So Dave asked if I would find witnesses for him, hence my trip to the nursing home."

"Once the DA gets the official toxicology report, I'm sure Dave will be exonerated, but if finding witnesses helps in the short run, so much the better. I'll give Reilly a call to see if he's heard anything about the investigation he can share with us."

"Sounds like a plan."

"See you around noon, then?"

"You'd better believe it."

I stowed my cell phone in my purse along with copies of Dave's photo that Martha had faxed over. I was about to put on my coat when the bell over the door jingled up front and I heard Lottie say, "Abby's busy, Jillian. Wait. Don't go back there. Let me see if —"

The curtain parted and Jillian swept into the workroom, fairly bursting with excitement. Lottie pulled back one side of the curtain long enough to give me a *Sorry, there was no stopping her* shrug, then quickly dropped it again.

Jillian was dressed, as always, très chic. Her long copper-colored hair was pulled into a ponytail, held in place by a shiny yellow scrunchie, and she wore a fashionable bright orange belted trench coat, white jeans, and a pair of gold espadrilles with a wedge heel. She opened an enormous gold tote bag and began to pull garments from it.

"Wait till you see what I picked out for La Lila."

"Seriously, Jillian — you're not choosing Lila's clothing for her."

She seemed stunned that I would say that. "Yes, I am."

"You actually met with Lila Redmond to discuss her clothes?"

"Yes."

I studied my cousin for a long moment,

162

but her gaze never wavered. "When?"

"This morning in her hotel room."

I donned my peacoat and put the strap of my bag over my shoulder. "How did you get an interview with her?"

Jillian thought a moment, then shrugged. "I think she got tired of saying no."

Just because Jillian had pestered Lila until she agreed to see her didn't mean that Lila had agreed to let Jillian dress her. That was just my cousin being obtuse. But I held my tongue.

"Take a look at these frocks," she said.

"Sorry, Jill, but the fashion show will have to wait. I'm on my way to deliver flowers."

She peered into the box. "You're delivering that?"

"Yes, *that.* What's wrong with it?"

"It's so — linear." She began to fold up the dresses. "Where are you taking it?"

I picked up the box and started toward the curtain. "To A Window on the Square. And FYI, the arrangement is supposed to be linear to play up the shape of the vase."

"If you're going to A Window on the Square," she said, sliding the dresses into her tote, "I'll go with you. I love that shop. Then we can come back here and look at the dresses."

"I have an appointment afterward. Sorry."

163

I went through the curtain with my cousin on my heels.

"What kind of appointment? Doctor? Manicure? Hair? . . . I hope."

She hoped? I glanced at my reflection in a wall mirror as I passed through the shop. A straight bob is a straight bob. I didn't have time to fuss over it. "I have to interview some people at Whispering Willows."

I paused to let Lottie know I was leaving. She was on the phone at the cash counter taking an order and nodded as I waved good-bye.

Jillian opened the door for me and followed me outside. "Isn't Whispering Willows where they care for people with Alzheimer's?"

I nodded to a pair of ladies I recognized as regulars in our coffee-and-tea parlor as we started up Franklin toward Lincoln Avenue. "One of their facilities is."

Jillian sucked air through her teeth. "The interview is for Grace, isn't it? I knew something was wrong with her. She always forgets to give you my messages, and I've heard the memory is the first thing to go. Oh, Abby, what will you do without her?"

"There's nothing wrong with Grace. Her memory is fine." I knew that because Grace never forgot to give me Jillian's messages. I

164

just conveniently forgot to reply to them.

"Then why are you going?"

"To find people who remember seeing Dave Hammond there on Monday evening."

"Abby, think about *where* you're going. Do you really expect them to remember?"

"I hope so."

"Then I'll ride along so I can show you the dresses while we're in the car. I really need your opinion. You're not a fashionista, but you do have an eye for color."

She was nothing if not persistent. "I don't think you should go to Whispering Willows."

"Why? Crotchety old people love me."

"And there's a perfect example of why you shouldn't go. You can't call them crotchety."

"I'm not going to say that in front of them. *Sheesh.* Give me a little credit, Abs."

At that moment, Connor McKay came around the corner and headed up Franklin toward us. "Don't say anything to him," I warned my cousin.

"Not even hello?"

"Nothing."

She pretended to lock her lips.

Connor flashed his winning smile as he stopped before us. "Morning, ladies."

I gave him a cool nod. Jillian smiled with her lips pressed together. We separated to go around him, but he merely pivoted and began to walk with us.

"Do I sense a chill in the air?" he asked.

I didn't reply, and Jillian shrugged.

"So," Connor said, undeterred, "did you catch Cody on Louden's show today?"

"No comment," Jillian said, then glanced over at me for approval. To remind her, I made a quick motion of locking my lips.

"I see you have an official spokesperson now," Connor said to me with a smile.

When I still didn't respond, he said, "So how's your former boss doing now that the police have ruled the Lip's death a homicide? Is he nervous?"

That brought me to a stop. "If you think I'm going to talk to you after what you did, think again, weasel."

"Wow," he said with an embarrassed laugh. "What did I do to deserve that?"

"You want to know? Okay, first, during the press conference on the courthouse lawn, you asked the DA if Dave Hammond was the last person to see the Lip alive, obviously trying to stir things up. Then you engineered your television piece to make it sound like Dave lied about stopping at Whispering Willows after leaving Lipinski's office, knowing that would make him look guilty."

Jillian nodded enthusiastically.

"I'm a reporter," Connor said. "I chase down tips. It wasn't meant as a personal affront."

"Right. As if you weren't aware that Dave's my friend."

Jillian clucked her tongue at him.

"I checked with people at the home, Abby," Connor retorted. "He wasn't seen there on Monday evening."

"I'll bet you checked," I muttered.

Connor seemed affronted. "You don't believe me?"

Jillian said, "Is that why we're going out to Whisp— ?" She saw my eyes narrow into angry slits and immediately pressed her lips together, giving me a wide-eyed, innocent look.

"Is that why you're going out *where?*" Connor asked, turning his vivid eyes on her. "Whispering Willows?"

She glanced at me for help.

"Jillian," I said in an exasperated voice, "I told you we were going to A Window on the Square." I lifted the box in my arms. "We have a delivery to make. Let's go."

Still steaming, I walked away, with Jillian hurrying to catch up. Fortunately, Connor was smart enough to realize he wasn't going to get anywhere, and he didn't follow.

"Do you think he caught on?" Jillian

whispered, as we stopped at the intersection.

I glanced back to see Connor heading toward the courthouse. "Who knows? At least he doesn't seem interested. But the next time I tell you not to say anything, don't say anything!"

While we waited for the light to change, I looked to my right and saw workers installing decorative black wrought-iron balconies under the second floor windows of a narrow old building that housed Pete's Diner. It was a cozy place that served up a standard fare of Greek and American food. But the plain tan front had been painted a deep red with black trim and gold embellishments, and a new sign said COMEDOR DE PEDRO in gold script with the image of a bullfighter on either end. I had a feeling it was another sign of Cody-mania.

"What happened to Pete's Diner?" Jillian asked. "And who is Pedro?"

"*Pedro* is Spanish for *Peter*," I explained, as we detoured up Lincoln Avenue half a block to the east to check it out. "And Comedor de Pedro means 'Peter's dining room.' "

"Comedor de Pedro. How classy and Continental."

"It's still Pete's Diner, Jillian." I pointed

to items on the menu posted near the door. "Moussaka, lamb, roasted potatoes, gyros, lemon rice soup . . . it's the same menu."

She pulled out a chair at one of the black wrought-iron bistro tables now arranged in front and sat in it. "I feel just like I'm in Madrid."

"You've never been to Madrid."

"Magazines, Abby. Who needs to travel when we have magazines? Oh, look across the street! A French coffee shop. Ooh-la-la!"

I turned to see. Overnight, the Daily Grind had become La Journalier Routine. Underneath the new name, apparently for those who didn't read French, was the word COFFEEHOUSE.

"If I remember my French," Jillian said, "La Journalier Routine means —"

"The Daily Grind." Imagine that.

While Jillian sorted through a rack of sale items at A Window on the Square, I delivered the arrangement, picked up a check in payment, then tried to slip out of the shop without my cousin. Unfortunately, she has excellent peripheral vision.

However, my misfortune of being stuck with my chatterbox cousin took a surprisingly fortunate turn. Not only does Jillian

169

have superior side vision, she also has nearly perfect recall for gossip. And on our way to Whispering Willows, she recounted gossip she'd heard from Lila Redmond that morning that shed a whole new light on the Lip's death.

Chapter Eleven

"What do you think?" Jillian asked, after displaying the last of four knit dresses she'd unrolled from her giant tote bag.

"I like them, but it's what Lila likes that counts, right?" I answered, playing along with her fantasy. "Are you sure that's her style?"

"She'll love them. Do you know she travels with her own personal secretary? Can you imagine what a help that is? I'm thinking of hiring one for myself."

Jillian pulled out her cell phone and recorded a voice message. "Note to self. Interview secretaries."

"Why do you need a secretary? You're not that busy."

"I will be once word gets out that I dressed La Lila. I'm thinking of having a frank discussion with her about her hair. Lila brings her personal stylist with her — Marietta — but the woman gives her the same hairdo over and over — like yours does. Except this morning, Lila was so upset, she sent her stylist scuttling from the room before she could finish silkifying."

" 'Silkifying' isn't a word. And what's wrong with having the same hairdo every day?"

Jillian patted my shoulder. "Don't feel bad, Abs. Not everyone is blessed with imagination. But getting back to Lila's story, what happened was, she thought she was going to appear with Cody on TV, but then she got a call saying he was going on with his lawyer instead. Can you imagine all the work it takes to prepare for a TV appearance — and then to have your boyfriend decide to go on without you? That's a deal breaker in my book. I hope she dumps him."

"To be fair, Jillian, it wasn't all Cody's fault. His lawyer advised him to do that."

"No, he didn't. If his lawyer said that, then he's a liar."

"And you know this because . . . ?"

"Because I heard Lila's end of the phone conversation. Cody shut her out to punish her."

"For what?"

Jillian's smile was secretive. "You're not going to believe it."

"Try me."

172

"Well," she said, pushing up her coat sleeves and turning to face me, "it seems the Lip made advances."

"What kind of advances?"

"You know. He put the moves on Lila. Propositioned her, in fact."

"No way."

"Abby, I swear it's true. I heard Lila defending herself to Cody. She said that the Lip cornered her when she was alone and propositioned her. When she turned him down, he groped her and tried to kiss her."

"When did this happen?"

"Okay. Here's the story. They first met Lipinski last Friday when he flew out to LA to see them. Then on Saturday, they all flew back here together, and his chauffeur picked them up and took them to his house on Lake Michigan to relax until the hearing. That's when it happened, but Cody didn't find out until after they left court on Monday. Lipinski went back to the hotel with them to have lunch and discuss strategy, but Lila refused to join them. Afterward, Cody and Lila had a huge argument about it and that's when she told him why she didn't want to be anywhere near the Lip.

"And really, who could blame her? The man was revolting. Greasy hair, phony smile, lizardlike eyes . . . Anyway, Lila

173

regrets telling Cody because he's been nasty to her ever since. He's acting like it's her fault. Apparently he's insanely jealous. Lila can't even look at another guy without him having a tantrum. Seriously, can you believe Cody treating Lila Redmond like that? He has to be up-the-wall and over-the-top crazy. He was a nobody six months ago and now he's acting like *she's* the nobody."

Jillian sat back with a huff. "Poor thing. To suffer the Lip's groping and then to be punished for it! You'd think Cody would've fired Lipinski instead of taking it out on his girlfriend."

"Fire his attorney right before the hearing?" I asked. "Cody wouldn't be that crazy."

I pulled into the nursing home's parking lot and turned off the motor, still sorting out Jillian's startling news about the Lip. Accosting his client's girlfriend was sinking to new lows. But why would Cody punish Lila? Why take it out on the victim and let Lipinski off the hook? Had Cody decided that firing his lawyer and starting from scratch with a new law firm would cost him too much time and money?

On the other hand, maybe he hadn't let the Lip off the hook. If Cody was jealous enough to punish Lila Redmond for Lipinski's misconduct, what was to stop Cody from taking his fury out on Lipinski, too?

That was where my thought process ran into a wall. How could a celebrity, even a minor one, have slipped into Lipinski's building without being seen? Cody's fans trailed him everywhere.

"Are you coming?" Jillian asked, tapping on my window. "The elder-geezers won't keep forever."

When we entered Whispering Willows, Nadine was the only one in the reception area; she was talking on the phone behind the counter. She glanced up, saw me, and waved us over.

"Remember," I whispered to Jillian, "don't use any negative words. They're *seniors*."

"We already had this conversation, Abby."

"Right, and then you called them elder-geezers."

Putting her hand over the phone, Nadine said to us, "You have to sign in." She slid a guest book toward me. "The rules have changed."

By her tightly pursed lips, I had the distinct impression she was blaming me. I signed for both Jillian and myself, and indicated that we were there to visit Mrs. Hammond.

"She's in the recreation center," Nadine whispered.

Perfect.

"What do you want me to do?" Jillian asked, as I led her up the long hallway.

"Smile and don't say a word."

"Seriously, Abby, I want to help."

Could I trust my cousin to be tactful and not insult any of the patients? It sure would make the job go faster with both of us working the room.

I took copies of Dave's photo out of my purse. "If you really want to help me, take one of these photos and start with the people on the right. Go around the room, show the photo, and ask if they know who Dave Hammond is. If the answer is yes, ask whether they saw him here Monday when he came to see his mom. Got that?"

She nodded.

One of the nursing staff came up to me with a friendly smile. "May I help you?" The little silver tag on her green uniform said *Kim.*

"We're here to visit Mabel Hammond," I said.

"Mrs. Hammond is sitting by the window on the far side of the room. And you are?"

"Abby Knight, and this is Jillian Knight-Osborne. We're friends of the family."

176

"You're sisters?" Kim asked.

"Cousins," Jillian corrected. "First cousins, to be exact. Our fathers are brothers, giving us the same genetic —"

I nudged her. Kim didn't want our life stories, but she was eyeing the papers in our hands, so I turned mine so she could see the top photo. "If you don't mind, Kim, we'd like to show a photo of Attorney Hammond to your residents. I'm here at Dave's request to find someone who can verify that he was visiting his mom Monday evening."

"That'll be fine," Kim said, "but you should know that two detectives were here yesterday afternoon for the same reason."

The detectives were hot on Dave's trail. "Would you mind telling me what you told them?"

"I told them I don't work evenings — my shift is over at four o'clock — and that I can't imagine Dave having anything to do with a murder."

"Do you know if anyone else here reported seeing Dave Monday?" I asked.

"No one that I spoke with did, but you're welcome to talk to the patients in the center."

"Great," I said. "What about those still in their rooms?"

Kim gave me a sad smile. "I'm afraid their conditions are such that they wouldn't be of any help. But if you need anything else, I'll be just up the hallway."

"Thank you." I glanced at Jillian, who was gazing into the open doorway of a patient's room. "Let's go, Jill."

She was oddly silent as we walked toward the back of the building. "Are you okay?" I asked her.

She glanced at me, blinking back a mist of tears. "I don't want to get Alzheimer's, Abby."

"I know."

"I don't want you to get it, either."

A rare admission. "Thank you, Jillian."

"Someone has to remember what an adorable child I was."

I took my notebook out of my purse, tore off a sheet, and handed it to her. "Write down the names of everyone who claims to have seen Dave."

"I am so on it." She pulled out a pen and headed for four people sitting at a card table and working a jigsaw puzzle.

I watched her talk to the group for a few moments, and when no one jumped up and ran screaming from the room or otherwise seemed upset by her questions, I started on the left side. I paused to chat with Dave's mom, but sadly it wasn't a good day for her. It had been a year since I'd last seen her, but she didn't remember me at all. How heartbreaking it had to be for Dave. Was that perhaps the cause of his distress?

Fifteen minutes later, Jillian and I met at the back of the room. "Any luck?" I asked.

"No." Jillian handed me the blank paper.

"Me neither." With a frustrated sigh, I tucked the paper and notebook back into my purse and surveyed the patients. Where was the woman who had called me?

"Can we leave now?" Jillian asked. "I feel like I need to cry, and if I cry, I'll ruin my makeup, and if I ruin my makeup, I'll have to —"

"I get it, Jillian."

As we walked down the hallway toward the front door, we met Kim coming out of a patient's room. "How did you do?" she asked.

"We struck out," I told her. "But maybe you can help me with something. I got a call at work yesterday evening from a woman who said she was from Whispering Willows, but I couldn't find her today. I assumed she was a patient, but she could be one of the staff. Do you have any idea who it might be?"

"What time was the call?" Kim asked.

I thought back to my conversation with Kathy. "Around seven thirty."

"Then it wouldn't have been a visitor," Kim said. "You can talk to Lauren. She's a nurse here, too. You'll find her in the break room right now, first door on your right, behind the reception area. And also there's Kelly, a student nurse. She works three evenings a week, and I believe she was on duty Monday evening. I'll give you her number. I'm sure she won't mind if you call."

"Thanks, Kim. I appreciate your help," I said.

"Dave's a good man," Kim said, scribbling Kelly's number on the back of a business card. "He's always been kind to his mom and to all of us. I hope you find your witness."

We stopped at the break room to see Lauren, only to find that someone had beat us to it.

"Connor McKay!" Jillian hissed.

I dragged her away from the doorway before Connor could glance around. "Let's get out of here," I whispered, and we fled across the lobby and out the door.

"I guess he caught on after all," Jillian said breathlessly.

180

■ ■ ■ ■

At fifteen minutes after eleven o'clock, I dropped Jillian at her car in the public lot, then pulled into an empty space to phone Dave with my report. When his cell phone went straight to voice mail, I called his office next, but Martha said he hadn't yet returned from the police station.

"It's been over two hours, Abby," she said. "What could they possibly be asking him that they haven't asked before?"

"They're probably going over his previous statement, trying to see if he changes it. Is Dave still determined to represent himself?"

"Of course. The stubborn mule. I know it's not my place to advise Dave, but I told him he'd better consult with another attorney, because there's no way Melvin Darnell will be fair with him. Darnell doesn't like to lose cases because he thinks it costs him votes come election time, but he's lost more than a few cases to Dave, which makes Dave his enemy."

"So much for our justice system," I said.

"Sorry, Abby. I know I'm preaching to the choir. Do you want me to have Dave get in touch with you when he comes back?"

"Yes, please. Have you figured out what's

been bugging him lately? Why he hasn't been himself?"

"He doesn't want to talk about it and told me to quit asking, but I think I have it figured out. He's been very forgetful lately, probably because of all the pressure he's been under, but I think he's afraid that he's developing Alzheimer's disease, too."

"Oh, no! Poor Dave. I'm sure it's just the stress he's been under."

"Me, too. Don't tell him I told you."

I assured Martha I would keep mum, then sat in my car thinking about Dave's situation. Naturally, because of his mother, he would fear Alzheimer's. Add to that the stress of his job, the pressure of winning Andrew's case, and now the probability of Darnell's singling him out as a prime suspect, and it was no wonder he was depressed.

But was that, indeed, what was going on? Was Darnell focusing solely on Dave and instructing his detectives to ignore other leads? It would help immensely to know for sure. I'd love to be able to tell Dave he wasn't being targeted. What a relief it would be for him.

Wait! I knew someone who could provide illumination: Deputy Prosecutor Greg "I'm Too Sexy for My Court" Morgan. I glanced at my watch. Forty-five minutes before my date with Marco. If Lottie and Grace could cover for me a little while longer, I'd have time for a quick chat with my courthouse snitch.

I stopped at Bloomers to see how the ladies were doing and learned that business had been slow and that Grace had broken her eyeglasses.

"Silly old things," Grace said, holding up the broken lenses, "but I'm blind as a bat without them. The optician agreed to squeeze me in if I can be there by twelve thirty, if you don't mind taking a later lunch, dear."

For a second, all I could do was blink at her, as my romantic interlude with Marco went up in smoke. But seeing her squinting hopefully at me, I couldn't very well put her off.

"Sure, Grace. I have to make a quick trip over to the courthouse to see Greg Morgan about the Lipinski case first, if you don't mind."

"Of course," Grace said.

"Has there been any word from Dave yet?" Lottie asked.

"Martha said he's still being interviewed. And unfortunately I wasn't able to find anyone to corroborate his alibi at the nursing home."

"What about the woman who called here for you?" Lottie asked.

"I couldn't find her," I said. "Jillian and I asked all around. Then Connor McKay showed up, so we left. And by the way, if McKay should come by here, please don't tell him anything. I let it slip about Dave visiting his mom and now I think I've set loose a monster."

"You haven't had a very good morning, have you, sweetie?" Lottie asked.

I shook my head. The afternoon didn't look promising, either. "Did any orders come in while I was out?"

"Two," Lottie said. "I took care of them and finished the ones still waiting on the spindle."

Only two. The day was sliding downhill fast.

Grace tapped the face of her watch. "If you want to be back in time for me to make my appointment, Abby, you'd best step lively. Tempus fugit."

"You're right," I said, and headed toward the curtain. "I need a bouquet of flowers to bring with me. What do we have over-stocked?"

"Gerberas. Are they for the Courthouse Hottie?" Lottie asked.

184

Courthouse Hottie was one of Lottie's nicknames for Greg Morgan. She used to believe Morgan was the perfect man for me, until she realized that Morgan believed he was, too. Perfect, that is. "Only if he tells me where the investigation is going."

"You still think the DA's gonna try to pin the Lip's death on Dave?" Lottie asked.

"I don't know. I just want to make sure we're ready if he does."

Lottie turned back to Grace. "What was that you said about a tempest?"

"Tempus fugit," Grace said. "It's a Latin phrase meaning time flies."

"Time flies," Lottie repeated as she hurried into the workroom behind me and got on the computer. A few minutes later she said, "I've got one!" and cackled with delight as she hurried back through the curtain.

As I wrapped the bouquet in cellophane, I heard her say to Grace, "Yep, time flies, all right. As Groucho Marx once said, 'Time flies like an arrow; fruit flies like a banana.' "

"Whatever are you talking about, Lottie? Bananas don't fly."

"Come on, Gracie," Lottie beseeched. "Think about it. What do fruit flies like to eat?"

"Fruit."

185

"Yeah, and what are bananas? Fruit. So fruit flies like bananas. Get it? That's *my* quote about time."

Stony silence. That wasn't good.

I tiptoed to the curtain and peered out just as Grace assumed her lecture pose. "As Benjamin Franklin said, 'Dost thou love life? Then do not squander time, for that is the stuff life is made of.' " Then she straightened her shoulders, lifted her chin, and glided into the tea parlor.

I jumped back as Lottie pushed the curtain aside and came into the workroom muttering, "She just had to have the last word, didn't she?"

"You know Grace doesn't like to be topped."

"She doesn't like to be stumped, either." At that, Lottie broke into a grin. "And I did stump her, didn't I?"

The temperature had risen over the course of the morning, and with the sun out, I decided to skip the coat. I was warm enough in a scoop-necked, long-sleeved yellow T-shirt with a black-and-white tweed cropped jacket and black jeans. So, with the bouquet in hand, I dashed across the street to the courthouse's back entrance, where I was stopped by a guard I hadn't seen before.

He was around forty years old, had a bald pate complemented by a thicket of black hair growing from each nostril, a big gut that hung over his belt, skinny legs, and a haughty attitude. I showed him my driver's license, but he was more focused on my open jacket and the hint of cleavage that my scoop-neck T-shirt revealed.

"State your business," he said.

I pulled my jacket together with my free hand and held out the bouquet so he had something else to ogle. "I'm here to deliver flowers."

"To who?"

To *who*. I knew I shouldn't — I tried to hold back — but when he repeated his question and aimed it at my chest, it just came out. "It's to *whom*, and the whom is Deputy Prosecutor Greg Morgan."

"Well, then, Miss Manners," he said frostily, "remove your jacket, give me the flowers, then step through the scanner."

I handed him the bouquet. "I didn't have to remove my jacket last time."

"It's not my fault if the other guard didn't follow orders." He pointed to my chest. "Off."

I glanced around to see if there were witnesses, which there weren't, so I gave up trying to argue, slipped off my jacket and

187

handed it through to him. He nearly dropped it because his gaze was now glued to the front of my T-shirt, one of the banes of being well-endowed.

Giving him a glare, which he didn't see, I stepped through the scanner and snatched my belongings out of his hot paws. "And just so you know, Miss Manners teaches etiquette, not grammar."

"So maybe you should sign up for her class so you'll know it ain't polite to correct a person's grammar."

Touché.

Turning my back on the guard, I donned the jacket, then hurried toward the wide staircase with the bouquet. I took the first flight at a run, stopped to catch my breath, then went slower on the second flight so I'd have it together by the time I entered the prosecutors' suite. There I encountered the head secretary, a skinny woman in her thirties who favored thin, blue-tinted glasses and talked in a high, nasal voice. She was hard at work on her computer, filling in the next day's calendar.

"I have a floral delivery for Attorney Morgan," I announced.

"Leave it on my desk," she said without looking over at me.

"Is Mr. Morgan here? I'd like to deliver it

myself."

She heaved a sigh, then reached for the phone. "I'll check. Who shall I say is calling?"

She knew who I was. I'd delivered flowers there before. "Abby Knight, in the flesh, not calling."

"Abby Knight is here in the flesh," she twanged tonelessly. She listened a moment, then replaced the receiver and turned back to her computer. "Mr. Morgan has an appointment in fifteen minutes. You'll have to be quick."

As I headed toward Morgan's office, my phone beeped. I glanced at the screen. Marco was texting. He'd have to wait.

CHAPTER TWELVE

The deputy prosecutor's tiny office seemed to be made out of manila file folders. They were piled in large stacks on a row of filing cabinets against the wall, spilled out of cartons on the floor, and swallowed up the desk. The room was so full of files that Morgan was lost in their midst.

He was sitting on an old wooden swivel chair in front of a beat-up oak desk, his carefully manicured fingernails, neat haircut, charcoal pin-striped Hugo Boss suit, and gray silk tie at odds with the scarred wood floors, cracked plaster walls, and mildewy corners of the high ceiling. As always, Morgan looked model perfect, his chestnut brown hair glistening with blond highlights, his baby blue eyes framed by long, dark lashes, and his smile too white to be natural.

He saw me and got a big grin on his face, his chair creaking as he rose. "Abby! What a pleasant surprise. And you brought flowers for me. Gee, it's not even my birthday." He held out his hands and wiggled his fingers impatiently, as if to say, *Gimme, gimme!*

Greg Morgan was the only man I knew who would assume that a bouquet of daisies was for him. If I didn't need his help, I wouldn't give them to him, just for his smugness. At least I could pretend I'd brought them for another reason. Lucky for me, Nikki was dating Morgan.

"I had to come over, anyway, so I thought as long as I was here, I'd drop these by in case you wanted to surprise Nikki tonight."

"Oh." His smiled faded as he sat down.

Now I'd embarrassed him. I would have to come up with something to make him happy again. The easiest way was to stroke his gigantic ego, so I put the bouquet on his desk and said, "By the way, Nikki said you two had a great time Sunday. She really enjoyed herself."

He gazed at me skeptically. "She did? Are you sure?"

Not the reaction I'd hoped for. What *had* Nikki told me about Sunday? I knew they went somewhere, but nothing was coming to mind. I pushed on, hoping he wouldn't press me for details. "Did you hear that Dave Hammond had to go back for another interview with your boss this morning? Actually, he might still be there."

Morgan suddenly became busy, shuffling through some papers so he wouldn't have to meet my eyes. "No, I hadn't heard."

Yeah, right. I knew how courthouse staffers gossiped. I sat down on the straight-backed wooden chair opposite his desk so we'd be at eye level. It was harder for him to ignore me that way. "Yep, a second interview. What's that about? Darnell can't possibly believe Dave had a hand in Lipinski's death. Can he?"

At that, Morgan leaned back and clasped his hands behind his head, the old chair's springs groaning beneath him. "Up to your old tricks, I see."

"What tricks? I was just wondering what Darnell was thinking."

Morgan smiled at me, saying nothing. He wasn't making this easy.

"So how *is* the Lipinski investigation coming?" I asked. "Any new leads?"

"Abby," he said with a sigh, sitting up, "I wish I could satisfy your curiosity, but you know the rules."

"Rules are meant to be broken, Greg, at least where friends are concerned. It's not like you haven't helped me before."

Morgan put his finger to his lips to warn

192

me to be quiet, then got up and closed his door. "The last time I helped you," he said, returning to his desk, "I got called on the carpet for it."

"Oh! I didn't know."

"Yeah, well, I can't let it happen again. I'd like to keep my job."

"Look, I'm sorry I got you into hot water, but I also don't want to see Dave Hammond railroaded. You know that could happen, Greg, so stop rolling your eyes. Surely you can tell me whether Dave is the prime suspect. No harm in that, is there?"

Morgan picked up his pen and examined the tip. "Can't do it."

I leaned closer, staring at him so he'd feel uncomfortable. "You know what I think? That if Darnell wasn't targeting Dave, you'd tell me not to be concerned, that he was just one of many people being interviewed."

Morgan narrowed his eyes at me. "Either change subjects or this conversation is over."

"Okay, how's this? Have you ever been up against Ken Lipinski in court?"

"Yes," he answered warily.

"Then you know how he operated. There's a reason the man was disliked by most of the attorneys in town. Lipinski played dirty. He was a scoundrel. Dave can't be the only lawyer who's ever had important documents taken during a hearing where the Lip was involved, so he shouldn't be the only suspect. If the detectives would just talk to the lawyers in Lipinski's other cases —"

"He didn't have any other active cases, Abby."

"What? That's not possible. The guy was always busy."

"He cleared his calendar so he could focus on Cody Verse's defense."

I sat there, stunned.

"So if there's nothing else —" Morgan said.

"He cleared his entire court calendar?"

"Yes. And why wouldn't he? This case was catapulting him into the national spotlight. Who could blame him for dumping the lesser cases?"

Not Morgan, apparently. But knocking out all the lawyers Lipinski might have been up against meant that Dave needed more than just reliable alibi witnesses; he also needed to find a suspect with as strong a motive as he had. Hmm. An idea was forming.

Morgan set his briefcase on the desk and began to put files inside, then paused. "So Nikki actually enjoyed the college basketball game?"

That's what they'd done on Sunday! "She

194

said it was incredible, Greg." As in, incredibly boring. As in, she'd rather scrub toilets.

He shook his head. "She had a strange way of showing it."

"Forget about Nikki for the moment, Greg. Lipinski's death was ruled a homicide, right?"

"That's common knowledge."

"I remember Darnell saying that Lipinski died from a lethal mix of drugs and alcohol. Wouldn't that make it a premeditated murder?"

Morgan paused, as if about to say something, then continued to stuff the briefcase.

"Let's say you just agreed with me. Then Dave would've had to take the drug or drugs to the meeting and get it into the Lip's drink without him noticing. So, besides the fact that Dave wouldn't have done anything like that, he'd also have had to have access to the drugs involved, right? So why don't you have the cops search his home and office? I guarantee they won't find any evidence, because *he didn't do it!*"

Pressing his lips together, Morgan snapped his briefcase shut. He wasn't going to give an inch. What could I do?

"Wait, Greg," I said, as he started toward the door. "I won't ask you anything else. Just please, as Nikki's best friend, give me one little hint as to why Dave is a suspect."

He stopped, his back to me, his hand on the doorknob. Then he turned and said very quietly, "Do you know what prescription medicines Dave's mother is taking?"

I shook my head.

"Then maybe you should find out."

I hurried out of the courthouse carrying a knot in my stomach the size of a basketball. How could I have forgotten about Dave's mom? If Mrs. Hammond was taking the same medicine that was used to kill the Lip, Dave was in hot water for sure.

I made my way through the multitudes gathered on the lawn, detouring around an area where blankets had been spread for picnic lunches as though it were summer already. All around me people huddled together, cupping warm drinks or shivering as they ate sandwiches, hoping to see their idols or to be caught on television by one of the roving reporters. On the wide front steps of the courthouse, mimes, jugglers, and unicycle riders took turns performing, while teens swarmed over the cement planters, watching for the limo convoy, obviously ditching school.

My phone beeped again as I made my way toward Franklin, reminding me I had unanswered text messages. Before checking them, I called Martha to see if she'd heard from Dave, but got a recording. The texts were from Marco, and the last one sounded urgent: CALL ASAP.

I hit speed dial number two, and Marco answered on the second ring. "Sunshine, where are you?"

"On my way back to Bloomers. Why? What's going on?"

"I hate like hell to do this, but I'm going to have to postpone our lunch date. I wanted to catch you before you headed this way. Rafe is in trouble."

"What kind of trouble?"

"I don't know yet. He said he needed to see me before he left for work, and he'd explain when I got there. He's at Down the Hatch, so I'm on my way there now."

"Why couldn't he tell you over the phone?"

"Who knows? This is Rafe we're dealing with."

Why did I get the feeling my ring was involved? "I hope he's okay."

"Me, too. And I'm sorry about our date, babe. *Really* sorry. You don't know how sorry."

"You'll make it up to me," I said, waiting at the curb for cars to pass.

197

"I keep trying."

"Is that why you texted me earlier?"

"No, I hadn't heard from you and wondered if you'd had any luck at the nursing home."

"I couldn't find one alibi witness, Marco, not even the woman who'd called me at the shop. I haven't talked to all of the staff yet, so I'm not giving up hope. The detectives have already been there, by the way. I stopped by Greg Morgan's office to see what I could pry out of him, and he said that the Cody Verse lawsuit was the only active case the Lip had, which makes it less likely that other lawyers are suspects. Then Greg hinted that Mrs. Hammond's medicine was the same as the drug they found in Lipinski's stomach, which would be another reason the detectives are focusing on Dave. And they're definitely focusing on him, Marco."

"The tox report must have come in," he said as I dashed across the street. "I asked Reilly about that earlier, and he seemed to think they wouldn't get it for another week."

"If they didn't have it, why would Morgan tell me I should find out what meds Mrs. Hammond was taking?"

"He must have felt that would help you somehow, possibly just to let you know what the detectives' working theory is."

"It's time to start another working theory, Marco, such as Cody Verse as the killer."

"Any evidence to back that up?"

"No, but how about a jealousy motive?"

I stopped outside Bloomers to recount Jillian's tale about the Lip making moves on Lila, and Cody's reaction to it. "You know how jealousy can make people do crazy things, and it sounded to me like Cody was pretty far out there when it came to being jealous. Maybe he slipped a drug into Lipinski's drink to make him sick, not intending to kill him."

"Okay, let's test your theory. First, Cody would need access to the drug that was used."

"He's a celebrity, Marco. I don't think that would be a problem. He probably has a personal physician on call."

"Fair enough. Second, he'd have to have the opportunity. Was anything mentioned about him being at Lipinski's office that afternoon?"

"Don't know."

"Then we need to find out. Third, do you trust that Jillian's gossip is accurate as to what transpired between Lila and Lipinski, and then later between Cody and Lila?"

"Jillian definitely has an ear for gossip, but

you're right — she also has a tendency to exaggerate."

"Fourth," Marco said, "someone in an irate state would be more likely to punch, shoot, stab, or strangle. Adding a drug into a drink is a deliberate act that takes forethought and quite a bit of cunning."

"True, but I still think Cody should be investigated."

"I'm not discounting your theory, only putting it to the test. And if we're talking about a jealousy motive, Scott Hess should be on the suspect list."

Several people were passing by, laughing, so I wasn't sure I'd heard correctly. "Did you say Hess?" I whispered.

"Yep. Just about everyone in town knew who the Lip was, but I'm betting few knew who Hess was. His name was never on the billboards with Lipinski's, or mentioned in any radio or TV spots that I've ever heard. Maybe Hess was tired of working in his boss's shadow. Maybe he wanted some of the fame, too.

"I'm sure Hess was aware of the dispute over Dave's missing evidence," Marco continued, "and no doubt he knew Dave had filed a complaint against his boss. Hess could have easily learned that Dave was coming in for a meeting at the end of the day. Maybe he saw a window of opportunity. All he had to do was stay in the building after the staff went home, or use his key to come back later. If Hess had access to any prescription medicines, he'd have the means, motive, *and* opportunity."

"One hitch, Marco. How would Hess know that Dave's meeting would last past office hours?"

"He'd have to stick around the office to see."

I glanced up when Lottie opened the door. "Sorry to butt in, sweetie," she said, "but Grace needs to leave for her appointment and the parlor is jammed."

I signaled that I'd be right in. "Marco, I need to go."

"And I'm just pulling up behind the bar. I'll get back to you later."

I spent the next half hour refilling coffee cups, brewing tea, and serving Grace's cranberry scones. The parlor crowd was just starting to thin out when I got a phone call from Dave.

"Dave, thank goodness you called," I whispered, so customers couldn't overhear. "I was concerned. What happened at your interview? Why were you there so long?"

"Take it easy, Abby. I wasn't questioned

the whole time. I did a lot of sitting and waiting."

"Tell me what happened."

"It's obvious Darnell is trying to build a case against me. Thus far, he's basing it on three things. That no one at Whispering Willows can corroborate my alibi. That there is bad blood between Lipinski and me over the missing exhibit. And that I was allegedly the last one to see him alive. All he needs is the means and he'll have his case."

"Is he checking into the meds your mom is taking?"

"Yes. How did you know that?"

"Greg Morgan let it slip. Did he tell you what drugs were in Lipinski's stomach?"

"He wouldn't tell me anything, but I seriously doubt whether the tox report is back. It's too soon. He's speculating. He's got Martha under the lamp now, and I imagine my wife will be called next. He may call you, too."

Me? The one who let it slip to McKay about Dave going to visit his mom? I'd have to try to stay under the radar. "Thanks for the heads-up, Dave."

"It's time for us to be proactive, Abby. If the detectives won't look into other leads, then we'll have to do it for them. Do you want to talk to Marco about the two of you working for me? I'd call Marco myself, but I need to get back to the office. My afternoon appointments will be coming in soon and no one is there to greet them."

"Of course we'll work for you. And just briefly, I did talk to people at Whispering Willows today, but I couldn't find anyone who saw you. I couldn't even find the person who phoned me. I haven't interviewed all of the staff yet, but I will. A reporter showed up, so I left."

"Good move. Whatever you do, Abby, try to keep the press out of this. If they find out that the police are investigating me as the prime suspect, my business could disappear overnight. I'd be a pariah."

"I won't let that happen, Dave." Even if I had to stuff McKay's mouth with stockings and handcuff him inside my closet. On second thought, Nikki's closet.

"Can we meet at my office tomorrow morning?" Dave asked. "Say around eight thirty?"

"We'll be there."

I hung up, then dashed across the room with the coffeepot to pour refills for the remaining customers. A few minutes later, Grace walked in wearing a pair of glasses with frames that were thin rectangles of black with ornate silver corners.

"Sweet," I told her. "They go great with your hair."

"You don't think they're too young for me, do you?" she asked, starting a fresh batch of coffee. "The frames were in stock."

"Not at all. You look very fashionable."

Lottie came in to admire the new frames and let us know she was leaving for lunch, so I could take over for her in the shop. In between customers, I phoned Marco to give him a brief rundown on Dave's interview and ask, "Do you have a problem with a meeting at Dave's office at eight thirty in the morning?"

"Nope."

"Great. Are you still at the bar?"

"Yep."

Hmm. He was being awfully short. "With Rafe?"

"Yep."

"Is he in trouble?"

"Oh, yeah."

"Did he get my ring back?"

"Nope."

"Marco, Rafe has to get it back before the dinner at Cinnamon's parents' house tonight!"

"That's why he's in trouble. He says Cinnamon took the day off work to have her hair and nails done. He won't see her until dinner and claims he doesn't know where her salon is."

"She took the entire day off for hair and nails?"

"You don't really expect me to answer that, do you?"

"Rafe has her cell phone number. Why can't he call her?"

"He says she turned off her phone."

"Then what are we going to do?"

"I'm thinking of shipping him back to Ohio — tonight."

In the background I heard Rafe say, "It's your fault for sending me to Bindstrom's in the first place."

He had a point.

Apparently, Marco didn't agree. The two argued for a few moments, and then Marco said to me, "I'll pick you up at six thirty, okay?"

"Okay. But Marco —"

Too late. He'd hung up.

Now what was I supposed to do? Show up at Cinnamon's parents' house and bite my tongue as she flashed my ring around? Watch Francesca Salvare turn several shades of magenta when she figured out that Rafe couldn't possibly have afforded it? Cringe as Francesca cast a wistful glance at my bare right hand?

I drummed my fingers on the counter, considering my options. Finally, I pulled out the Yellow Pages and searched for beauty salons.

As Grace liked to say, if you wanted something done right, you had to do it yourself.

CHAPTER THIRTEEN

It took me a mere six phone calls to learn that Cinnamon had booked herself an afternoon at the Olive Tree Beauty and Day Spa, three blocks west on Lincoln. So as soon as Lottie came back, I grabbed my coat and purse and headed out to lunch, or so they thought.

Across the street, a group of five teenage boys were performing a rap for the large crowd hanging around the courthouse, so instead of my usual shortcut across the lawn, I took Franklin to Lincoln, turned the corner, and headed west. On my way I passed Bindstrom's, now sporting bright green awnings and a newly painted gold-leaf door — when had that happened? — and was reminded that I would have spared myself all this aggravation if I'd picked up the engagement ring myself.

At the end of the block, I crossed the street and saw Jingles cleaning the window of the corner drugstore. The old-fashioned store boasted establishment in 1954 and looked like it hadn't been painted since. But now, in place of the faded and peeling lettering above the door that had said PHIL'S D UGS, it had a glossy black rectangular sign that said PHARMACOLOGIE in a shiny gold font that screamed "hip and modern."

I paused to peer through the window and saw the familiar crowded aisles, and cracked black-and-white tile floor. The only thing new was a sign in the window advertising Cody Verse posters for ten dollars.

"How's it going, Jingles?" I asked.

"Goin' to the dogs, Miss Abby," he said in his slow, deep voice, shaking his head. "Goin' to the dogs."

The Olive Tree was a recent addition to our downtown landscape, having opened less than a year ago in an old three-story cement-block building renovated to look like an ancient Grecian temple. Entering the main floor through a doorway flanked by stone columns, I was greeted by the sound of splashing water and warbling birds.

I glanced to my right and found the source — a floor-to-ceiling birdcage filled with tiny songbirds flitting about the branches of an artificial tree. Opposite the entrance was a small waterfall tucked into what appeared to be a grotto but was actually the reception counter.

Behind the counter was a young woman with long blond hair, wearing a white Grecian-style gown. She stood perfectly still, her elbows at her sides, her arms bent so her hands stuck straight out in front of her, palms upraised, fingers forming the letter O. Her eyelids were closed, so she was either meditating or sleeping on her feet. Behind her was a tall perch on which sat a white cockatoo, which began to squawk as I approached.

"Hush, Zeus." The blonde raised her eyelids to half-mast and asked in a voice a little above a whisper, "Do you have an appointment?"

"No, I'm looking for a friend of mine. Her name is Cinnamon . . ."

I didn't know her last name.

"Cinnamon is in the olive grove right now," the receptionist said without missing a beat, "but we never interrupt clients when they're in the grove unless it's an emergency."

"Do you actually have an olive grove in here?"

"The olive grove is what we call our massage salon."

If I hadn't known better, I'd have sworn the woman was sleep-talking. "So Cinnamon is having her massage right now?"

"That's typically what happens in a massage salon."

I was in a hurry. I didn't need an attitude. "When can I talk to her?"

The woman's eyelids fluttered upward to see the clock on the wall. "She booked for an hour massage, but that includes a matcha tea break. In about thirty minutes, she will be guided into the beauty salon to begin her facial, so let me see . . ."

"Can I talk to her before the facial?"

"Not unless it's an emergency. Is it an emergency?"

I glanced at my watch. "Getting close."

Apparently that didn't cut it. "In one hour, she will begin her hair appointment. You may speak with her prior to that appointment."

I hated to wait that long. I'd been gone long enough as it was. Still, did I have a choice?

Suddenly the cockatoo left its perch with a great flapping of wings and landed on my shoulder. I froze, fearing it was about to peck me.

"Zeus, off," the young woman ordered, snapping her fingers. The bird lifted its wings and flew back to its perch, where it kept a beady eye on me.

"What was that about?" I asked.

"He was checking out your earrings."

I fingered the tiny dangling crystals hanging from my earlobes. "Why?"

"He loves sparkly things. He's been known to pluck earrings right off people's ears."

"Even pierced ears?"

She lifted her shoulder. "Zeus doesn't care. You wouldn't believe the stuff he's hidden in the grotto. If you'd like to wait for Cinnamon, please have a seat in the garden." She pointed to a stone bench in an area filled with potted silk flowers and more artificial trees, reached by a faux flagstone path.

Not knowing what else to do, I followed the path to the bench and sat down beside a woman reading a magazine, who shifted uncomfortably, glanced at me, then grumbled, "With what they charge here, you'd think they could pad these benches."

I waited a while, then checked my watch. Tempus was really fugiting now. Maybe I could book the bed next to Cinnamon's and talk to her while we were getting massages.

I walked up to the grotto again and looked at the menu of services posted on the faux stone wall. I saw the price of a full-body massage, and blanched. Yowzers. That stone bench should have been padded in spun gold. How could Cinnamon afford a whole day here? On a waitress's salary? Were tips that good?

The young woman had gone back to her nap, so I cleared my throat and waited for her to open her eyes. "Do you have any appointments open right now for a —" I located something more in my price range. "Neck and shoulder massage?"

She ran her finger down a column in the appointment book, as though searching for a spot to squeeze me in. By the looks of all that white space, I didn't think there would be a problem.

"I can schedule that. Your name?"

"Abby."

"Credit or debit, Abby?"

I had to pay up front? I dug through my purse, pulled my debit card out of my wallet and handed it to her. She ran it through, handed it back, then hit a small gong on the counter. A moment later another young woman clad in the same style of gown, her feet bare, came up front, checked the appointment book, then smiled at me.

"Hello, Abby," she said in a whispery voice, making me wonder if voice quality was one of the job requirements. "My name is Natalia and I'll be your masseuse." She led me up the hallway behind the grotto. "I see this is your first time here. I hope you'll be pleased with our services." She parted a curtain of leafy silk vines. "Here we are. The olive grove."

At that moment, Zeus soared over our heads, through the vines and straight into the massage salon, where he landed on a branch of one of the artificial olive trees and proceeded to watch me.

"Zeus, you bad boy," Natalia said. "You know you're not supposed to be back here."

Holding my hands over my earlobes and keeping an eye on the bird, I followed Natalia across a spacious, carpeted, softly lit, cafeteria-sized room filled with the scent of lavender and the soothing sound of tinkling wind chimes. It seemed the perfect setting for a relaxing conversation between customers — until I saw the gauzy curtains that formed walls around each table, and then I came to a stop. That wouldn't do at all. Walls, even of the gauzy variety, weren't conducive to a conversation.

"Is something wrong?" Natalia asked.

Just about everything. "I — thought I dropped an earring."

We padded on. Scanning the row of curtained rooms ahead, I saw only one pair of bare feet and guessed that was Cinnamon's masseuse. We were headed toward the area beside it.

Natalia pulled aside the curtain and let me enter. "You'll need to remove your shoes, and all clothing and jewelry from the waist up." She pointed to a twig hook on the back wall. "You may hang your clothes there and leave your jewelry on the tray on the side table. Cover it with that silk square, in case Zeus gets in again. Your hair wrap is on the bed."

She walked to the head of the massage table. "After you've undressed, lie on the bed on your stomach with your face in this opening and cover yourself with the sheet. When you're ready, hit the gong on the side table." With that she slipped out, drew the curtain, and said, "Zeus, come!"

Her command was followed by the beating of wings and rustling of the leafy vine curtain.

I stood for a moment considering what to do. Barging into the next bed area wouldn't work. I'd either have to call it quits now and ask for a refund or hope for an opportunity to catch Cinnamon alone later. Hmm. Maybe her tea break. I'd have to send my masseuse on an errand.

Next door, I could hear Cinnamon mur-

muring, "Oh, that's good. You're right on that big knot. Carrying all those heavy trays isn't easy on my neck. Oh, yeah. Keep doing that."

Hmm. I had a few knots to work out, too. Maybe having a neck massage would help me figure out a better plan.

I covered my hair with the white terry wrap, placed my earrings in the Oriental-style black tray to the left of my bed, and put the red silk square on top. I was about to take off my sweater when it dawned on me that Cinnamon would have been instructed to remove her jewelry, too, and with a full-body massage, I assumed that applied to her rings as well.

Meaning that my diamond engagement ring was probably, at that very moment, sitting in a tray about eight feet away.

I bent down to peer under the curtain. The cubicle on the other side of Cinnamon's appeared to be empty. Maybe I could sneak into it and take a quick peek at my ring through the curtain on the other side.

At that moment Cinnamon murmured something, to which her masseuse said, "Mineral water? No problem. I'll be back in a few minutes. Don't move."

Crouching, I watched bare feet disappear across the carpet and heard the flutter of

215

the vines as the masseuse left the olive grove. With wind chimes tinkling soothingly, I slipped out of my cubicle, tiptoed past Cinnamon's, and stepped quietly into the next one. Standing at the head of the empty massage table, I eased the curtain between the areas back half an inch and peered through.

Cinnamon lay facedown on the table, covered by a sheet. In a tray on the side table right next to the curtain where I stood was a thick silver rope chain, a pair of silver chandelier earrings — and my engagement ring, fully exposed! The red silk square lay folded beside the tray. Obviously, she hadn't been warned about the white-winged raptor.

Even in the dim light, my ring was just as beautiful as I remembered it. Seeing it a mere twelve inches away, I knew I had to touch it, maybe even try it on for size, and make sure she hadn't scratched it.

I stretched my arm around the curtain and let my fingertips trace the warm gold circle. From the corner of my eye I saw a large white blur and glanced up to see Zeus perched on the curtain rod above, staring hard at my ring. The bird had managed to slip back into the grove.

I shielded my ring and glared up at him.

No, you don't, you thief. You're not making off with my diamond.

At that moment, Cinnamon shifted on the bed and murmured to herself, "How freakin' long does it take to bring a freakin' glass of water?"

Not long. Her masseuse would return at any second. I had to get out of there.

Zeus flapped his wings as if to show his impatience. The bird was waiting for me to leave!

"Natalia," I heard someone call from beyond the vine curtain, "I think Zeus got into the grove again."

Go, Abby!

A moment later, I was standing beside my massage table, my heart pounding hard. Whew. That was close. Then I noticed my right hand balled into a fist. I uncurled my fingers and there was my ring.

Oh, no. What had I done? Now Cinnamon would discover it missing and panic. The police would be called. They'd conduct a search. I'd be found with the ring — my ring — but they wouldn't know that. I'd be accused of theft. How would I explain myself?

Calm down, that little voice of reason whispered. *It can't be a theft if it belongs to you.*

I glanced up and saw the cockatoo watching me. *Stupid bird! See what you caused?* What should I do? Keep it? Hope the cops didn't find me with it? Or if they did, hope I could explain it rationally and pray that word didn't get back to my parents and Marco's mom? Fat chance. Not with the news-hungry media hovering outside. I could just imagine the reporters seeing police cars outside the salon and rushing over to find out the cause.

Headline: FECKLESS FLORIST FINGERS RING!

What if Cinnamon sued the salon because they couldn't find the ring? What if they went out of business because of me?

I heard the vines move and knew one or both masseuses were coming. Quickly, I dove for the bed, then remembered I still had my sweater on. Yanking it off over my head, I tossed it toward the hook and it caught. But I'd dislodged the hair wrap and there was no time to tighten it. I flopped onto my belly, pulled the sheet over me, then placed my face in the hole in the bed, holding my breath as I clutched my diamond in one sweaty palm.

"Here's your water," a voice said. "Let me help you sit up. You might be a bit dizzy from having all those toxins released."

Cinnamon's masseuse, not mine. I let out my breath. Then I heard the rustle of a sheet and pictured Cinnamon sitting up, blinking, and accepting the cup of water. How long would it be before she looked over at the tray?

At that moment, Natalia called from the other side of the curtain, "Are you ready, Abby? It's been a long time . . ."

Oh, no! She called me Abby! What if Cinnamon had heard her?

"Sorry," I said. "I forgot to hit the gong." *Crap.* Why hadn't I disguised my voice?

Natalia came into my room. "Your hair wrap is coming loose. Let me fix it for you."

She rewrapped my hair and then, after applying a soothing oil to her fingers, began to knead the muscles across the tops of my shoulders. Despite my anxiety, I couldn't help but feel some of the tension flow right out of my body. And, frankly, having my ring back in my possession felt pretty darn good.

"That's better," Natalia said, working my shoulders. "You were really knotted up."

Imagine that.

Then I heard Cinnamon say, "Hey! Where's my ring? I put it right here on the tray."

Oh, no.

"How odd," Natalia said to me. "Your muscles knotted up right under my fingers."

There was a rattle of jewelry, and then the masseuse said, "It has to be here someplace." I braced myself for the explosion.

"I'll be right back," Natalia told me. A moment later I heard her whisper, "Anna, what's happening?"

"Cinnamon's engagement ring is missing," the other masseuse whispered back.

Excuse me, *my* engagement ring.

"Zeus must have it," Natalie whispered. "I'll go look for it."

Zeus! That was the answer. Blame it on the bird. I was saved!

The other masseuse said, "Cinnamon, I am so sorry this happened. The cockatoo must have taken it. He likes sparkly objects, which is why we don't like him back here. He usually hides his treasures in the grotto, so I'm sure Natalia will be right back with it."

I highly doubted that. I brought my hand under the table so I could remove the ring. Was it right to let them search all over for it? Was it fair to make Cinnamon suffer the pangs of guilt for losing such an expensive ring? Should I confess now before she called the cops?

A few minutes later I heard the vines

rustle, and then Natalia said to Anna, "I couldn't find it."

The other masseuse sighed heavily. "I don't know what to say, Cinnamon, except I'm so sorry. I guess you'll want to file a police report so you can claim it on your insurance."

Explosion time. I scrunched my eyes shut and clasped my ring so tight it cut into my palm. *Speak up, Abby,* that little voice told me. *Tell them you found it. They'll think the bird dropped it in your cubicle.*

I was about to get up off the table when I heard Cinnamon say, "Don't worry. It's not real. I got it at the drugstore."

My eyes flew open. I uncurled my fingers and turned the ring to examine it. From the side I could see it was missing the etchings, but the shape and size of the diamond were a match.

"Wow, you had me fooled," her masseuse said.

She wasn't the only one.

"My dad made me put the real diamond in his safe so I wouldn't lose it," Cinnamon said. "Who knew he'd be right?"

CHAPTER FOURTEEN

My engagement ring was in Cinnamon's dad's safe? What was I supposed to do now? Even though we were having dinner with her parents, I didn't have a clue where they lived. Marco hadn't told me. I didn't even know who her dad was. I'd never felt so clueless in my life.

I let Natalia finish my neck massage as I tried to determine my next move, but as it stood, I couldn't think of a way to get the ring back without involving Cinnamon's father. And once he knew, and had explained the mix-up to Cinnamon, who would undoubtedly tell her mother, it would be only a matter of time until Francesca Salvare heard. And that meant she would be not only hurt that we hadn't revealed our plans to her but also embarrassed in front of Cinnamon's parents. I didn't even want to think about what my parents would say when they learned we hadn't told them about our engagement.

It was three o'clock when I left the Olive Tree and started back up Lincoln, still pondering my dilemma. Was there a way I could swear Cinnamon's father to silence? Would he be sympathetic to my plight if I explained how controlling Marco's mom was? Could I bribe him with flowers?

I turned onto Franklin and glanced up the block to see a police car parked in front of Bloomers. My stomach fluttered anxiously. What now?

Instead of passing by Down the Hatch, I ducked inside, relieved to find it not busy yet. "Where's Marco?" I called to Gert.

"In his office. Want me to get him?"

"Tell him there's a squad car at Bloomers. I'm on my way there now."

I left Marco's bar and started toward my flower shop. As I approached the shop, Connor McKay stepped out of the passenger side of one of several news vans parked across the street and came toward me. Just wonderful.

"Looks like some excitement at Bloomers," he said with a big smile. "What's up?"

"Off the record?" I asked.

He replaced his smile with a serious frown. "Whatever you want."

"I'm not positive," I said, casting a glance over my shoulder, "but the cops may have uncovered my plot to sell your liver on eBay."

Connor stared blankly for a moment, then realized he'd been had and scowled.

I smiled, then opened the door and stepped inside the shop to find Lottie, Grace, and Sergeant Reilly standing at the cashier counter, talking in hushed voices. That was never a good sign.

Sean Reilly was an attractive forty-year-old police sergeant who carried an air of confidence about him without the posturing so many cops adopted. He had intelligent hazel eyes, nice facial structure, brown hair starting to show a bit of white on the sides, and a sturdy body that lacked the typical gut-hanging-over-the-belt physique. He'd been a rookie under my dad and a good friend to Marco and me, but at the moment I wasn't exactly thrilled to see him. I knew his visit wasn't for pleasure.

Hearing the bell jingle, they turned toward me. "Don't panic, sweetie," Lottie said, putting her arm around my shoulders. "Sergeant Reilly just came to deliver a message."

"The detectives would like to talk to you," Reilly said.

Exactly what I'd wanted to avoid. "Sorry,

Reilly. No can do. I've been away from my shop too much today. Tell them to e-mail me their questions."

"If you're worried about Bloomers," Lottie offered, "we're on top of things here."

"It's not that," I said. "I simply don't feel like being interrogated."

"It's routine Q and A," Reilly said. "Nothing to worry about."

"What's routine about being stuck in a cement-block room with detectives firing questions at me so they can pin a murder on Dave?" I folded my arms in front of me. "No, thanks."

"I came over to escort you personally," Reilly said, sounding offended.

"I appreciate the gesture, Reilly," I said, "but even if I were inclined to cooperate, there's a reporter standing outside who is dying to know why you're here and would love nothing more than to get a photo of you putting me in your squad car."

As he swung to see what reporter I was referring to, the door opened and Marco came into the shop. He glanced at the four of us. "What's going on?"

Reilly hooked his thumbs in his belt and nodded in my direction. "Detectives want to talk to Abby. She's being difficult."

"*I'm* being difficult?" I said. "I'm not the

one trying to railroad Dave. Why should I cooperate?"

"Give me a minute," Marco said to Reilly, and led me toward the curtain, pausing when he caught sight of my mom's tee tea cart. "What is that?"

"Mom's new art piece. Know any golfers who drink tea?"

He shook his head in disbelief as we continued into the workroom. He put his hands on my shoulders and gazed into my eyes. "Think about this, Abby. If you refuse to talk to the detectives, they'll assume you're hiding information to protect Dave."

"What if I say something that hurts him? I've already done that once."

"If you tick them off, they could declare you a material witness and jail you. Imagine them coming to get you here and cuffing you in front of your customers."

Definitely didn't want that. I sighed and stepped up close to him, laying my head against his chest as he put his arms around me. "I just have a bad feeling about it."

"Come on, Fireball," he urged. "Detectives don't scare you. What's behind this sudden case of nerves?"

"Dave said a few things after the hearing that could hurt him."

"Like what?"

"Like that Lipinski was going to be sorry for what he did. If you take that out of context, it could be interpreted as a death threat."

"Then don't take it out of context." Marco lifted my chin to gaze into my eyes. "You're smart, Abby. You'll figure out how to work the interview to your advantage. You're not going to let them bully you."

I knew it was a pep talk, but strangely, it worked. I stepped back and straightened my shoulders. "You're right. They're not going to bully me."

"Now you've got it."

"I'm my father's daughter. I'm not afraid to stand up for what's just. If anyone's going to do the interrogating, it's me."

"There's that tough Irish lass I fell in love with."

Yeah, well, I was a tough Irish lass when I blabbed to McKay, too. And suddenly the qualms came back. "Would you come with me? Just to the station? For moral support?"

He put his arms around me. "Of course."

I gave him a hug. "Thank you. It'll only take me a few minutes to freshen up. Okay if we go out the back way? McKay is hanging around out front."

Marco cracked his knuckles, his gaze turning steely and determined. "I'll get rid of him."

Right. I could see those headlines now: BLOOMERS' BEAU KNUCKLES NEWS-HOUND. "Thanks, that's so sweet, but let's do this quietly. Would you let Reilly know our plan?"

I headed toward the tiny bathroom in back, calling over my shoulder, "By the way, you don't happen to know the name of a good safecracker, do you?"

"Do I want to know why?"

"It's more a question of need-to-know. I'll tell you on the way."

We eluded McKay and the crowds all around the courthouse square by snaking up alleys, and arrived at the police station ten minutes later. On the way, I gave Marco an abbreviated version of the events at the Olive Tree, after which he insisted there was no way we were going to break into Cinnamon's father's safe. He did think we might try appealing to him, though.

A policewoman came to escort me into one of their two torture chambers, otherwise known as conference room A, so I squeezed Marco's hand for reassurance, then took a deep breath and followed her. My anxiety level surprised me. I couldn't remember feeling this nervous when my own life was on the line. Perhaps I'd been too naive then to appreciate my peril.

The conference room was a windowless rectangular box with yellowed, peeling ceiling tiles, grungy white walls, and a black-and-white asphalt floor that was stained and cracked from wear. In the room was a standard government-issued steel desk, a long metal table with a cheap pecan veneer, eight hard, metal folding chairs, and an old coffeemaker on a stand in the corner, with about an inch of black sludge inside. Beside it were packets of a chemically produced sweetener, some lumpy powdered white stuff that substituted for cream, and flimsy foam cups guaranteed to partially disintegrate when they came in contact with hot liquid. It was all part of the torture.

"Would you like some coffee?" she asked.

"No, thanks. I'm good."

As I took a seat on a folding chair, the door opened and Detective Al Corbison stepped inside. Corbison was a paunchy, middle-aged, bald man with tobacco-stained teeth and no sense of humor whatsoever, a condition I'd discovered while being investigated in the murder of a law school professor. He was alone, which I took as a good omen. Two detectives made a more formidable foe.

"Miss Knight," he said in a gravelly voice. "Thanks for coming in."

Time to take charge of the situation. I sat forward and folded my hands on the table. "Thanks for giving me a chance to talk to you."

He gave me a quizzical glance as he put his file on the table and sat down. He pulled out a recorder and placed it beside the file. "If you don't mind, I'm going to tape our interview."

As if I had a choice. "Good idea, Detective." I smiled to unnerve him.

He started the machine, then stated his name, the date, and my name for the record, after which he said, "Would you describe your relationship with David Hammond?"

I was determined to make my answers as innocuous as possible. "I clerked for him when I was in law school, as you know."

"Do you work for him now?"

"Come on, Detective," I said, as if we were old buddies. "You're well aware that I own Bloomers Flower Shop."

"It's for the record," he reminded me. "Does David Hammond's former secretary work at your flower shop?"

"Yes. That would be Grace Bingham."

"Didn't David Hammond represent you

in the law school murder case?"

"Yes, and he did a great job, too. You guys weren't able to pin it on me." I smiled again. "Not that you didn't try."

Corbison pinched his nostrils together, as though forcing himself not to rise to the bait. Or maybe to avoid a sneeze. "Did Hammond also represent your boyfriend at one time?"

"If you're referring to Marco Salvare, yes. Another great job, by the way." Where was he going with his questions?

"And isn't it true you helped investigate that case for Hammond?"

"Okay, I see where you're going now. You're establishing that Attorney Hammond and I are good friends. Yes, we're friends, Detective, which is why I can say with total honesty that he wouldn't hurt a fly."

"Thank you for your opinion, Ms. Knight," he grumbled. "Are you doing any work for Hammond now?"

After that little barb, I was going back to my simple answers. "No."

"I understand you went out to Whispering Willows to question the staff and residents about Hammond's visit on Monday. Is that true?"

"Yes."

"Wouldn't you consider that working for

Hammond?"

"I did that voluntarily. He hasn't hired me to do any work for him." Yet.

Corbison opened the file and glanced at the first page. "What was the occasion of your trip?"

"Attorney Hammond was afraid — no, wait, wrong word. Erase that. He felt you might be zeroing in on him and wanted to make sure he had alibi witnesses."

"I hope you had better luck than we had. We couldn't find anyone to back up his story."

I knew he was waiting for me to tell him what I'd found, but I didn't want to admit to failure, so I said nothing.

Corbison glanced up. "Well?" he asked impatiently. "Did you find any?"

"Not yet, but I haven't questioned everyone."

"I didn't think so." He turned a page in the file. "Let's move on. Did you have occasion to speak with Hammond after the hearing on Monday?"

There it was — the topic I'd dreaded. "Briefly."

"Did he talk about the hearing?"

"Briefly."

"Did he mention a missing exhibit?"

"Briefly."

"What did he say about it?"

I paused to think back, remembering Dave's grim expression as he met me in the courthouse lobby. *"That bastard Lipinski took one of my exhibits. . . . It's my most crucial piece of evidence, Abby. It's Andrew's hand-written memo to Cody Verse containing the lyrics he wrote for the winning song, with Cody's written reply making some suggestions on them. Without that evidence, Judge Duncan may very likely rule in the defendant's favor and dismiss the case. Lipinski knew that. He should be disbarred for this."*

"He said Lipinski took his exhibit, and then he explained what the exhibit was."

"Did Hammond say he witnessed Lipinski take it?"

"I don't recall him saying that."

"Did he say the missing exhibit could damage his case?"

"He mentioned something to that effect, but what lawyer wouldn't worry about his case in those circumstances? How would you feel if an important piece of evidence went missing? Wouldn't you be concerned? Wouldn't you take legal steps to mitigate the damage?"

"In what way would the missing exhibit damage his case?"

"Attorney Hammond could explain that

better than I could."

"Did you hear Hammond make any threats against Lipinski?"

"He said Lipinski should be disbarred for taking the exhibit."

"That seems to be a pretty tame reaction, considering you just told me how concerned he was."

"I don't think any lawyer would feel being disbarred was *tame.* Besides, Attorney Hammond is not a vicious man. He doesn't make threats. All he said was that Lipinski *should* be disbarred."

"Yet Hammond proceeded to file a complaint with the bar association that day in order to start the process. So wouldn't you consider his statement a threat?"

I had a sudden recollection of standing just outside Dave's office after the hearing, listening to Dave vent his frustrations.

"I'm sorry, Dave."

"Not as sorry as Lipinski's going to be."

Now, *that* could be considered a threat. But I definitely wasn't going to tell Corbison. "Absolutely not. His statement was more about what *should* happen legally. No threat there as far as I can see."

"Did Hammond express any concern over how his client would react to the missing exhibit?"

"Of course. Attorney Hammond cares about every one of his clients. Andrew Chapper is no exception."

"Did Hammond tell you he scheduled a meeting with Lipinski for that same afternoon?"

"No, but I was in his office when he instructed his secretary to set it up."

"What was his mood at the time?"

"He was giving instructions. I guess you could say he was in an instructional mood."

Corbison didn't appear to think that was amusing. "Was he still angry?"

"Well, hey, wouldn't you be?" I smiled, trying to break the tension in the room.

"You didn't answer the question."

I shrugged. "Well, I'm sure he was, but I don't want to say positively. I'd be speculating."

"What do you think happened at their meeting?"

"I don't know what you want me to say, Detective, because I'd be speculating again."

He motioned with his hand. "Speculate away."

"I'm guessing the two lawyers discussed the hearing."

"Did you ever witness Hammond losing his temper?"

"Never. He's very easygoing."

Corbison leaned forward. "But he wasn't easygoing on Monday, was he?"

"He was a lot calmer than I'd have been."

"You know what I mean, Ms. Knight."

"If you're asking whether I think Attorney Hammond was so angry that he killed Lipinski during the meeting — no way."

"Hammond filed a complaint to have Lipinski disbarred. That's not something lawyers normally do to each other, is it?"

"I'm not a lawyer. I really couldn't say."

"You worked for a lawyer. And, as I recall, you went to law school — for a time."

Ouch. He knew that smarted. "Let me ask you something, Detective."

"I'm not finished with my questions."

How about that? We had something in common. "Do you have any hard evidence to tie Attorney Hammond to the crime scene?"

"That's privileged information."

"Does that mean you don't?"

"No, that means you don't get to know."

Corbison was getting snarly. I had to get back in his good graces. "Look, I'm not a rookie anymore when it comes to investigating murders, Detective. I want you to catch Lipinski's killer as much as you want to, and I'll do whatever I can to help, including steering you toward people who have real

236

grudges against Lipinski — Cody Verse, for instance."

The detective folded his arms over his paunch. "Lipinski's client?"

"Lipinski's *famous* client" — I leaned forward, as though we were best friends sharing confidences — "who was infuriated when he found out that Lipinski made advances on his girlfriend, Lila Redmond."

Now I had Corbison's attention. He pulled a pen from his shirt pocket. "When did this happen?"

"The weekend prior to their hearing, while Lipinski hosted them at his lake house."

"Did you witness it?"

"Someone told me about it."

He opened his notebook, ready to write down the details. "Go ahead."

"During their weekend stay, Lipinski tried to force himself on Lila, and she rebuffed him. Knowing that Cody is insanely jealous, she kept it from him until Monday, after the hearing, when Lipinski invited them to lunch. She refused to go and told Cody why. Apparently, Cody is insanely jealous anyway. In fact, Cody was so angry, he wouldn't let Lila appear with him on the morning cable show. He brought his new lawyer instead."

"How did you hear about this incident?"

This was where it got tricky. I didn't want to give Corbison Jillian's name because her knowledge was secondhand, which made it unreliable. Plus, she'd probably come across as a flake. "To be honest, Detective, my information is triple hearsay, but you can ask Lila Redmond about the incident."

Corbison stopped writing. "Triple hearsay?"

"Yes, but that doesn't mean it's not true."

"How do I know you're not making this up?"

"Talk to Lila, or her hairstylist. Better yet, investigate Cody. Get him in here and ask him about it. If he's innocent, he'll be happy to share it with you, right?"

Corbison finished writing, then closed his notebook and the file, ready to dismiss me. But I wasn't finished.

"And then there's Lipinski's young associate, Scott Hess, who would've had the perfect opportunity to kill Lipinski by staying behind when everyone went home for the day."

Corbison leaned back and clicked his pen. "I suppose you've already figured out a motive."

"Envy. Lipinski had fame and fortune, but Hess didn't even have his name up on the sign in front of Lipinski's law office. Had you even heard of Scott Hess before he took over Cody Verse's defense? Now he's appearing on television with Cody, and they both seem inordinately pleased with the arrangement. Maybe they even schemed together to kill Lipinski."

Corbison shot me a skeptical look, so I said, "Have you verified both alibis?"

He opened the file and flipped through a few pages, as though searching for the answer. At last I had him thinking.

Suddenly another image flashed in my mind — Andrew Chapper's grandfather, irate, bearing down on Dave, his big hands clenched at his sides.

"Is Andrew's case being thrown out?"

"Calm down, Mr. Chapper. The case hasn't been dismissed."

"I didn't bring this to you so you could let that devil-in-disguise Lipinski outsmart you."

Then, gripping Dave's coat, he'd raved, "You can't let that fraud Cody Verse get away with his sneak offense. You can't let Lipinski win this battle."

Corbison closed the file and scooted back his chair, ready to rise. "Okay, Ms. Knight, thank you for your time."

"Wait. Have you interviewed Andrew Chapper's grandfather?"

Corbison gave an impatient sigh. "Yes, we

talked to him."

"Are you aware of the confrontation Mr. Chapper had with Attorney Hammond just after the hearing, where, in full view of everyone in the courthouse lobby, he grabbed Attorney Hammond's lapels and began ranting about Lipinski and calling him names? If I were investigating this case, I'd want to know just how volatile he is, because his behavior Monday was definitely out of the norm. And if you think about it, he has more to lose in this lawsuit than Attorney Hammond does."

"Wouldn't that apply even more so to Andrew?" Corbison volleyed back.

Oops. He was right, and Dave would never want me to implicate his client. I had to back off that one.

"Come to think of it," Corbison said, "didn't Andrew Chapper cause a scene at the memorial service Cody gave for Lipinski?"

"That wasn't a memorial service. It was a chance for Cody to sell CDs. Besides, everyone knows Andrew is angry at Cody; otherwise he wouldn't have filed the suit. No surprise that he displayed some of his frustration in public. That doesn't mean he'd take it out on Lipinski. He's smart enough to realize that Cody would merely hire another attorney.

"But think about Cody's behavior, Detective. If a person wanted to throw suspicion off himself, giving a so-called memorial performance for his victim would be a good way to do it, wouldn't it?"

"If I were Cody and had just killed my lawyer," Corbison said, "I would suddenly remember something I had to do back in LA." He stood up. "And yet Cody is still here. But thank you for sharing." He nodded to the policewoman, who opened the door for me.

"Wait! I can explain why he's still here. It's all about publicity. Cody gets way more media exposure in New Chapel than back in LA, where minor stars are a dime a dozen . . ."

The policewoman took my arm.

Frustrated, I walked to the doorway, then paused to give it one last try. "Will you at least check out Cody?"

"Don't worry, Ms. Knight," Corbison replied indifferently. "I'll look into it."

That was doubtful. But Marco and I certainly would.

CHAPTER FIFTEEN

I found Marco standing just outside the station talking on his cell phone. He ended the call and gave me a long glance, as though trying to get a read on my emotions. "How did it go?"

"I did okay, but I couldn't shake Corbison off Dave's trail. He didn't seem very taken with my alternative-killer theories."

"They're focused on making a case against Dave. That was him on the phone. The cops just did a search of his office and house and discovered a bottle of his mom's prescription medicine in his bathroom medicine cabinet."

"Dave's mom stays with him on occasion," I said, as we made our way back to Bloomers. "It's perfectly reasonable for him to keep a supply of her medicine there."

"It's reasonable, but if her medicine matches what was found in Lipinksi's blood, they'll have all they need to make a case against him."

"Did the tox report come back?"

"We still don't know, but if the DA wants to indict Dave, the lack of a tox report won't stop him."

"The report would clear him later, though, wouldn't it?"

"That's not the danger, Abby. If Dave is indicted, think what it'll do to his reputation."

Exactly the concern Dave had expressed. I contemplated that dreary scenario as we headed up the alley behind Franklin Street. Neither of us spoke until we reached Bloomers, and then Marco said, "I'm going to get everything in order at the bar so I can start investigating right after our meeting tomorrow. Will you be able to get away to help me?"

"It'll be tough. I feel terrible leaving Lottie and Grace alone again, even though I know they'll be one hundred percent in favor of me helping Dave. I'd ask Jillian to fill in, but I'm afraid my assistants would stage a rebellion. Maybe we can figure out a way for you to investigate during the day, when the bar is quiet, and for me to work at night after the shop closes."

"Let's discuss our options when we meet with Dave in the morning. We still have to get through this evening."

Mentioning my engagement ring at such a time seemed petty, considering Dave's predicament, yet it was another problem that had to be tackled. I glanced at my watch. "If we're going to talk to Cinnamon's dad in private, we'd better get there early. What time is dinner?"

"Dinner's at seven, so I'll swing by at six. The Howards live up north, near Lake Michigan, so that will give us plenty of time to get there."

And decide on a strategy.

At ten minutes past six o'clock that evening, Marco and I were zipping north on Interstate 49 in his green Prius, following the little arrow on his GPS that was leading us toward Lake Michigan. Marco looked so yummy-hot in his brown leather jacket over a marine blue crewneck sweater and tan pants, his dark hair gleaming in the glow of the streetlights, I found myself wishing we could turn around and go back home. But this dinner couldn't be avoided, not if I hoped to get my ring back tonight.

"Let's plan what to tell Mr. Howard," I said.

"We need a plan?"

"Unless you know how to crack open his

safe, yes."

"Can't help you with the safe, but I figured you'd want to do the talking." Marco glanced at me. "You know, so you can work your feminine wiles on him."

"You're not seriously suggesting I flirt with the man, are you?"

"No, I don't want you to flirt. Just be cute and sympathetic so he'll take pity on us."

"Cute and sympathetic. So *that's* the definition of feminine wiles."

"You know what I mean."

Men have no understanding of our complex female natures. "So basically you want me to smile perkily through my tears as I limp across the room on my newly sprained ankle to explain to Mr. Howard that his future son-in-law gave his daughter a diamond ring he can't afford and didn't own to begin with, but he will replace it with something inexpensive once he saves up some money."

"I'd leave out the inexpensive part."

I batted him on the shoulder. "That's not funny."

Marco laughed. "I was kidding. Just tell him the truth."

"And what will your part in this drama be?"

"Supportive."

Wonderful. It was all on my shoulders. "Are you sure you've never cracked a safe?"

Half a mile short of the lake, Marco turned off the highway and headed east, following a two-lane road into a residential area that bordered Indiana Dunes State Park. The ginormous houses, some of which had docks right on the lake, were testaments to what money could buy.

"Marco, I don't think your GPS system knows where it's going. This is a classy neighborhood and Cinnamon — well, she isn't."

"I'm using the address Rafe gave me."

We wound through the hilly subdivision until we spotted the address on a mailbox at the curb. Marco stopped and we both gazed up the long, brick driveway to the hilltop house.

"Damn," Marco whispered.

"Ditto. But I take back what I said earlier. Not everything in this neighborhood is classy."

The Howard house was a massive white stone castle, complete with turrets and a tower that served as the front entrance. Rapunzel would have felt right at home. All it lacked was a moat.

Marco gunned the motor up the hill, pulled past the tower, parked, and came around to help me out. The gesture was appreciated because I was a bit unsteady on my five-inch stilettos, even though they'd seemed like a great idea when I bought them. At five feet two inches, I welcomed any additional height. I'd discovered the brown suede heels on a final-clearance rack and snapped them up, thinking they'd make me feel tall. Instead, they made me feel that I was about to break one or both ankles. It was the price one paid for being fashionable.

I pulled the belt of my trench coat tighter, then took Marco's arm. Underneath my coat, I was wearing a wrap dress in a green-and-brown geometric print, very retro, deeply discounted, and totally figure forgiving, which mattered to a busty short person. And although I'd felt sexy when I tried it on, I didn't feel that way now, as I clutched Marco's arm and made my way unsteadily up the brick-edged driveway to the tower.

We were greeted at the massive wooden door by Al Howard, a short, unattractive man who I guessed was in his early sixties, around Grace's age, and much older than I'd imagined Cinnamon's father would be. She also looked nothing like him. Al had a narrow fish face, small, close-set eyes, thinning hair dyed an unnatural flat black, and a loud voice that, when he talked, came out like barks. Was he her stepfather perhaps?

He invited us inside the tower, where I stared around in amazement as Marco helped me out of my coat. We were in a garish, marble-surfaced great hall, filled with expansive paintings of frolicking nudes, freestanding life-sized animal sculptures, gold-leafed furniture, a humongous multicolored crystal chandelier that was larger than my closet, and a double-sided, curving, white marble staircase with gold banisters that rivaled anything Hollywood could offer. Clearly, the Howards had money and liked to prove it, but not tastefully.

I couldn't imagine how Marco's mom, a widowed woman living within very modest means, would react to the excess. On the other hand, my mom's golf tee tea cart might have found a home.

"Great to meet you both," Al said, with a vigorous shake of Marco's hand, and then mine. "My wife will be down in a jif. Has to put her face on first. You know how women are, right, Mark? Cinnamon and Rafe will be along soon. She had to stop at my club first to get something from the safe."

What? The safe was at his country club? I discreetly tugged on the back of Marco's jacket to be sure he had caught that. "Are you a member of the country club in New Chapel?" Marco asked, as Al took my coat and hung it in a closet by the door.

"Sure am. I'm a golf nut. Couldn't live without the country club membership."

Oh, yeah. Mom's tea cart would be perfect here.

"But I'm talking about *my* club," Al continued. "Dirty Al's." He snapped his fingers and a man in a white jacket hurried through a doorway, bearing a tray with flutes of bubbly on it.

Wait. What? Dirty Al's? As in *Dirty Al's Gentlemen's Club?* Cinnamon's father owned a striptease joint?

"Have some champagne," Al said. "Moët and Chandon. Got a case yesterday. You wouldn't believe the price. If you want me to hook you up with my liquor source, Mark, just let me know." He elbowed Marco and winked at me, and then his gaze dropped to my breasts.

I reached for a flute, turning away so he couldn't leer. If I hadn't needed my ring back, I might have poked him in the eye. Seriously, Dirty Al's? Poor Francesca. She had no idea of the surprises in store.

Something metallic clanked, and Al said, "Here comes the little lady now."

I turned to see a forty-year-old version of

Cinnamon coming down one side of the staircase. She, too, had on a wrap dress, a silver one, but it was a lot less wrapped than mine, and probably ten times more expensive. Her straw blond hair was piled artfully on top of her head to show off her dazzling, teardrop-shaped dangling earrings — diamond, no doubt — and her unnaturally full lips were coated a shade of red one note away from black.

The clanking was caused by the stack of platinum bracelets on each wrist, which coordinated with her heavy platinum necklace set with pavé diamonds that vee'd straight into her impressive cleavage. She, too, wore a pair of five-inch heels, in a leopard print with silver spikes, but unlike me, she had no trouble walking in them. She was holding something that resembled the fuzzy end of a dust mop, until it raised its head and gazed at me with alert black eyes. At the dog's yap, she stroked its head and said, "Ginger loves meeting new people."

Ginger and Cinnamon. I was beginning to see a pattern.

Al put his arm around her. "Abby, Mark . . . my wife, Pepper."

Didn't get much worse than that.

"So you're Rafe's brother," Pepper said,

250

giving Marco a slow once-over that was more of a caress. "I see a strong resemblance between you and Rafe. People say that about me and Cinn, too. Everyone thinks we're sisters."

"Say, doll, why don't you give Abby a tour of the Sugar Shack?" Al suggested.

Pepper rolled her eyes at me. "Sugar Shack. How silly. He knows it's Casa Paprika. You'll see why when we get to the second floor."

Forget the pattern. That was just stupid.

"While you're showing Abby Casa Paprika, Mark and I are gonna have cigars in the den. Right, Mark?" He nudged Marco with his elbow.

Marco enjoyed cigars about as much as he did being called Mark. To keep him from leaving, I clasped his hand. We needed to get Al alone, and soon. "Why don't we hold off on the tour until your mom arrives, sweetheart? I'm sure she'll want to see Casa —" No, I just couldn't say it. "This gorgeous home, too."

"We'll give the missus her own tour," Al said. "Pepper loves to show off her house. Don't you, doll? Pepper comes from farm stock. Before she hooked up with me, she lived in a barn."

"You old silly," Pepper said, giggling. "I

251

didn't *live* in a barn. There was a barn on the property."

"So how did you two meet?" I couldn't resist asking, although I suspected I already knew.

"We met at Al's club fifteen years, one month, and three days ago," Pepper said, running her hand up his shirtfront as she gazed adoringly at him. "I auditioned for him."

Called that one.

"I'm still awed by how successful he is," Pepper gushed. "A genuine entrepreneur and a community leader, too."

Puh-leez. Her husband owned a strip joint.

"Come on, Abby," Pepper said. "You've gotta see my kitchen. It's something else."

"Some*place* else, she means," Al called, as Pepper started up the marble hallway toward the back of the house. "As in someplace she hardly ever visits." Both of them laughed on cue. It felt rehearsed.

Al motioned for Marco to follow, then practically trotted through open double doors into what appeared to be a den. From the foyer I could see brown leather sofas flanking a fireplace and a monstrous flat-screen TV above it.

Before Marco left, I handed him my champagne glass and whispered, "Talk to him. Be cute and sympathetic."

Marco gave me a scowl, then stepped through the doorway, so I wobbled after Pepper. She took me through the mansion like a paid tour guide, while I hoped against hope that Marco was convincing Al to give us the ring.

We had just concluded our circuit of the humongous paprika-colored master suite, complete with king-sized heart-shaped bed covered in black satin, when the doorbell chimed.

"More guests!" Pepper said to the dog, who gave a tiny yap. "We're so excited to meet Rafe's mom. Aren't we, Ginger? We've been looking forward to it all day."

I had a feeling Pepper and Ginger were going to spice up Francesca's day, too.

By the time I made my way to the top of the staircase, Pepper was halfway down and Francesca was having her hand shaken vigorously by Al, with Marco standing at her elbow. I wanted to hurry so I wouldn't miss a moment of the two women meeting, but I couldn't move fast because of the blasted shoes. How did Pepper manage? Maybe I needed lessons.

Marco's mother was wearing a classy black skirt and a cream-colored silk blouse with black pumps, her glorious dark hair waving prettily about her face and a richly colored scarf tied around her shoulders. I couldn't help but admire her, especially in contrast to Pepper.

"Here's my wife now," Al said, as Pepper tap-tapped toward them.

Francesca turned with a smile that froze into place. Her eyes widened as she took in Pepper's ensemble, and then she placed one hand over her heart, as though to catch her breath.

Pepper extended her hand, then spoke loudly, as though Francesca was deaf. "I'm — so — pleased — to — meet — you, Fran — cesca." She glanced at Marco. "She understands English, right?"

"I'm pleased to meet you, too," Francesca said politely.

"Wow," Pepper said. "Your sons sure take after you in looks. I was telling Abby earlier that everyone says me and Cinn could pass as sisters."

"Your boys could pass as sisters, too," Al said to his wife, and then both of them slapped their thighs and laughed uproariously. "It's an inside joke," Al said. "Pepper's sons are performers. They bill themselves as Jude and Babs . . . you know, as in Judy Garland and Barbra Streisand." He elbowed

Marco, who uttered a simple "Ah!" as if it now made sense.

Francesca was too stunned to reply. She caught sight of me coming toward the group and quickly held out her arms to embrace me. "Abby, *bella*," she cried, enfolding me in a hug. She whispered in my ear, "I'll never forgive Rafe for this."

I gave her a sympathetic squeeze.

"Pepper's gonna take you on a tour, Francesca," Al said, clapping Marco's mom on the shoulder. "Say, does anyone call you Frankie? Helluva lot easier on the tongue."

Marco's mother gazed at him in total stupefaction. I'd never seen her rendered speechless before.

Totally unaware of her reaction, Al said, "Abby, Mark, let's go start on the appetizers."

"C'mon, Francesca," Pepper called. "You gotta see my kitchen. It's something else."

Which prompted Al to play out his half of their stale joke about some*place* else. While they performed, I took the opportunity to whisper to Marco, "Any luck?"

He handed me my glass. "No opening."

"What are we going to do? Cinnamon and Rafe will be here any minute!"

Marco straightened as Al came up and put his arms around both of us. "Ready for shrimp? No pun intended, Abby." He elbowed Marco and winked at me. Rather, at my breasts. Once more and he'd be wearing an eye patch.

Time to be blunt. "Mr. Howard, there's something we need to discuss."

"Excuse me, boss," a tall man in a white waiter's coat said, stepping out of a doorway at the back of the house. "Phone call."

"Take a message," Al said.

"It's Cinnamon."

"All right, I'll get it in the den." He smiled at us. "Help yourself to the food, right through that doorway on the other side of the hall."

Moving fast on his short legs, he swept up a portable phone in the den, then walked out of sight with it. But we could still hear his end of the conversation.

"What's the problem, Cinn? Hey! Don't cry. What's that? You broke up? You gotta be kidding . . . Okay, just come home. Forget about the ring. Come home so we can get this straightened out."

"They broke up!" I whispered to Marco. "We'll never get the ring back now."

"Patience," he whispered.

"What do you mean? Do you have a plan?"

Marco took my elbow and steered me into the dining room. "Don't say anything about the ring until we find out what happened."

We detoured around the long, marble-topped mahogany table set with crystal, china, and silver to reach a huge serving table against the far wall that was loaded with platters of fruit and cheese and an enormous bowl of shrimp with a dipping sauce. Marco had just popped a fat pink shrimp in his mouth when Al entered the room.

"Kids!" he said, shaking his head. "That was Cinnamon. Seems she and Rafe had a falling-out. You know how young love is. One minute they can't get enough of each other, the next minute they're enemies. Anyway, I told her to come back here and I'd help them patch it up. I'm getting good at that. After all, I've had four wives to practice on."

I wondered how many more wives it would take for him to get it perfect.

Al dipped a shrimp in cocktail sauce and stuffed it into his mouth. "Have one, Abby," he mumbled, sauce in the corners of his mouth.

"No, thanks. I'm not a shrimp fan. Too many legs." I took a cocktail pick and stabbed a cheese cube. No legs.

257

"So," Al said, "what was it you wanted to talk to me about?"

"Nothing that can't wait until later," Marco said.

"I got time now." Al took another shrimp and crunched into it.

I could sense he wasn't going to drop the subject until we gave him something, so I discreetly squeezed Marco's hand, which was our signal to play along. "I noticed you don't have a tea cart in here —"

"Abby," Marco said in a warning tone.

"— and since you're such a golf nut, I thought I'd mention that there's a one-of-a-kind golfer's tea cart for sale in my flower shop."

"A what?" Al asked.

"Abby," Marco said, "not now."

"No, wait," Al said, holding up a bejeweled hand, "I want to hear about this one-of-a-kind cart."

I knew that would get his attention. "You'd love it," I said. "It's a unique piece of artisan furniture designed for the discriminating wealthy golfer and his wife who love to entertain. How perfect would it be for your amazing collection of furniture? You might even consider surprising Pepper with it. She'd be the only woman in the county to own one."

"Only one, huh?" Al said, rubbing his chin. "Maybe I'll drop by and take a look at it. Where's this shop?"

"Bloomers is on the town square in New Chapel," I said, "two doors down from Marco's bar, Down the Hatch."

Al tilted his head to look up at Marco, who stood a good head taller. "So you own a bar, too, huh?"

"Yes, sir, I do," Marco replied.

"How about that? You oughta drop by my club sometime, check out my bar —" Then, as though I couldn't hear, he added quietly, "And the girls." He elbowed Marco.

I elbowed Marco, too.

"Speaking of Dirty Al's," Al began, only to be interrupted by a clanking of bracelets when Pepper, Ginger, and Francesca returned. Fortunately, Marco's mom seemed to have recovered from the shock of meeting the Howards. Her cheeks had regained their healthy color, and her smile had found its way back . . . until Al announced that he and Pepper had decided Cinnamon and Rafe should hold their reception at his club.

And Francesca asked, "What club would that be?"

CHAPTER SIXTEEN

"Let me be sure I understand, eh?" Francesca said, smiling so hard I could hear her teeth grinding. She touched the gold cross that she wore at her neck, as though drawing strength from it. "You want to hold *my* son's reception at your gentlemen's club?"

It wasn't so much a question as it was a challenge. Marco moved closer to her, probably to restrain her in case she attacked.

"Al's got a great big banquet room on the second floor," Pepper said proudly, "and lots of staff to serve the food and drinks."

I wondered if the staff would be wearing formal G-strings for the occasion.

"Hey, it's free," Al said with a shrug, "and we've got plenty of room for all five hundred guests."

"Five *hundred?*" Francesca managed to say without choking.

"That's our side," Pepper said. "We

weren't sure how many you wanted to invite."

Cinnamon chose that moment to burst into the castle and slam the door behind her, causing both of the Howards to spring into action.

"Hey, Cinnabun," Al said, scooting out of the dining room, Pepper and Ginger close behind. "Come say hi to Mrs. Salvare and —"

"I don't ever want to hear the name Salvare again!" Cinnamon shouted. "I *hate* Rafe!"

We heard shoes pounding on marble steps, and then a door slammed somewhere above us, echoing loudly in the great hall below. That was the problem with castles. Noisy.

Francesca said to us, "I think it's a good time for us to leave, no?" I wasn't about to disagree, but Marco tried.

"They made a meal for us, Mom."

She narrowed her eyes at him. "I will say only two words to you, Marco. Dirty. Al's." Then she marched out of the dining room.

Pepper had followed Cinnamon upstairs, leaving Al at the bottom of one side of the staircase, calling, "C'mon, Cinn, this can be worked out! You'll see." He turned as we came into the hall and shrugged. "Kids.

261

What can ya do with 'em?"

"Cinn, honey, open up," Pepper called in a sweet voice, tapping on her daughter's door. When that didn't produce the result she wanted, she pounded on the wood and screeched, "Open this friggin' door!"

"Daddeeeeeeee," Cinnamon wailed from far off. "I want Daddeeeeeee."

"Go take care of your child," Francesca said, suddenly becoming helpful, although she did manage to get her point across. Cinnamon *was* a child. "We will make it another time, eh?"

"Are you sure?" Al said, looking relieved.

"Believe me, it is not a problem." Francesca offered her hand. "Please give my thanks to your wife for her hospitality."

With that, Francesca tossed one end of her scarf over her shoulder and marched toward the door. Marco retrieved my coat; then we said our good-byes and followed. Once outside, Marco helped me into the trench coat and held out his arm to support me, but instead, I took off my high heels and walked the rest of the way on bare feet. Cold, yes, but I'd had enough haute couture for one night.

Francesca was waiting by the car. "We will not speak of tonight outside the family."

Then she gave me a fierce hug. "Thank you, Abby."

"You're welcome . . . for what?"

"For not being like them." With a shudder, she got into her car and rolled down the window. "Now I will go kill my last-born."

As I slid into the Prius, Marco took out his cell phone and called Rafe. "Mom is on her way to find you. You'd better be sick or dying, because she's going to tear you a new one."

Marco listened to Rafe as he buckled his seat belt and started the engine, then hit the speaker button so I could hear. "Rafe, would you repeat that?"

"I said Cinnamon wants a huge, pull-out-all-the-stops wedding!" Rafe said. "Do you know that the groom's parents are supposed to pay for all the liquor at the reception? Can you imagine what Mom would do to me if I told her she had to pay for five hundred guests? So I told Cinnamon we'd just elope, and she went ballistic on me. What's wrong with eloping?"

"Nothing," I said, "unless your bride has her heart set on a big, traditional wedding. And by the way, five hundred is just the Howards' side."

"Did you know Cinnamon's dad wants

the reception held at Dirty Al's?" Marco asked.

"He's her stepdad, and yeah, she told me about that when we got to the club. But before you start yelling, I didn't know Mr. Howard owned that kind of business. Holy crap, Marco, Mom would string me up by my thumbs before she let us hold our reception there."

"Yep," Marco said.

"Is my ring still in his safe?" I asked.

"No, we took it out," Rafe said. "Then we argued about the wedding, and she threw it at me. Almost put out my eye."

"Wait. You *have* my ring?" I cried. "It's in your possession right now?"

"Oh, right," Rafe said sheepishly. "I guess you want it back."

He guessed? "Where are you?" I asked.

"I just pulled up in front of Marco's apartment."

"Okay, we'll be right over," I said.

"Rafe," Marco cut in, "meet us at Abby's instead. Leave now, before Mom gets there."

Marco glanced at me as he tucked his phone into his pocket. "Unless you'd rather ask for the ring in front of my mom."

"Good thinking, Salvare."

Within fifteen minutes, Rafe had dropped

off the ring and was on his way back to take his licks with his mom, and Marco was opening a bottle of wine in my kitchen, preparing a little celebration, while I put on some slow jazz, lit a few candles in the living room, and dashed into the bathroom to brush my teeth.

When I returned, Marco was holding two glasses of red wine. I took one of the glasses and said, "We need a special toast for the occasion."

Marco thought for a moment, then touched his glass to mine. "Here's to the woman who's right for me in every way. I consider myself one helluva lucky guy to have found you. You really are my sunshine."

Aw. Coming from a man of few words, that meant a lot. "Thank you, Marco. I feel the same way about you, and I've never felt that way about anyone before."

We sipped, and then Marco set both glasses aside so he could take me in his arms. As we danced to the sexy voice of Sade, Marco murmured with his lips against my ear, "We've waited a long time for this moment."

"I know."

He took the ring from his pocket, and held it up. "Still like it?"

"I adore it."

We stopped dancing so he could take my left hand in his. Marco slid the ring onto my finger, then lifted my hand to his lips and kissed each finger before turning my hand over to kiss my palm. It was a gloriously happy moment that I'd never forget in a million years.

He pulled me into my arms. "I love you, Abby."

"I love you, too, Marco."

Every cell in my body vibrated with passion as Marco swept me up and carried me to the bedroom to finish our celebration.

Shortly after midnight, as I was saying good-bye to Marco, who had to go to work, Nikki came home from her evening shift at the hospital. "Hold up, Marco," she said, heading straight for the computer in the living room. "You might want to take a look at what I found on the Internet before you leave."

"What did you find?" I asked.

"A blog site devoted to Ken Lipinski."

"A fan club?" I asked, following her.

"Not quite." Nikki sat down, logged on, and typed an address in the search box. A Web site popped up. Marco and I leaned down to look over her shoulder.

" 'I hate my ex to death dot com,' " I read.

"It's Darla Mae Brown's blog site," Nikki explained. "She's the Lip's ex-wife, but she took back her maiden name. She's an LPN and used to work at the hospital. One of the X-ray techs still stays in touch with her and told me about it. Look. Here's her last blog."

" 'Fifty Ways to Cleave His Liver,' " Marco read.

I scrolled down a few posts and stopped. "Look at this. She devoted an entire entry to killing him by mixing sedatives with alcohol."

"Here's another one," Nikki said, pointing out the title. " 'Hang 'em High. Ways to Make Murder Look like Suicide.' Can you believe that? And every post is like that — all ways she'd like to see the Lip die."

"She's going on the suspect list," Marco said. "I'll take a closer look at that site tomorrow." He gave me a kiss, then headed for the door. "See you in the morning, Buttercup."

At the door, he called, "Nikki, check out Abby's hand."

Nikki stopped reading and swung to gaze at me. "Did you get the ring back?"

I dangled my left hand in front of her. "I got it back."

Marco closed the door on our excited screams as we hugged and jumped up and

267

down and hugged some more, behaving just like Tara and her friends.

Men weren't comfortable with high emotions.

I was so excited about finally having my engagement ring that I woke well before the alarm rang the next morning. I hopped out of bed and danced over to Simon, who was sitting on my dresser, staring at me like a vulture who'd just spotted breakfast. Scooping him into my arms, I twirled him around, singing, "Good day, Sunshine," until he wiggled free, leaped to the floor, and took off for the kitchen. He wasn't comfortable with high emotions, either.

I admired the diamond while I fed Simon, ate breakfast, showered, dried my hair, dusted my freckles with mineral powder, and applied lip gloss. Regrettably, before I left, I had to take the ring off and string it on a gold chain to wear around my neck so no one would see it. I wore a button-down shirt under my tweed cotton pullover so the lump wasn't noticeable.

I arrived at Bloomers early enough to finish five orders and still make it to Dave's office by eight thirty. Marco was already there, coffee in a paper cup in one hand, lounging in one of the chairs opposite

Dave's big oak desk. In his tight jeans and leather jacket, dark hair waving onto his collar, he looked so handsome I wanted to crawl onto his lap and smother him with kisses.

Dave had left his office, so I took the opportunity to give Marco a good-morning kiss, pull out the chain, and show him the ring. "See? Close to my heart." I tucked it back inside before Dave returned, then sat in the other chair, smiling blissfully.

"Happy?" Marco asked, reaching out to take my hand.

"Can't you tell?"

"Wish I could've stayed the night."

"Me, too. Did Rafe survive your mom's wrath?"

"I went straight to the bar after I left your place, and when I got home Rafe was asleep, not stuffed into a garbage bag. So I guess he survived."

Dave came in and sat down. "Coffee, Abby?"

"No, thanks. I've had my fill this morning."

"Marco told me about Lipinski's ex-wife's blog site," Dave said, taking out a fresh legal pad. "Martha is checking into getting a copy of their divorce decree and property agreement from the clerk's office. I want to see what kind of settlement the woman got. Knowing Lipinski, he probably hid assets from her. The man knew all the tricks. It can make for a lot of bitterness."

"It would give Darla Mae a motive for murder," Marco said. "And she's a licensed nurse, so she probably has access to drugs."

"She already spelled out how to use them to kill the Lip," I said. "I'd say she's an excellent suspect."

Marco took out his small black notebook and wrote Darla Mae's name in it. "I'll do some digging on her this morning, maybe pay her a visit."

"Can you wait until lunchtime so I can go along?"

He glanced at me and gave me that little grin he reserved just for me. "Sure."

My heartstrings went *thwang.*

"Next up," Marco said, "Cody Verse. I'll let Abby tell you why."

I related Jillian's tale about Lipinski's advances toward Lila, and Cody's subsequent jealous behavior.

"It's enough of a motive to warrant further investigation," Marco said, writing Cody's name in the notebook.

"Scott Hess has probably instructed Cody not to talk to anyone," Dave said. "You'll have to work around that."

"Not a problem," Marco said. "I'll interview Lipinski's secretary. She'll know if Cody or any of his entourage was there."

"Hess may have instructed Lipinski's secretary not to talk as well," I said.

"Don't worry. I can get around that, too." Marco glanced at me, the corner of his mouth lifting in a coy smile.

A tad smug of him to say so, but true nevertheless. Few females could resist the Salvare charm.

"What about Lipinski's office staff?" I asked. "There might be a minefield of motives among his employees."

"I'd be surprised," Dave said. "Lipinski treated his staff well."

"Really?" I said. "I've always heard how greedy he was."

"Not with his people," Dave said. "Any attorney who handles such a high volume of personal injury cases has to have a crackerjack support team, and that takes well-paid assistants."

"I'll talk to as many of his staff as I can when I go see his secretary," Marco said, jotting down more notes. "I'm hoping someone will be able to provide details about the crime scene" — he glanced up at Dave — "unless there's a chance of getting a copy of the prosecution's evidence list."

"No chance, I'm afraid. Not with me being a suspect," Dave said.

Greg Morgan would know what was on the evidence list, but I'd have to torture him to make him talk . . . or maybe Nikki could do a little undercover work for me. In any case, I kept those thoughts to myself. Dave would definitely not want to know.

"We're also considering Scott Hess as a suspect," I said.

"Motive?" Dave asked.

I explained Marco's envy theory to him. "Hess had ample opportunity. All he had to do was stay behind when the staff left for the day. Marco, maybe someone on the Lip's staff can tell you whether Hess is on any kind of meds."

"I doubt you'll have any luck approaching Hess himself," Dave said to Marco. "If he smells an investigation, he'll clam up."

"I'll head over to Lipinksi's office as soon as we finish here and see what I can find out," Marco said.

I glanced at my watch. Drat. Not enough time to go with him. As much as I wanted to help, I couldn't keep leaving Lottie and Grace in the lurch, or ignore my business. I had assistants to pay, bills to meet, food to eat, and the occasional drastically reduced pair of five-inch weapons of mass distortion to buy.

"Anyone else to add to the list?" Marco asked. "Is there a conflict of interest if we investigate your clients, Dave?" I asked.

"All fetters are off, Abby," Dave said. "Investigate whomever you want. If you find something that points to my clients, I'll have to withdraw from the case. But let's not worry about that unless we have to."

"Then we should talk to Andrew's grandfather," I said, rubbing a calf muscle I pulled while wearing the aforementioned weapons. "He strikes me as a very unstable person."

"Herbert Chapper suffers from post-traumatic stress disorder," Dave explained to Marco, "from his tour of duty in Vietnam. Any kind of stress can set him off, and I know this lawsuit is affecting him, so take that into account if you're going to interview him."

"Has he ever been treated for PTSD?" Marco asked.

"For years," Dave said. "He's on an antidepressant and attends weekly therapy sessions at the VA clinic, but he's getting worse instead of better."

"Sounds like a loose cannon," Marco said, writing down the information.

273

"He is most certainly a loose cannon," Dave said, "but maybe a bit too loose to commit a premeditated murder."

Martha came in with a stack of documents. "Bonnie at the clerk's office was kind enough to fax these over and save me a trip to the courthouse dungeon." She placed them on Dave's desk, then said to us, "Dave represented Bonnie in her divorce. Got a nice settlement for her, too, which is why she's always gracious about helping."

"Thank you, Martha," Dave called, as she returned to her desk. He glanced through the papers, found the document he wanted, and read over it. "As I suspected, Darla Mae Lipinski got the raw end of the deal. All she received in the settlement was her jewelry and her ten-year-old car. He got their mansion, vacation home, BMW — the list goes on. It's a wonder she didn't end up owing him money."

"Why would a judge grant such an unfair settlement?" I asked.

"Darla Mae signed the agreement," Dave explained. "They didn't have a hearing."

"Shouldn't her lawyer have advised her not to sign? Or did Lipinski pay him off?" I asked.

"She went pro se," Dave replied.

My mouth fell open. "She represented

herself? Against Lipinski? Is she crazy?"

"I'm sure Lipinski manipulated her," Dave said. "Probably told her he'd make mincemeat out of her if she tried to fight him. I've seen that happen with lawyers going through divorces. They use their legal knowledge to their advantage. My guess is Darla Mae signed the papers to get him off her back."

"What a dirty rotten scoundrel," I said, feeling my temper rise. "How could he have done that to a woman he once loved? You know, the more I learn about Lipinski, the more I understand why someone would want to —"

Marco put his hand on mine. "Keep your objectivity, Abby."

Keep it? When it came to Lipinski, I'd never had it.

"Do you have an address for Darla Mae?" Marco asked.

Dave flipped through the papers, then called, "Martha? Address for Darla Mae?"

"I'd be surprised if Darla Mae did it," I said. "She blogs openly about ways to kill Lipinski. It's too obvious."

"Let's investigate her before we make a judgment," Marco said. "Stay objective, remember."

I remembered. And at the moment my

objective was to *not* stick out my tongue at him.

Martha bustled in and put a memo on Dave's desk. "Darla Mae's address."

Dave handed Marco the memo, then checked his watch. "I have to go to court in a few minutes. Anything else we need to discuss?"

Marco jotted down the address, then reviewed his list. "That should do it for now. We've got plenty of people to talk to. Darla Mae Brown, Cody Verse, Lipinski's office staff, Scott Hess, Herbert Chapper — I'm also adding Andrew Chapper." He glanced at me, anticipating my objection, but I held my tongue. He obviously had his reasons for including Andrew. I'd just wait and let him be proved wrong.

The phone rang and Martha answered it in the outer room. A few seconds later she stuck her head in the doorway. "Connor McKay on the line regarding Andrew. He says you'll want to talk to him. Should I take a message?"

"I'll take the call," Dave said.

"I'll bet that rat followed me here," I said. "Be careful, Dave. Conner is sneaky."

Dave pressed the button to put him on speakerphone. "How can I help you, Mr. McKay?"

"Hot off the press, Counselor," McKay said with gloat in his voice. "Thought you'd want to know that one Andrew Chapper has just been arrested for resisting arrest, public intox, and, last but not least, carrying a concealed weapon, a forty-five Magnum with — according to Andrew himself — a bullet meant for Cody Verse."

Dave took him off speakerphone to say to us, "Just what I needed." He waited a second, then picked up the handset and said, "I have no comment." He hung up and let out a heavy sigh. "Looks like I'll be making a stop at the jail, too."

I watched Marco write Andrew's name in his notebook. Sometimes holding one's tongue saves one from looking like an idiot.

CHAPTER SEVENTEEN

Marco and I left Dave's office at eight forty-five and headed back to Bloomers together. At that time of morning, the town square was filled with the usual businesspeople hurrying to their offices and shops, in addition to the mobs of Cody Verse fans that had set up camp on the courthouse lawn.

"Can you be ready at noon to interview Darla Mae?" Marco asked.

"Sure. It's my lunch hour. And you can fill me in on what Lipinski's staff has to say. Just don't turn on too much charm, okay? I don't want to have to fend off any frisky females."

Stopped at the corner in front of Bindstrom's Jewelry, Marco put an arm around me and kissed my cheek. "The only fending off you'll need to do is with me, Fireball."

He didn't need to worry about that happening.

Mr. Bindstrom came out the door just as

we were about to kiss. "Morning," he called.

"Morning," we replied, putting a respectable distance between us.

The jeweler stood outside studying his display windows, so Marco and I exchanged a discreet kiss, then headed in different directions. I turned onto Franklin and went toward Bloomers, keeping a sharp eye out for McKay, while Marco headed for the public parking lot.

Back at Bloomers, I found everything in perfect order, ready to open for the day. Grace handed me a cup of coffee and pointed me toward the workroom, where Lottie was creating a huge floral arrangement for the New Chapel Savings Bank's lobby as the bank prepared to celebrate its fiftieth year in business.

The glossy black Oriental-design vase, which had a base diameter of eighteen inches and a height of two feet, was filled with a riot of spring and summer flowers in a trio of red, orange, and pink: red amaryllis, scarlet geraniums, orange gerberas, dark pink gerberas, midpink peonies, glory lilies, magenta anemones, orange broom, and brilliant red stock, with a backdrop of green hellebores and dark green bergenias. The entire arrangement stood four feet high and nearly three feet wide, a perfect centerpiece for a large, elegantly appointed lobby.

I leaned over to inhale the fresh, sweet aromas. "Outstanding, Lottie."

"Thanks, sweetie. Fill us in on your meeting."

I did, quickly, because it was almost nine o'clock. And as soon as Grace turned the sign in the door to OPEN, our regular morning customers flocked in, eager to find out what kind of scones she'd made for the day.

"Raisin oatmeal," I heard her announce. This was greeted by applause. The coffee-and-tea parlor had become Grace's stage.

The phone rang and Lottie answered it at the desk, then took down an order. More orders waited on the spindle. Everything in my life was finally coming together. My flower shop was still afloat. My fiancé was not only extremely sexy, but also sensitive and supportive. My assistants were the best in the world. My parents were happy. I had my ring back . . .

The bell over the door jingled and a female voice called, "Abs? Yoo-hoo! Are you in the workroom? Have I got a surprise for you!"

And then there was Jillian.

She swept through the curtain and paused, turning so I could see her long, crimson wrap-sweater with one end draped over her shoulder, beneath which were a creamy white cashmere pullover and matching wool slacks, ending with glossy red ballet flats. She plunked her huge gold tote bag down on top of the worktable, scattering stray leaves and rose petals, and heaved a satisfied sigh. "I'm glad I caught you in. You, too, Lottie," she said, catching my assistant trying to slip out of the room. "You'll want to stay for this."

Lottie sheepishly returned, giving me a look that said, *What is she cooking up now?*

I folded my arms. "What's the surprise?"

"Well," she said jauntily, "as you both know, I'm Lila Redmond's fashion consultant."

"Jillian," I said with a sigh, "how long are you going to keep that up?"

"As long as La Lila needs me. Anyway, I've decided to bring all three of you up to speed on the current fashion trends so you don't embarrass yourselves in front of Lila or the media."

"How are you going to do that?" I asked skeptically.

"By holding a workshop. I thought noon today would be the perfect time."

"I have to be somewhere at noon, Jillian."

"And I have to run the shop while Abby's out," Lottie said with a shrug.

Jillian clucked her tongue. "That's too bad, Lottie, because your hair . . ."

Lottie was just about to leave, but at that she said, "What about my hair?"

"It's so" — Jillian waved her hand in the air — "nineteen eighties."

Lottie came back to the worktable, patting her short, brassy curls. "What's wrong with that? The nineteen eighties were good years."

"Have you walked down the hair aisle at the drugstore lately?" Jillian asked with as much tact as she could muster. "Have you seen all the products designed to *straighten* curls?"

Lottie seemed to deflate. "I guess I haven't paid any attention."

Jillian put her hands on her slender hips and gave Lottie a slow once-over, shaking her head. "And then there's all that pink. Pink sweatshirt, pink sneakers, pink lipstick, pink earrings." Jillian sighed. "Pink barrettes."

Lottie stuck out her lower lip. "I like pink."

"So do I," Jillian said. "The trick is to use it as your accent color, not your lifestyle."

Lottie glanced down at her outfit in dismay. "Oh."

I couldn't bear to witness the destruction of a good woman's self-esteem, so I said sternly, "Jillian," only to have her hold out a palm to halt me.

"Bup-bup, Abby." She turned toward Lottie. "I can help you, Lottie, and I'll do it for free. I won't even tell you how much a private consult like that would cost."

"Hmm," Lottie said, as though doing a quick mental calculation.

Jillian sat Lottie on a wooden stool and pointed at some distant, imaginary place. "Imagine walking in the front door of your house with a new look, your husband stopping dead in his tracks, his eyeballs bulging. 'Lottie? Darling? Can this gorgeous woman really be you?'"

Somehow I couldn't picture salt-of-the-earth Herman, wearing his old, tattered sweat suit, parked in front of a television tuned to a basketball game, calling Lottie darling. Toots, yes.

But Lottie straightened on the stool, her eyes wide, as though she could actually see it.

"Imagine," Jillian said, making a frame with her hands through which to view Lottie, "walking outside and having the cameras across the street catch sight of you. 'Hey! Someone get a shot of that stunning creature. She must be one of Lila Redmond's actress friends.'"

"Actress friend?" Lottie asked, totally caught up in the fantasy.

"You've heard that Cody Verse is coming to the square tomorrow evening to judge the preliminary round of a talent contest, haven't you? The mayor announced it this morning. And you want to be ready when those cameras turn on, right? Just think how proud your sons will be when you show up on TV looking like a model."

Lottie sighed dreamily, sinking her chin onto her palm. "Oh, yeah."

Jillian's eyes twinkled gleefully as she glanced at me. "Sure you don't want to join us?"

I motioned for her to meet me in the corner. "Why are you doing this?"

"I'm just trying to help."

I narrowed my eyes at her. "What's in it for you?"

"When women see Lottie's transformation, my business will soar."

"Won't it soar when they find out you're Lila's consultant?"

Jillian shook her head. "I had to sign a confidentiality agreement."

Right.

"Now, as for Grace . . ." Jillian said, returning to Lottie's side.

The curtain parted and Grace stepped

into the room, head held as elegantly as a queen's. "As for Grace," my assistant said, using her most formal English accent, "she is perfectly content fitted out like a proper sixty-two-year-old British subject, isn't she?"

Jillian opened her mouth to argue, but at Grace's steely gaze she backed off. "So, Lottie," she said, turning to her willing victim, "I'll be back with everything we need for a makeover." She gave her a quick hug. "Won't it be fun?"

A regular circus.

Marco picked me up in front of Bloomers at noon and we took off for Darla Mae's, following his GPS's route south from the town square.

"How did it go at Lipinski's office?" I asked, applying a generic lip gloss that Jillian wouldn't have approved of.

"I had a productive conversation with Lipinski's secretary, Joan."

"She was willing to talk to you?"

"Not at first. She's a private person and still steadfastly loyal to her boss. Plus, Joan fears repercussions if Scott Hess finds out she talked to me. She needs her job. Luckily, Joan wants to see the killer caught as much as we do, so once I explained my objective, she opened up as much as she would allow herself to."

"And just how did you explain your objective, Charm boy?" I teased.

Marco's mouth curved into a playful grin. "By using the Salvare magic — and a little good fortune. Hess wasn't in the office. He's touring the three-county area with Cody Verse while Cody promotes his CD."

"Does our envy motive bear out?" I asked.

"I asked Joan why Hess's name wasn't on the sign out front, and she said Lipinksi hadn't felt Hess was ready. When I pointed out that Hess has been there for five years, she said she couldn't answer for Lipinski. I asked if Hess had ever expressed any feelings about the exclusion, but apparently he wasn't in the habit of discussing personal business with the staff.

"I did get Joan to allow that it was possible for Hess to stay in the office after hours without the staff knowing, but she said he drives to work — he lives too far to walk — so she would have noticed his Grand Am in the parking lot when she left. She said there were only two cars in the lot, Dave's and the Lip's, at closing time."

"Hess could have returned to the office after Dave left."

"Sure. Joan said Lipinski and Hess were

the only ones who had keys to the building."

"What about Hess having access to drugs?" I asked.

"She wasn't able to answer that. When I asked about Dave's meeting with her boss, she said she could hear the men arguing when she left for the day. She said it was heated but not to the point where she feared it would get violent. She said she felt terrible telling the detectives that Dave was the last one she saw in the office with Lipinski because she knew what they would think. She was upset when I told her the detectives were focusing on Dave."

"What about Joan as a suspect?"

"Airtight alibi. And I think she actually liked working for Lipinski."

"Did you mention Lipinski's encounter with Lila?"

"No. I doubt she'd have any knowledge of that."

"Secretaries know a lot more than you think. It's worth a try."

"I did ask if Cody had been in to see Lipinski Monday afternoon, and she said no."

"So that lets Cody off the hook."

"Nope. He's on the hook until we know exactly how Lipinski's drink was drugged. Joan verified that he kept a decanter of bourbon in his office, which means someone could have tainted it before he poured from it."

The monotonal voice of the GPS system kicked in. "Prepare to turn left."

"Wouldn't the killer be taking a big risk by poisoning a whole bottle?" I asked, as Marco moved into the left lane. "What if Lipinski had poured a drink for Dave or for one of his clients? Or what if he'd given the bottle to someone on his staff?"

"An inexperienced killer might not think of that, and a sociopath wouldn't care."

"Then are we dealing with a sociopath? Because it seems like an inexperienced killer would be caught right away from evidence left behind."

"Inexperience doesn't necessarily mean stupid," Marco said.

The GPS said, "Turn left in one hundred feet." Marco put on his signal.

"It seems that it would have been easier for Scott Hess to slip a drug into Lipinski's decanter than for Cody," I said. "Hess could have gone to the office over the weekend, while Lipinski was entertaining at his lake house."

"Hess definitely had the opportunity, and we've established a possible motive, but until we know what drug was in the glass, we won't know whether he had the means."

Marco brought the Prius to a stop, waiting for traffic to clear so he could turn. "I asked Joan if she knew what the detectives had taken from Lipinski's office in the way of evidence. She said all she saw them remove was a gift basket, the bourbon decanter, and the empty glass found near his body. So I think it would be wise to go back to Lipinski's office tomorrow to talk to the secretary who discovered him to see what she remembers about the crime scene. Joan said she had taken time off because of the shock of finding the body. Do you want to go along?"

"If you can wait until noon."

"I've been waiting for you all my life, Abby. What's another few hours?"

Smooth.

Marco turned into the entrance of a mobile home park and followed the guidance of his GPS up a narrow, dusty lane jammed with tiny trailers. Some of the homes were well cared for, with patios outside, and even decorative awnings, while others were rusted and run-down.

Up the road one mile farther was a much nicer park, where the mobile homes sat on decent-sized lawns and had gardens, decks, and bump-outs that gave them extra room inside. But Darla Mae, once the wife of a wealthy lawyer, who had resided in the mansion where her ex still lived, didn't have a home in the nicer park.

"You have reached your destination," said the voice.

Darla Mae lived here, at lot number thirty-one, in a peeling, rusty, gray trailer that was about the size of my bedroom. To me, that spelled one big fat motive.

As we walked up to the door on the side of her trailer, an old man in faded blue overalls lumbered past. Seeing us, he paused to say, "If you lookin' for Darla Mae, she at work."

"Where does she work?" I asked.

"County home, where the old folks is at," he said, then continued on.

"Do you have time to go see her?" Marco asked, as we got back in the car.

I glanced at my watch. Ten minutes past noon. Jillian would be busy transforming Lottie into . . . something, and I really didn't want to witness it. "Let's go."

The county convalescent home was a low, flat, yellow-brick building that had been a hospital in its previous life, long before my time. When local officials finally got around to building a hospital in town, the old one became a home for ailing senior citizens who couldn't afford private care. I'd never been inside, but I'd heard the building was in poor condition.

A set of revolving doors took us into a large, square waiting room that smelled of pine disinfectant and urine. Beneath humming fluorescent light tubes in the ceiling, I saw a small oak desk and chair near the entrance and a pair of stained, lumpy brown sofas against two outside walls, accompanied by a smattering of side chairs and a few occasional tables with artificial green plants on them. Other than an elderly gentleman in a three-piece suit sitting in a chair in the corner and staring out the side window as though watching for someone to come pick him up, we were alone in the room.

Marco pointed out a sign hanging on a door at the back: VISITORS MUST STOP AT THE DESK.

Fine, except that the desk was unattended. A brass buzzer on top had a label taped to it that said PUSH FOR ASSISTANCE. Marco pressed the buzzer several times, as we waited. After several minutes, we decided to try the telephone on the desk, except it had no instructions on what to dial for help.

Marco tried dialing "0" but got a busy signal.

"I feel like we've stepped into a horror movie," I whispered.

"Let's try the door," Marco said, but I was already on my way across the room to talk to the elderly gentleman.

"Excuse me," I said.

He turned slowly, his gaze traveling from my face up to my hair as though he'd never seen a redhead before. "Yes, ma'am?" he asked in a trembling voice.

"Sorry to bother you, but there's no one at the desk —"

He smiled sadly. "Yes, ma'am."

"— so should we wait? Will a receptionist be here shortly?"

"Yes, ma'am." He turned to stare out the window again, so I returned to Marco.

"He says we should wait."

Marco took my elbow and guided me toward the door. "Thank you, sir," he called.

"Yes, ma'am," the old gentleman replied.

We were about to open the door when a woman about Lottie's age stepped out carrying a cup of coffee. She had short, curly brown hair and wore a blue two-piece nurse's uniform. She gave a start when she saw us. "Can I help you?"

"Yes, ma'am," the old gentleman called.

"Not you, Norris," she called with a laugh. "Poor guy," she said to us. "He used to be a banker, so every day he dresses for work in that same suit, then waits for the bus to come pick him up. Sometimes he'll stand on the stoop outside. He never leaves, of course."

"That's so sad," I said.

"Not to Norris," she said. "He's perfectly happy there. I'm Pat, by the way. Who are you here to see?"

"Darla Mae Brown," Marco said, showing her his private investigator's license. "It's regarding her ex-husband. Is it possible for us to speak with her, at least to introduce ourselves?"

"I guess it'd be okay," Pat said, "as long as you don't take up too much of her time. We're short-staffed here. County budget doesn't allow for much help."

"We'll try to keep it brief," Marco assured her.

"Up the hallway to the end. You'll see a door that says PHARMACY on it. She's in there."

Darla Mae had access to a pharmacy.

Through the doorway we found a wide, linoleum-tiled hallway lined with people in wheelchairs parked opposite a bank of windows that looked out onto a terrace.

Some were chatting; others sat staring at their laps or through the windows; the rest were napping. The ones who were awake stopped what they were doing to stare at us as we passed.

"Hi," I said, smiling at them. "How are you?" They continued to stare. Under my breath, I said to Marco, "This sure is different from Whispering Willows."

A nurse in a cheerful print uniform stepped out of a doorway at the far end, shut the door, inserted her key in the knob and locked it, then turned, saw us approaching, and smiled.

"We're looking for Darla Mae Brown," Marco said, as we stopped in front of her.

"Then today is your lucky day, handsome," she said in a pleasant Southern drawl.

Darla Mae was a skinny woman in her early forties with bouffant brown hair streaked — make that striped — with blond highlights. Her hairdo engulfed her head, which was small and rather elfin. She had enormous brown eyes with sagging purple bags underneath, leathery skin stretched over prominent cheekbones, a small mouth, a pointed chin, and a long, scrawny neck. I imagined her as a young woman with more meat on her bones and suspected she'd been pretty. Now she just appeared hard.

Marco showed her his ID. "Marco Salvare. I'm a private investigator. This is Abby Knight, my assistant."

"You're the florist from Bloomers!" Darla Mae said, turning a smile on me that showed a tooth missing on one side. "I know all about you, honey. You've been in the newspapers a lot this past year. Look at you, such a bitty, pretty thing to be helping the cops catch nasty ol' killers."

Bitty *and* pretty. I liked this woman.

She put her hands on her hips and studied us. "So what do we have here? A private investigator and a killer catcher. I guess you came to see me about Kenny's murder, didn't you? Thing is, I already answered all the detectives' questions, so I'm pretty much talked out."

"Could you spare ten minutes to answer a few more questions?" Marco asked, turning the full force of those soulful brown eyes on her.

"Give me a reason why I should," she said.

"We're not happy with the direction the police investigation has taken," Marco replied. "We think they're focusing on the wrong individual."

Darla Mae cocked her head to one side. "So what you're sayin' is, you want them to focus on me instead?"

Marco gave her that ultra-appealing half grin, one corner of his mouth curving up in a way no woman could resist. "Interesting way of phrasing it."

"I don't beat around the bush, honey."

"Then I won't, either," Marco said. "We're looking for information that will help us point the police in the right direction. What that direction is, I can't say."

She smiled cannily. "Something led you in my direction."

"Your blog," I told her.

"Then you already know what you need to know," she answered.

Marco glanced at me, but I didn't have a clue as to what she meant. "What do we know?" I asked.

"That I killed Kenny."

Wow. That was easy.

CHAPTER EIGHTEEN

"You might want to shut your piehole, honey," Darla Mae said to me. "You'll be attractin' flies shortly."

"Did you just admit to killing your ex-husband?" I blurted, as Marco's shocked gaze shifted from Darla to me, letting me know that perhaps I should have held my tongue.

"Let's go up the hallway and sit a spell," Darla Mae said. "I know you got questions."

Understatement of the year.

She took us into a room filled with orange plastic chairs, metal-legged tables, and a row of dispensers for soda, water, and candy. Darla Mae sat down and patted the chair next to her, gazing up hopefully at Marco. He sat beside her, so I pulled out a chair and faced them both. If she did any more patting, it would not be on Marco.

"Fire when ready," she said.

"Are you taking responsibility for the

death of your ex-husband?" Marco asked.

"Listen," she said, "I've been blogging about ways to kill him for months. I put the blueprints out there for the world to see — and someone took me up on it."

"Did you put a drug in Ken Lipinski's drink?" Marco asked.

She gave a careless shrug. "I might as well have. I gave the killer the idea, didn't I?"

And didn't seem sorry about it, either.

"Did you tell the detectives what you told us?" Marco asked.

"About being the instigator? Yep. All they said was not to leave town. So I said, 'How could I leave town? That SOB ex-husband of mine took all the money. Why do you think I blog about ways I'd like to kill him?' " Darla Mae laughed.

"Do you have any idea who actually killed your ex-husband?" Marco asked.

"Nope," she said, "but at one time I could've written a book about all the people that wanted to."

"Who would be at the top of your list?" Marco asked.

Darla Mae leaned back with a frown. "Hard to say. I haven't been in Kenny's life for a while. When we were hitched, there was a list of lawyers and judges as long as my arm. Talk to Kenny's secretary. She'll know who's been threatening him recently."

"I talked to Joan this morning," Marco said. "She didn't mention anything about threats."

"That's Joan. She's very loyal," Darla Mae said. "Hard for her to admit Kenny was that much of a jerk."

"What about your ex-husband's associate, Scott Hess?" Marco asked.

"Scott's a competent attorney," she said, "but I don't think he got a fair shake. Kenny couldn't stand for anyone to step into his spotlight. You've never seen Scott's name in the news, have you, even when he won a case? Kenny had to take credit for every single victory. His office, his win. Didn't matter if it was a crappy judgment, either. Kenny was all about Kenny."

"Do you think Hess is capable of murdering your ex-husband?" Marco asked.

Darla Mae's face scrunched up as she pondered the question. "Scott's a gutsy guy and pretty smart, but gutsy and smart enough to pull off a murder? I don't know. Besides, why would he want to kill the golden goose? Kenny fed him clients."

"Maybe he wanted bigger clients," Marco said. "With Ken gone, Hess would inherit them, wouldn't he?"

"Only if they trusted Scott," she replied.

"With Kenny alive, at least Scott was guaranteed a decent income — nothing like what Kenny made, of course. No one could top Kenny when it came to making money — or hanging on to it. He was the cheapest SOB I've ever met."

"Why did you marry him?" I asked.

"He was nice-looking, smart, and wanted to become a big name in law. I thought he'd be a good provider." She shrugged. "That was it, I guess."

"How long were you married?" Marco asked.

"Let's see. We got hitched after Kenny got his bachelor's degree. I was already working as an LPN . . ." She counted to herself, then said, "Twenty-three years."

"Why did you represent yourself in the divorce?" I asked.

" 'Cause that slime-bellied snake in the grass said he'd kill me before he let another lawyer get a look at his finances. He told me I'd come out better letting him draw up the papers. I knew I was getting screwed, but he got so ugly about it, I finally signed the danged thing. Everyone knew Kenny was greedy and sneaky, but they didn't know how mean he could be. I could tell you stories . . .

"But that isn't why you came. To think,

300

though, I worked all those years to put him through law school, made sacrifices that gutted me, only to have him leave me when someone with money came along." Her expression hardened. "That fool left me for an heiress, as if he ever had a chance with a woman of her caliber."

"This is the first I've heard of an heiress," Marco said, writing in his notebook.

"It never came to anything," Darla Mae said. "Kenny represented her in a big divorce case. When he saw how much she was worth, he wined and dined her right under my nose. He honestly believed she was wild about him. She played him for a fool to get herself a free divorce."

"Does she live around here?" Marco asked.

"As far as I know, she went back to Barcelona. That's where she was from."

"I need to ask you some standard questions now, if that's okay?" Marco asked.

She glanced at her watch. "You'll have to make it quick, honey."

"Where were you Monday until around eight p.m.?" Marco asked.

"Right here. You can check with the on-call doc about that. Monday is his day to make rounds, and I assisted."

"Would you give me his name, please?"

Marco asked.

"Even better, I'll give you one of his business cards." She fished in her pocket, brought out a stack of cards, shuffled through them, and pulled one out. "Here you go."

Marco pocketed the card. "Do you have access to the pharmacy?"

"You saw me coming out of it. Someone has to dole out all the pills every day."

Pat stuck her head into the room. "We need to get the patients back to their rooms."

"I'll be right there." Darla Mae turned back to Marco. "Listen, sugar, if you have more questions, you're going to have to come back when I get off work. I'll tell you right now, though, you'll be wasting your time. I'm not sorry Kenny's gone, but if I had actually ended his life, I'd have taken down the blog that told how I did it. I may have been stupid when I let Kenny push me around, but I've gotten a lot smarter since then."

Marco put away his notebook and extended his hand. "Thanks for your time."

As soon as we stepped out the door, I drew a breath of fresh air and shook off the melancholy that had crept over me while we were inside. As we walked toward the Prius, I said, "I think we can cross Darla Mae off the list."

"Not yet."

"Really? I thought she was pretty frank about her feelings."

Marco opened the car door for me. "Doesn't mean she was completely forth-coming."

"You don't think she gave us the whole truth?"

"Most people don't. Not in the first interview, at least. Did you catch her comment about having made sacrifices for Lipinski that gutted her? That's a powerful statement. It makes me wonder what kind of sacrifices he asked of her."

"I wouldn't even begin to know how to investigate that."

Marco got into the car and shut the door. "What kind of big sacrifices do men ask of women?"

"To give up their jobs."

Marco glanced at me. "That was quick."

Probably because it was a topic Marco and I needed to discuss. What would happen to our respective businesses after we married? We both knew that with him working nights and me days, something had to give or we'd never see each other. But for me to abandon my flower shop was unthinkable. If Marco felt the same about his bar and his PI work, we'd have a problem.

I shrugged. "I'm just saying . . ."

Marco reached for my hand. "I wouldn't ask you to give up Bloomers, Abby."

"I wouldn't ask you to give up your jobs either, Marco."

We had a problem.

After a thoughtful pause, Marco said, "I'll dig up Darla Mae's work history. Maybe I'll find a clue there." He started the engine. "What else would be a sacrifice?"

"Having children."

Marco gave me another glance — children was another subject we'd tiptoed around — so I added, "Before they're financially or emotionally ready."

"I don't think Darla Mae and the Lip had any children," Marco said, "but it'll be easy to check out. Anything else?"

"The reverse situation — not having children. If one spouse really wanted them, it would be a huge sacrifice."

"We'd have to ask Darla Mae about that one. I don't know any other way to find out."

"I might." I pulled out my cell phone and dialed Nikki's number, catching her still at home. "Hey, Nik, I need more information

304

on Darla Mae. Can you talk to your source and see if she knows whether Darla Mae ever had kids, didn't have kids, wanted them, didn't want them — that kind of thing?"

"I'll see what I can do," Nikki promised. "By the way, did you hear that Cody Verse is going to judge a talent contest here in town? So . . . remember that baton-twirling routine we did as kids?"

"Yeah, I remember the routine. I have the scars on my head to prove it."

Nikki, at the budding age of ten, had watched a college bowl parade and decided we needed to become baton twirlers. With her long arms and legs, she'd been a natural. But a short, impatient redhead who was unable to catch a spinning shaft of metal wasn't. I spent most of that summer ducking and running.

"Besides," I told Nikki, "no one would even know what a baton twirler is nowadays."

"Then how about a piano duet of 'Heart and Soul'?"

"Bye, Nik." I ended the call and said, "Nikki's on it."

As I tucked my phone into my purse, Marco pointed across the highway and to the west. "See that?" he said. "Lipinski's office and parking lot are visible from here. Darla Mae would have been able to tell when he was there alone."

"And done what about it? Jogged to his office on her break, carrying a bottle of pills? Besides, the Lip wouldn't have given her the time of day."

"Not necessarily. Think about the kind of man the Lip was, Abby. If Darla Mae had called him just before closing time on Monday, asking for his help, I'm betting he would have stayed late to see her. It would have stroked his ego to have her come to him for assistance."

"I'm sure it would have. The thing is, I didn't get any bad vibes from Darla Mae, and you know I usually do when someone is guilty."

"I'm curious about something," Marco said. "When did you start noticing these vibes? Was it before or after you got hit on the head by your baton?"

"Are you making fun of my vibes?"

Marco's mouth curved devilishly. "What do you say we pay Mr. Chapper a visit?"

"Now there's a guy with bad vibes. I'd really love to go, Marco, but I'd better get back to Bloomers. Can we make it after five o'clock instead?"

Marco reached over and looped a finger

under the chain just inside the neck of my shirt, drawing out the ring so he could see it. Then he tugged me toward him for a kiss.

I took that as a yes.

As Marco dropped me off in front of Bloomers, I noticed a bunch of young people lined up in front of a large tent, as though waiting for admission. The jugglers and acrobats were back, too, performing for the people in line, along with the ad hoc brass band, which was playing a very bad rendition of a John Philip Sousa march while parading back and forth in front of the courthouse. All of it was being filmed by cameramen.

I approached Bloomers cautiously. I wasn't usually afraid to enter my flower shop, but now I found myself peering through the window first to see if I could spot the transformed Lottie — just in case I needed to brace myself. It was always better to be prepared. I'd learned that lesson from my mother's art. But the only people I saw were a pair of women browsing among the gift items.

"Aunt Abby!"

I turned to see Tara and her three friends dashing across Franklin in their pink rapper outfits. "Aunt Abby," she said breathlessly, "did you hear about Cody agreeing to judge the talent contest?" At the mention of Cody's name, they bounced up and down in excitement. "We just signed up for it."

"Aren't you supposed to be in school?" I asked.

"The teachers let everyone who wanted to enter the contest take time off," Tara said. "My mom drove us downtown."

Why hadn't teachers been that cool when I was a kid?

"We're going to perform our rap," one of her friends said. "If we win, we get to meet Cody in person."

"We're not sure which one to do," another friend said. "We have to rehearse them first."

"If we can find a *place* to rehearse," Tara said, swinging back to look at me with big, hopeful eyes. "Like your coffee-and-tea parlor."

"Tara, I'd love to help, but we always have customers in the parlor."

"It'll be after hours." She gave me a hug. "Please? The first round is tomorrow."

"Please?" her friends echoed, their hands folded together in supplication.

"We'll help out in the shop after school," Tara volunteered, receiving eager nods from her fellow rapperettes.

Cool. Extra hands in the shop. "What time

308

could you be here?"

"I can be here at three o'clock," one of the friends said.

"Me, too," Tara said, "except on Monday." She made a face. "Piano lessons."

"I can be here at four," another friend said, "after ballet lessons."

"I can be here at four, too," the last one said. "I have band practice after school."

"Can you serve coffee and tea?" I asked them.

"Yes!" they said in unison.

"Okay," I said, "so how about two of you work in the parlor starting at three o'clock, followed by the other two at four. Then after five o'clock, the parlor is yours — as long as an adult is with you."

Leaving me free after three o'clock to work on the investigation.

"We've got that covered," Tara said. "My mom is going to come down at five today, and the other moms will take their turns starting tomorrow."

"You certainly came prepared," I said.

"We want to win the contest," one of the girls said.

"So show us what to do," Tara said. "We'll start right now."

"I'll let Grace handle that." I held the door open for them. "Head for the parlor, girls."

I followed behind them, still waiting for a glimpse of Lottie. Grace was making a fresh brew behind the coffee counter and glanced up in surprise when the four girls surrounded her, chattering excitedly.

"Grace," I said, stepping through the circle, "how would you like to have some help in the afternoon?"

"That would be lovely," Grace said, smiling at them. She was such a trouper.

"Would you be able to show them what to do this afternoon?"

"Absolutely," Grace said. "First, Tara, would you perform introductions, please?"

Tara pointed around the semicircle. "Sarah. Beth. Jamie. This is Mrs. Bingham."

"Hello, Mrs. Bingham," they said in unison.

"How fortunate you're wearing your lovely pink caps," Grace said. "We won't need to pull your hair back. Would you like to wash your hands, please, so we can get started?"

"Are you okay with the girls helping?" I asked Grace while the girls were washing up. "I thought it would free you up to work in the shop so that I can spend more time on Dave's case."

"It's a splendid idea, love," Grace said. "It will also allow me the opportunity to mold these girls into well-mannered young women, something I find sadly lacking these days." She glanced around at the doorway, then said conspiratorially, "Have you seen Lottie yet?"

"No. She wasn't in the shop. How did her makeover go?"

Grace thought for a moment, then said, "As Sir Francis Bacon put it, 'There is no excellent beauty that hath not some strangeness in the proportion.' "

Strangeness? Uh-oh.

"But you should judge for yourself, love." Grace turned my shoulders toward the doorway. "Lottie's back."

Lottie was ringing up a purchase at the cash register. "Thank you, ladies," she said, handing the customers a receipt. "Visit us again." She saw me and stepped around the counter, pivoting to model her new look. "Well? What do you think?"

That the horror movie had followed me to Bloomers. At least I had the presence of mind not to drop my jaw again.

Starting at the top, Lottie's brassy golden-red curls were now starched and straightened into a layered bob that stuck out all around her head at a forty-five-degree angle. Her thick, pale eyebrows had been plucked into sharp, maple brown tents. Her eyelids sported supershimmery olive green shadow, and her eyes were heavily rimmed with black kohl eyeliner, giving her a Cleopatra look. Her round face had acquired instant cheekbones through shading in a dark bronzer topped with swipes of peach shimmer, and her lips were a glossy persimmon.

Then came her outfit. Instead of her usual small pink hoop earrings, she now sported huge chandeliers made of silver that brushed the tops of her shoulders and must have felt like lead weights dangling from her lobes. The earrings were accompanied by at least four heavy silver chains that filled the V-neck of her olive green knit baby-doll top — not a good look for a woman of Lottie's size unless she was pregnant.

Over the green shirt she wore a ruffled black sweater vest that was short in back and hung to her knees in front, and in place of her jeans she had on a pencil skirt in a black pinstripe, with black high-heeled platform shoes that gave her the appearance of having clubfeet. Lottie was a big woman. She didn't need added height.

Thank goodness I was an expert at disguising my feelings. "Who is this fashion plate?" I cried, putting my hands to my face. "Lottie, I can't believe the transformation.

A. Mazing!"

She giggled like a girl. "Aw, come on, it isn't that much of a change."

Yes, it was, and not a good one. I wasn't sure what Jillian had had in mind at the outset, but I doubted this was it. I found myself hoping Lottie's husband, Herman, was taking his heart medicine faithfully. He'd need a reserve of it tonight.

"What do *you* think of it?" I asked her.

"Well," Lottie said thoughtfully, "I'll admit it takes some getting used to, and it's going to be a lot of extra work because I have to starch my hair every morning and use a straightening iron on it, but Jillian promised I'd be the trendiest woman on the square." She turned carefully on her club-footed shoes so I could get a 360-degree view. "Who says a woman my age can't wear the latest fashions?"

Many, many smart people.

Tara and her friends were hard at work when I left the shop a little after four o'clock that afternoon. Grace had worked with the girls for the first half hour, then monitored them for the next, so that by the time I was ready to go, they were bustling around the parlor on their own, refilling coffee cups, pouring tea, taking orders for scones, and chatting with customers, who thought they were delightful.

The system seemed to be working out as I'd hoped. Lottie was in the workroom, now in her bare feet — having ditched the Frankenstein heels — finishing up the floral pieces needed by the end of the day, while Grace manned the shop. Marco had arranged to have his head bartender take over for him, so he was waiting in his car when I slipped out the front door. Making sure Connor McKay wasn't lurking nearby, I jumped in the passenger seat and we took off.

On our way to the Chappers' house, Marco filled me in on his phone conversation with Dave, who reported that Andrew was still in jail because his grandparents didn't have the bail money to get him out. Dave had petitioned for an emergency bond reduction hearing, which would be heard before the status hearing the next morning, leaving Andrew in jail overnight.

"That should put his grandfather in a foul mood," I said. "I hope he doesn't freak out like he did after Monday's hearing. Did I tell you he grabbed Dave by the lapels and got right in his face to yell at him? I was ready to call for security."

"I'll handle Chapper," Marco said. "I've

314

dealt with his kind before."

"That works for me. What else did Dave tell you?"

"That was it. But I have some bad news to report from the home front."

"What?"

"Rafe and Cinnamon are back together."

"No! I was hoping Rafe had finally come to his senses. I'll bet your mom flipped when she heard."

"Mom handled the news pretty well. I suspect she was prepared for it. I just hope Rafe keeps his promise to give the relationship six months before they tie the knot."

Marco turned onto a street a few blocks northeast of the town square and started searching the house numbers. The homes were one-story boxes on small lots with garages off an alley in back.

Marco pulled up in front of a brown house. "Just so you know, I called the Chappers to ask if we could stop by. I didn't think a surprise visit would be a good idea. I told them Dave hired us. They'll assume we're working on Andrew's case."

"What do we do if Mr. Chapper figures out that we're investigating the Lip's murder?"

"Play it by ear. He'll either cooperate or he won't."

"And if he gets violent?"

Marco pointed to his foot. I leaned over for a look as he pulled up one leg of his jeans, displaying a small .38 strapped to his ankle. "I'm ready for that eventuality."

CHAPTER NINETEEN

Andrew's grandmother was waiting for us at the door, and as we approached, I was struck again by the unhappiness that surrounded her like smog. Mrs. Chapper was a thin, washed-out woman with deep marionette lines that ran from nose to chin, and long, thick, salt-and-pepper hair pulled back with a clip to hang limply down her back. She wore a flowered-print blouse over brown knit pants that bagged at the knees from years of use, white socks, and tan canvas shoes, a look that would give Jillian screaming nightmares.

Marco showed her his ID through the glass storm door. "Marco Salvare. I spoke with you on the phone earlier. I hope you don't mind that I brought a helper."

I'd been demoted from his assistant?

She offered a tired smile as she admitted us. "I don't mind. Come in, please."

"Mrs. Chapper, I'm Abby Knight," I

volunteered, offering my hand. Hers was so fragile I was almost afraid to shake it. "In addition to being Mr. Salvare's *helper,* I'm a florist. I own Bloomers, on the town square. You might have seen it."

Color stained spots on her cheekbones. "I don't get into town much, but I'm sure your flower shop is very nice. Would you like to sit on the sofa? And please call me Tansy."

At least I think she said Tansy. Her voice was so low and soft, I tugged my ears to make sure they weren't plugged.

"Call Tansy," a bird squawked somewhere in the house. "Aw-w-wk."

Another bird. Wonderful. Didn't need to tug my ears to hear that noise.

We were standing in their tiny living room, into which had been stuffed a brown plaid sofa, matching love seat, coffee table, corner hutch packed with small ceramic figurines, and a blue lounge chair, where Mr. Chapper was stretched out, a beer in one hand, watching an old movie on an even older television set in the opposite corner. Perched on his shoulder was a large orange, blue, and green parrot. Not a cockatoo, thankfully, but I covered my earlobes nevertheless and gave him a warning glare.

"Herbert?" Tansy said, since he didn't seem aware of us. "This is Mr. Hammond's investigator, Marco Salvare, and his helper, Abby."

I had a sudden image of myself in curly-toed green shoes, helping Santa Claus pack his sleigh.

Mr. Chapper used a lever on the side of the chair to retract the footstool, then got to his feet and straightened as though called to attention. The bird flapped its wings to keep its balance, but remained on his shoulder.

"Herb Chapper," he said gruffly, sticking out his hand toward Marco. "Nice to meet you." He barely glanced in my direction — not surprising since I was a mere helper elf.

"Suppertime," the bird squawked, flapping his wings. "Call Andrew."

I braced myself for a reaction to the reminder of his grandson's predicament. But Mr. Chapper merely reached up to pet the parrot's head and say, as though to a child, "Not today, Petey. Andrew isn't here."

That wasn't at all what I had expected.

The parrot took off and circled the room twice, his wings brushing Marco's hair, which caused me to duck each time, while Marco remained unfazed, even when a feather landed on his head. Mr. Chapper scowled at me as he stretched out his hand to Petey, who landed calmly and walked up his arm to resume his shoulder perch. "Salvare, you're not afraid of birds, are you?"

"No, sir," Marco said.

Mr. Chapper gave me a look that seemed to say, *Wimpy elf*. He turned his attention back to Marco. "Military man?"

"Yes, sir. Army Rangers, sir."

I thought Marco was overdoing the military thing, but it seemed to work on Mr. Chapper, who shook his hand again, this time with a smile. "You have my respect, son. Rangers are tough. Brave. I was regular army, drafted straight out of high school. Straight into that potboiler Nam . . ." He didn't finish his sentence. His eyes seemed to glaze over as he stared past Marco.

"Herbert?" Tansy said sharply, then dropped her tone back to add, "Why don't you ask our guests to sit?"

He turned toward her. "What?"

"Ask our guests to sit," she repeated.

He stared at her for a moment, then snapped back to the present. "Sit down!" he commanded us. "Take a load off."

"May I bring you some coffee or tea?" Tansy asked, as we sat on the sofa.

"None for me, thanks," I said, and Marco also declined.

"Tansy." Mr. Chapper held up his empty bottle. She took it from him and left the room. I heard a loud squawk, but as Petey

320

was now grooming his feathers, I knew it wasn't him — unless he was a ventriloquist.

"I raise parrots," Mr. Chapper said, as though sensing my thoughts. "Intelligent birds. I've got just two at the moment. Sold one last week. They make perfect pets. Don't need to be walked. Great alarms, too. Squawk like the devil himself when they sense danger."

Devils squawked?

"I'm sorry to hear about Andrew being incarcerated," Marco said, which I thought was rather courageous of him, given Mr. Chapper's past behavior. Or was he fanning the flames?

"Boy's acting out because he's frustrated," Mr. Chapper replied, with a pound on the arm of his chair. The bird shifted on his shoulder but didn't appear alarmed. "No one seems to care that Andrew is the victim here. No one! They've all gone gaga over Cody Verse. Whole town is in an uproar because of that fraud. Look what he's done. Brought the devil media to town. Brought chaos to town. Calls upon that devil-in-disguise lawyer to cheat my grandson out of his rightful share of the winnings. A regular Armageddon!"

Marco took out his notebook and pen. "You're referring to Ken Lipinski?"

321

"Can't stand to speak the devil's name," Mr. Chapper cried. "He's where he belongs, burning in the fires of eternal damnation. I thank the Lord each day that the devil is gone. Good riddance to bad rubbish."

He seemed to be stuck on devil clichés.

"Have you met the lawyer who's taking over for Mr. Lipinski?" Marco asked.

"Hess? No, haven't met him. Can't be as bad as that demon boss of his, though."

Tansy came back with another beer. He took a long pull from the bottle, then leaned his head back with a sigh. I glanced at Marco and opened my eyes wide, as if to say, *This guy is loco.*

Tansy asked us again if we'd like something to drink, and when we declined, she glanced at her husband, who had closed his eyes and was breathing regularly, as though dozing. "This trouble with Cody has been extremely hard on us," she said quietly, taking the bottle from his hand and placing it on the small, oval coffee table in front of her.

Tansy settled on the love seat and for a moment simply stared at her hands in her lap. "Cody and Andrew were best friends, as close as brothers. Andrew didn't have any real brothers or sisters, you see, because his parents were killed in a car accident

322

when he was five, so his friendship with Cody went very deep. That's why Cody's betrayal cut him to the quick. And we were powerless to do anything to help, so we went to see Mr. Hammond."

"How has this whole ordeal affected your husband?" Marco asked.

She sighed. "He hasn't slept through the night since Cody won his contest. Herbert has always had a problem with . . . nightmares. Andrew's troubles have made them worse."

"Nightmares?" Marco asked. "Or flashbacks?" At Tansy's stunned look, he said, "It's okay. I know your husband has PTSD. How long was he in Vietnam?"

"Over a year." She glanced at Mr. Chapper to be sure he was asleep, then whispered, "He still refuses to talk about what he saw there."

After a sigh, she said, "Andrew has been such a dear, sweet boy, always looking out for our well-being. He's very talented, you know. You should hear the songs he composes. They're brilliant. That's why I wanted him to go to a music school. But Andrew thinks we won't be able to make it without his support, so he refuses to leave us.

"When we heard that Cody had won the top prize on that TV show, we thought surely he would acknowledge Andrew as the song's cowriter, and then Andrew would be able to use his half of the prize money for school. It just broke our hearts to see Andrew so disappointed."

Mr. Chapper sat up suddenly and pounded the arm of his chair, causing the parrot to grab on to his shirt with its beak to keep from falling. "That fraud Cody is a selfish pig. Andrew should've gotten half those winnings! It's unfair, damn it!"

"Herbert," Tansy appealed. "Please."

"He'll get his fair share, Tansy," Mr. Chapper said vehemently. He grabbed the remote and threw it across the room, making a dent in the wall. "Andrew's gonna get his fair share!"

That was what I expected.

Tansy waited until the storm had subsided, then said, "Herbert. Ten breaths."

His fierce gaze turned on his wife, and for a moment I thought he was going to throw Petey at her. Then he leaned his head back, closed his eyes, and inhaled through his nose to fill his lungs, then blew it out slowly through his mouth.

"It's a therapy tool," she explained quietly, as he continued the breathing exercise.

"Does your husband get therapy through the VA program?" Marco asked.

Tansy nodded. "Saturday mornings. He doesn't attend as regularly as he should, especially since the lawsuit was filed, but he's fairly good about taking his medicine."

That was his behavior *on* drugs?

"What kind of medicine?" Marco asked, ready to write it down.

"An antidepressant," she said. "Are you sure I can't get you something to drink?"

"We're fine," Marco said. "Do you know the name of the medicine?"

She picked at a piece of lint on her knit slacks. "I'm not sure. Limbitrol, I believe."

Marco made a note, then glanced over at Mr. Chapper, who had fallen asleep again. "Is your husband employed?"

"No. Herbert gets a disability check."

"Do you work outside the home?" Marco asked.

She brightened for a moment. "I used to own a cleaning service . . . but I had to sell it because Herbert wasn't doing well on his own. I fill in once in a while, when one of the crew is ill, but only if Andrew is here with Herbert."

What a life.

Mr. Chapper began to snore. At once, the parrot flew over to Tansy's shoulder and resumed grooming its feathers. One fell on Tansy's lap, and she picked it up and began smoothing it, brushing the soft tufts in one direction and then another.

"Did all three of you meet with Dave on Monday after the hearing?" Marco asked.

"Yes, we did," she replied.

"Did you come straight home after the meeting?" he asked.

"Yes," she said. "Andrew had to go back to work."

"Where does he work?" Marco asked.

"He has two jobs," she said. "He works as a tow truck driver on weekends and as a furniture deliveryman during the week."

"Does he work with a partner?" Marco asked.

"Not on the tow truck. He does with the furniture truck."

Marco noted it. "What time did he get off work that day?"

"Eight o'clock," she said quickly. "Just like always."

"Did Andrew come straight home after work?"

She nodded, keeping her gaze on the feather. Avoiding eye contact always made me suspect that someone wasn't telling the truth.

"After the meeting with Dave Hammond, was your husband at home the rest of the day?" Marco asked.

"What business is it of yours?" Mr. Chapper said suddenly, pushing his chair to an upright position. "I thought you came here to work on Andrew's lawsuit."

"These are routine questions, Mr. Chapper," Marco said.

"You want to explain how that pertains to Andrew's lawsuit?" he fired back.

"Your lawyer is concerned that if you and your grandson become suspects in the murder investigation, Andrew's chances of winning the suit would be zero," Marco said. "I'm trying to see that it doesn't happen."

Mr. Chapper pulled the footstool in and stood up. "Tansy, put supper on the table. Now."

"Herbert," she began, rising from the love seat, which caused the parrot to fly over to the TV set and perch on top, "they're trying to help."

"Supper, Tansy!" he snapped. "These people are leaving."

She meekly obeyed, glancing apologetically at us as she left the room.

"Mr. Chapper," Marco said, both of us getting to our feet, "you don't seem to understand how serious the situation is."

"And you don't understand the word *leaving,*" Mr. Chapper said curtly. "Or would

327

you like me to demonstrate it for you?"

"There's no need for that, sir," Marco said. He called, "Good-bye, Mrs. Chapper," then gave Mr. Chapper a brisk nod, ushered me to the door, and held it open so I could exit first, never taking his eyes off the man. As we headed for the car, the front door slammed shut behind us.

Marco didn't say anything until we were in the Prius, and then, as he started the engine, he said, "That guy is all over the place. A real mess. I feel sorry for all three of them."

"Do you think Mr. Chapper killed the Lip?"

"Right now, he's at the top of my list."

"I'm not sure I agree, Marco."

"You don't believe he'd kill for his grandson?"

"I didn't say that. I just can't picture him sneaking into Lipinski's office to drop pills in his liquor. Mr. Chapper seems the type to burst into the office and start shooting."

"Maybe so, but I have a feeling there's more to him than meets the eye. Did you see the stack of magazines on the side table beside his chair?"

There were magazines on the side table? Wait. There was a side table? "No."

"They were under his remote — before he

threw it. *Guns and Ammo. Modern Mechanics. A Basketful of Dreams.* I'm surprised you didn't notice."

"Are you sure they weren't Tansy's?"

"Hers were in a rack beside the love seat. Two on knitting and three on cooking."

I hadn't noticed a rack by the love seat. Had I been in a coma? "So you're picturing Herbert Chapper ordering a gift basket, then tampering with the wine, resealing the bottle well enough to fool the Lip, and delivering it to the law office without raising anyone's suspicions?"

"It's a working theory." Marco checked the time. "Do you want to see if we can catch Lipinski's staff before they leave work for the day? I'd like to talk to the person who accepted delivery of that gift basket."

"Sure. I'm free the rest of the day . . . and night, too, by the way."

Marco glanced at me, his gaze sultry. "What a coincidence."

We arrived at Lipinski's office at ten minutes before five o'clock, which didn't leave much time for questioning. As we drove into the parking lot, Marco looked for Scott Hess's Grand Am, but it wasn't there. "That should make things easier," he said.

We walked into the office and approached

329

the receptionist, a woman around Marco's age who brightened when she saw him. "Hello, again."

"Hello, Heather," he said, then added, "My assistant, Abby Knight," as though sensing that now was not a good time to refer to me as a helper. "Got time for a few questions?"

"Sure," she said, leaning her chin on her palm and smiling up at him as he pulled out his notebook. She still hadn't glanced my way. I was apparently invisible.

"What can you tell me about the gift basket Mr. Lipinski received the day of his death?"

"The one Cody Verse gave him?" she asked.

There was a surprise.

"Mr. Lipinski brought the basket back with him after he met with Cody at the hotel," she added.

"Did he open the basket?" Marco asked as he wrote.

"Sorry," Heather said. "I wouldn't know."

"Did he receive any other gifts on the day of or shortly before his death?"

"Yes. A package came in the morning mail."

"Will you describe the package?" he asked.

"It was about an inch thick and the size of

a mailing envelope — maybe eight by ten or nine by eleven. I thought maybe one of his client's children had made him something, because it was wrapped in a cut-up brown paper sack and tied with twine, like a kid would do. And Mr. Lipinski's name and address were in a thick childish print made with an orange marker."

"Return address?" Marco asked.

"There wasn't one," she said.

"Did you give the package to Mr. Lipinski?"

"No," Heather said. "Joan took it off my desk."

Marco stopped writing to repeat, "Mr. Lipinski's secretary took it."

"Grabbed it," Heather said, "like it made her mad. She said something under her breath that sounded like 'That witch.' "

Why had Joan neglected to mention that to Marco?

"What did she do with the package?" Marco asked.

"I don't know. Probably gave it to Mr. Lipinski."

"Excuse me!" I heard, and turned to see Scott Hess coming toward us from the door. "What do you think you're doing?"

"Let me handle him," Marco said quietly. Completely at ease, he waited until Hess stopped in front of us, then held up his ID. "Marco Salvare. I'm investigating Ken Lipinski's death. And you are . . . ?"

Ouch. Probably ticked by Marco's slam.

CHAPTER TWENTY

Hess turned red in the face as he glared at Marco. Drawing his shoulders back, he replied haughtily, "*Attorney* Scott L. Hess. And you can put away your ID. I know who you are, Salvare. What I don't know is why you're investigating when we have police detectives on the case."

"A few more investigators never hurts, does it?" Marco asked.

"Who are you working for?" Hess asked.

"Not important," Marco replied. "We're just looking for information."

"So am I," Hess said, edging toward belligerence. "Such as, who hired you."

"Attorney Dave Hammond," Marco said.

"And exactly what makes you think you can waltz in here and question my staff?"

"This is your staff?" Marco asked.

"Damn right it is. My law firm, too."

Marco turned to look outside through the

big glass doors. "Your name isn't on the sign."

Boy, was he pushing Hess's buttons.

Hess put his hands on his waist, cocked his head like a rooster, and got right in Marco's face. "You see anyone else in charge here, *Marco?*"

"I don't really care who's in charge," Marco said. "I'm looking for information and I'd greatly appreciate any help you can give me."

"Get your sorry ass out of this building before I call the cops," Hess snapped.

Heather's eyes got wide.

"There's no reason to get angry," Marco said. "I came peaceably."

"Just get out," Hess said. "I don't have time for this."

"Not a problem," Marco said. "But I've gotta tell you, man, in my line of work, when I see a person with an attitude like yours, I have to wonder what he's hiding. And that, in turn, *Scott,* makes me dig even deeper for answers." Marco gave me a nod. "Let's go."

"Hey!" Hess called. "Are you saying I've got something to feel guilty about?"

"*Do* you have something to feel guilty about?" Marco replied coolly, turning to face him.

Hess marched up to Marco, his chin jutting forward, his nostrils flaring, chomping hard on chewing gum. I knew that smell. Juicy Fruit!

"Are you insinuating I had something to do with Ken Lipinski's death?" Hess demanded.

I slid back a few paces. If they started punching, I didn't want to get caught in the cross fire, especially if Marco decided to make use of his jujitsu training. Just to be on the safe side, however, I inched my cell phone out of my pocket so I could call the cops if need be.

"If you didn't have anything to do with Lipinski's death," Marco said, "why are you afraid to talk to me?"

"Afraid? You don't know what you're saying, man."

"Then enlighten me."

"Why should I talk to you?" Hess threw his hands in the air, walked a few feet away, then came back. "You listen to me, brother. Ken brought me into this firm. He nurtured me. He was grooming me for partnership. Why would I kill him?"

"Well, let's see," Marco said. "He gave you the small, unimportant clients that freed him up for the big, splashy, multimillion-dollar cases that afforded him a house on the lake and a brand-new Bentley, while you're driving a nine-year-old Grand Am with bad tires."

Bad tires? I glanced out the window at the car in question. How did Marco manage to take in so many details in such a short span of time?

"And after years of working for him," Marco continued, "your name still isn't on that big sign out there, or on the office door. For that matter, it isn't on any billboard ads or in the phone book, either. For a man being groomed for partnership, that's odd, don't you think?"

"So what?" Hess challenged. "That doesn't mean I killed him."

"It means you got jack while your boss lived like a king, and that smells like a motive to me. See where I'm going with this?"

"You're talking nonsense," Hess ranted. "You hear me? Nonsense."

"Then let's talk about opportunity," Marco continued. "You had that in spades, with access to this building day and night. Which leaves one question. Did you have the means to kill your boss? I'm just starting to work on that one, so are you sure you don't want to talk to me, maybe clear up some misconceptions?"

"That's it!" Hess shouted. "Get out or I'll

slap you with a restraining order."

Marco held up his hands. "I'm on my way out." He took my arm and we proceeded outside to the Prius.

"Touchy little guy," Marco said, starting the engine.

"You really pushed his buttons."

"Yeah," Marco said with a satisfied smile. "Sometimes it's the only way to get people to reveal themselves."

"Did he reveal anything — besides his temper and brand of chewing gum?"

"He's clearly defensive about being the new man in charge, but he might just be combative by nature." Marco's cell phone rang. He flipped open the phone without checking the screen and said, "Salvare." He listened for several minutes, then said, "Sure, Dave. I'll be there."

He pocketed his phone and put the car in gear. "Dave hired a lawyer from Fort Wayne. He wants me to meet with the attorney tomorrow after the hearings in Andrew's cases."

"He hired a lawyer? Does that mean he got more bad news?"

"Yep. He found out that the DA is convening a grand jury next week."

"Holy cow, Marco. Darnell is really out to get Dave."

Marco checked traffic, then pulled out onto the highway. "Apparently Dave's fingerprints were found at the crime scene, and the missing exhibit was among papers on the Lip's desk."

"That's not much to build a case on. Everyone knew Dave and Lipinski met that afternoon."

"That's why Darnell wants a grand jury. You know how that game is played."

Did I ever. A shrewd DA didn't need much in the way of evidence, just good persuasive powers, which described Melvin Darnell to a T. "And Dave's attorney won't be able to get discovery until Dave is actually charged," I said. "We're going to have to ramp up our investigation."

"There's good news, though," Marco said. "Now that Dave has his exhibit back, Cody is ready to talk settlement. Andrew should get his share of the prize money after all."

"That has to make Dave feel better. Now I understand why Hess got so antagonistic when you mentioned Dave's name. He would have made a lot of money if that lawsuit had gone to trial."

Sitting in the last booth at Down the Hatch, Marco and I ordered sandwiches and beer and then discussed strategy. Working all evening wasn't how I'd hoped to spend my time with him tonight, but we didn't really have a choice. At least we'd be together.

Gert dropped off our beers as Marco put our plan into action. He phoned the physician who provided medical care to the county nursing home residents and got the doctor to verify that Darla Mae had made rounds with him Monday afternoon. However, he couldn't vouch for her whereabouts after five o'clock. He told Marco to talk to Pat, the other nurse on duty.

Next, Marco phoned the warden at the county jail and set up a visit with Andrew at seven o'clock that evening. It was something of a miracle that he was able to arrange it on such short notice, especially since it wouldn't even be during regulation visiting hours. Marco would only say that the warden owed him a favor.

Then, while I ate my Philly sandwich, he flipped through his notebook, found Lipinski's secretary's number, and called her. "Joan, this is Marco Salvare. Sorry to bother you again, but I have a few more questions for you. Do you have time to talk?"

While he was on the phone, I made a quick call to my sister-in-law to see how Tara's rehearsal was going.

"Their act is a little rough yet," Kathy

said, "but it's really cute. I think they actually have a shot at making the cut. We'll probably be here for a few more hours."

"How are the minirappers?" Marco asked, when I ended the call.

"Still rehearsing. Did Joan tell you anything new?"

"No. She was making dinner. I set up a meeting at eight o'clock at the coffee shop."

After we'd cleaned our plates, Marco suggested we make a suspect list to take to the meeting with Dave's attorney. I volunteered for secretarial duty — Marco's handwriting is impossible to read — and finished my beer while he went to get a legal pad.

I readied the pen, then began to write as Marco dictated from his notebook.

"Number one, Darla Mae, the Lip's ex-wife, is an LPN and works at a nursing home, with access to prescription drugs."

I wasn't happy about putting Darla Mae first, but it was Marco's list, not mine.

"Number two, Herbert Chapper, Andrew's grandfather, goes to a VA hospital for therapy for PTSD and is on Limbitrol, an antidepressant.

"Number three, Andrew Chapper, plaintiff in the lawsuit against Cody Verse, has access to his grandfather's meds.

"Number four, Tansy Chapper —"

"Wait, Marco. Tansy? Seriously?"

"We can't exclude her, Abby. She has access to her husband's medicine, too."

Couldn't argue that point. I put her down.

"Number five," he continued, "Cody Verse, rock star, using steroids, could also be on antidepressants to counteract the side effects."

"Okay, wait," I said. "Before we say he's on steroids, shouldn't we have some proof?"

"This is just a rough list. But just so you know, I found Cody's publicity photos from when he first applied to be a contestant on the *America's Next Hit Single* show on one of those celebrity Web sites and compared them with recent photos. The changes are dramatic. His head is bigger. His neck has almost doubled in size. His chest and arms are noticeably developed — all typical signs of steroid use."

"I remember noticing that when he was on TV. I didn't even think about it being from steroids."

"I notice it a lot in baseball players. Another point of note: People on steroids often get the jitters and can't sleep, so they're prescribed antidepressants and sleeping pills."

"Cody was definitely jumpy during his TV spot. So how do we find out whether he's taking antidepressants?"

"I'll have to work on that one." Marco took a sip of beer, then checked the time on his watch. "Ready to talk to Andrew?"

"You bet." I grabbed my coat and purse and followed Marco out of the bar.

It took more than ten minutes for us to go through all the security procedures at the county jail, then another ten in the tiny visitor's cubicle waiting for Andrew to show up. When he finally shuffled into the other side of the room, even in his prison garb and ankle cuffs Andrew was a drop-dead-gorgeous young man, definitely rock-star quality. With his slim build, wide shoulders, vivid blue eyes, clear skin, and shiny dark hair, he made Cody look like a wannabe.

Andrew took a seat behind the glass and bowed his head, one side of his dark brown hair falling over his left eye. I wanted to give him a big hug and tell him everything would be all right.

Judging by Marco's stern expression, however, he didn't find Andrew as sympathetic a figure as I did. He introduced himself and held his ID up to the glass, rapping with his knuckle to get Andrew's attention.

After giving Marco a sullen glare, Andrew

looked at it, glanced at me briefly as I was introduced, then dropped his head again. It wasn't until he heard that we were working for Dave that he showed a spark of interest.

"Have you seen my grandma?" he asked earnestly, leaning toward the speaking device in the glass. "Is she okay?"

Interesting that he hadn't asked about his grandfather.

"Your grandma is fine," Marco said. "We were there earlier today."

Andrew slapped the counter with his hands. "I should be home with her. I can't believe the cops put me in here, man. I didn't harm anyone."

"Sheer luck," Marco said sharply. "You could have killed someone. Drunk, resisting arrest, carrying a concealed weapon, and if that wasn't stupid enough, you told the cops the gun had a bullet in it meant for Cody Verse. What the hell were you thinking?"

Andrew ran his fingers through his shaggy hair. "I don't know! I was wasted."

"That's your defense?" Marco asked. "You were wasted?"

"I just get angry sometimes," Andrew said through clenched teeth.

"Now you know what happens when you get angry," Marco said. "You get stupid. You're going to have to be smart if you want to be a successful musician."

"Like that's ever going to happen," he muttered.

"Didn't Dave tell you that Cody wants to settle out of court?" I asked.

"Yeah. So?"

"You won, Andrew," I said. "Cody is basically admitting that you cowrote that song. You'll be able to go to music school now."

"I wish I had that choice," Andrew muttered, head down again.

"You have the choice of not going to jail," Marco said.

"Yeah, whatever," he muttered.

"Where did you get the gun?"

"It's Herbert's."

"Doesn't he keep it locked up?" Marco asked, pulling out his notebook.

"Yeah." Andrew began to trace letters carved into the counter with his thumbnail.

"What were you planning on doing with the gun?"

Andrew shrugged. "I hadn't really thought about it."

"Yeah, right," Marco said. "Hey. Look at me. What were you going to do with the gun?"

Andrew lifted his head and glared at Marco. "Why should I tell you?"

"I'm trying to help you, you numskull."

I gave Marco a surprised look. I'd never seen him question anyone that way.

"You won't believe me," Andrew said sullenly.

"Try me," Marco said.

Andrew glanced around, as though checking to see if the cop outside his door could hear, then leaned toward the speaker and said, "I wanted to punish Cody for betraying me. I wanted to put the gun to his head and make him beg for my forgiveness." He sat back smugly.

"Try again."

Then Marco waited, his steady gaze making Andrew shift uncomfortably, rake his fingers through his hair again, and finally mutter, "I was going to throw it in the lake."

Marco didn't say a word, just continued to gaze at him.

Andrew slapped the counter. "That's the truth, man! I wanted to get rid of it."

"Why?" Marco asked.

"I can't say."

"I think you'd better say."

He pushed back his chair with a frustrated huff. "I don't trust Herbert, okay?"

"What did you think he was going to do?"

"I just wanted to get the gun out of the house, that's all. Herbert scares me sometimes. I don't think he should have a gun.

345

But the cops pulled me over before I could get rid of it."

"The timing bothers me," Marco said. "Cody comes back to town, you go to court, your grandfather causes a scene, Lipinski dies, and suddenly you decide to get rid of the gun. See what I mean? It looks suspicious."

"Coincidence, I guess."

Marco gazed at him as though trying to figure him out. "Can you prove you weren't on your way to see Cody with that gun?"

"Yeah, by the direction of my car. I was way up north. I'd have to be going southeast to get to the hotel. The cops should've figured that out."

I saw Marco write in his notebook: *Check with Reilly re: direction of car.*

"Where were you Monday afternoon?" Marco asked.

"Delivering furniture."

"By yourself?"

"No, with another guy from the store. Call my boss if you don't believe me."

"What time did you get off work?"

"Five o'clock."

"Where did you go after that?"

"Home."

"You didn't stop anywhere?"

"No, why?"

346

"Your grandmother said you worked until eight o'clock."

"Not last Monday. I got off work early."

"Where was your grandfather when you got home?"

"In the kitchen. Grandma made an early supper that day."

"Was your grandfather home all evening?"

"Sure."

"Does he ever leave the house by himself?" Marco asked.

"When he goes for a walk."

Herbert took walks by himself. The Chappers lived on the south side of the railroad tracks, a good distance from the highway and Lipinski's law office — but if he followed the tracks due west, it might be only a half-hour trek.

I thought Marco would follow up on Andrew's answer, but he took a different tack. "Does your grandfather drive?"

"Not anymore. He almost got himself and Grandma killed once because of one of his flashbacks. Now he's afraid to drive."

"Do you know what medicine your grandfather uses?"

"Some kind of antidepressant. Whatever it is, it doesn't work."

"How so?"

"He still has big mood swings. He still gets

in rages . . . talks about killing himself. People shouldn't have to put up with that crap."

"Has he ever harmed your grandmother?"

"No," Andrew said, rubbing his arm in short, jerky movements. "He knows if he ever touched her, I'd take Grandma and get the hell out of there."

That surprised me. "You'd leave him on his own?" I couldn't help asking.

"Are you kidding? In a minute."

"Has your grandfather ever hit you?" I asked.

"Nah. Herbert treats me like I'll break. When he gets stressed, Grandma's the one who suffers. He should be locked up in a mental ward, but Grandma says she took a solemn oath to stay with him. You know, in sickness and in health?" He gave me a disgusted look.

Wow. When the Chappers took those vows, they sure didn't know what was in store for them. It was probably best that people weren't able to predict their futures or who'd be brave enough to get married? I glanced at Marco and he glanced at me. Was he thinking the same thing?

"Let's go back to Monday," Marco said. "Did your grandfather go for a walk that evening?"

"I don't know. I don't watch Herbert every minute."

"But earlier you said he was home all evening."

"I was in my bedroom recording a new song, okay? Check my computer. It logs the time and date I record. So I don't know whether he went for a walk."

"Your grandmother said he was home all evening."

"Then why are you asking me?"

"Why did you change your answer?"

"Because —" He hesitated. "I didn't want you to know I was in my room. How can I swear they were home if I say I was in my room all night? Now, how about telling *me* something? Like when I'm getting out of here?"

"Dave's going to court in the morning," I told him. "With any luck, you'll be out before noon."

"Do me a favor," Marco said. "When you get home, apologize to your grandparents for what you put them through. I don't care how you feel about your grandfather. Both of them took you in and raised you, and they deserve respect for that. Do you understand me?"

My cell phone vibrated. I took it out of my purse, saw that Nikki had texted me, so

I read her message while Marco wrapped up the interview.

As we exited the jail, I said, "You were awfully tough on Andrew."

"He needed it. The idiot could get jail time for what he did."

"Do you believe either of Andrew's stories about the gun?"

"He was drunk, we know that for sure. I'll check with Reilly about where he was picked up. That might help me decide. I'm also going to have another talk with Andrew's grandmother. I want to know why she told us Andrew worked until eight Monday night."

"I'd say it was to protect him, but she could've said he was home with her."

Marco opened the car door for me. "So why didn't she?"

"Maybe she simply forgot."

"Or maybe she didn't know where Andrew was."

"But Andrew said his computer would show he was there."

"Computer programs can be manipulated, Sunshine." He shut the door and went around to the driver's side.

I buckled my seat belt, reviewing Andrew's answers, the hurt behind his anger at Cody, and the bitterness that came through whenever he mentioned Herbert Chapper. "I don't think Andrew killed Lipinski. He wouldn't do anything that would cause him to be taken away from his grandmother. He's too protective of her."

"I think he's protecting his grandfather."

"Are you serious? The way he talked about Herbert?"

"Talking doesn't make it so. It could be an act."

"If that's an act, he fooled me. In any event, I might have been too hasty in dismissing Darla Mae."

"Why? What happened?"

I showed him Nikki's text message: *D M had abortion 17 yrs ago.*

"That might be the sacrifice she was talking about," Marco said.

"But only if she was forced into it. That would make a difference."

Marco checked the time. "It's almost eight o'clock. Let's meet with Joan, and then we'll track down Darla Mae and find out."

I tried to stifle a yawn, but that never worked. "Okay," I said, covering my mouth.

He reached over to run his thumb under my chin. "Tired?"

"Beat. But I'll survive. This is important."

"You don't have to come with me, babe."

"I want to be there."

"Tell you what. When we get to the coffee shop, you relax with a cup of tea or cocoa — or whatever. I'll question Joan. If you think of anything that I missed, you can jump in."

"Okay." I yawned again. "I don't know how you do it, Marco. You work at the bar all day, then do your private eye work at night. You have to be exhausted by the end of the week."

Marco didn't say anything.

We pulled into a parking space near the coffeehouse, La Journalier Routine, and got out of the car. "What happened to the Daily Grind?" he asked.

"You're looking at the French version."

"Because of Cody being in town?"

"Cody and the television crews."

"Unbelievable."

"The realty next door to Bloomers is getting a face-lift, too. New paint and awnings, new sign. . . . In some ways Cody's visit has been good for New Chapel. The town square is starting to look like a movie set."

"You don't have to worry about me getting the Cody bug."

That was one worry I wished I had. Of all the businesses on the square, his bar needed upgrading the most. Marco had bought the old place a year ago and kept promising to redo it, but never found the time. Secretly, I suspected he liked the 1960s decor.

Marco took my hand as we walked toward the coffeehouse. It felt good to walk beside him, to have his warm, strong fingers entwined with mine. I wondered how it would be to have our lives just as tightly entwined . . . if we ever saw each other.

"I'm going to sell Down the Hatch," he said suddenly.

Then he opened the door and we stepped inside.

CHAPTER TWENTY-ONE

My head was still buzzing from Marco's startling announcement as he led me to a table and introduced me to Ken Lipinski's secretary. Joan was probably in her mid-fifties, with light brown hair, small, shrewd brown eyes framed by lots of fine wrinkles, a mouth that didn't appear given to smiling, and a jowly face. She wore a gray sweatshirt jacket over a white turtleneck, gray sweatpants, and running shoes, as though she'd paused during a run for a caffeine fix.

"Nice to meet you," Joan said somewhat stiffly. "I've ordered flowers from your shop many times."

At least that's what I think she said. It was hard to hear over the voice in my head saying, *Marco's going to sell his bar?*

Sure, it would ease up his schedule and give us more time together, which was my biggest complaint with our relationship — or lack of one. But I just couldn't let him do it. He'd told me once that he'd always dreamed of having his own business, and I knew he was proud of owning Down the Hatch. He might end up blaming me one day for squashing his dream.

"Abby?" Marco said, indicating the chair he'd pulled out for me. He gave me an inquisitive glance. I forced a smile and took my seat.

We ordered coffee, and then Marco eased into his questions by asking Joan how Lipinski's staff was coping with his death.

"Scott doesn't quite have a handle on things yet," Joan said tactfully. "He'll have to grow into it, I suppose."

"I had a conversation with Heather yesterday," Marco said.

"I heard," Joan replied, but I couldn't decide whether her tone was accusatory or not. Her expression and voice remained the same. "She told me about it."

"Did she tell you about my conversation with Scott Hess?" Marco asked, as the waitress served our beverages.

"Yes, she did."

"Hess didn't want me inquiring into your boss's death."

Joan stirred sugar into her coffee, tasted it, then laid the spoon carefully alongside her saucer. "Scott isn't the easiest person to talk to."

Said the pot about the kettle.

"It went beyond that," Marco said. "He was extremely defensive, and that always raises red flags with me. Do you think it's possible that Hess had something to do with it?"

Wow. That was blunt.

Joan studied Marco, as though weighing her answer. "I'm not qualified to answer that."

"I understand you're accustomed to shielding your boss," Marco said, "and Hess is now your boss, but you're still with me on wanting Lipinski's killer found, aren't you?"

Joan looked down, as though ashamed. "Of course. I'm sorry if I've given you a different impression. This is — difficult for me." She gave Marco a fleeting smile. "The staff calls me Mother Hen, and I guess I can be a bit overly protective."

"All I ask is that you be honest," Marco said.

"I know."

"Then let me ask you again. Do you think Hess had anything to do with your boss's death?"

"I wish I could say no, but . . . he did have a nasty argument with Mr. Lipinski. It was just before Mr. L's trip to Los Angeles to meet with Cody Verse."

"What was the argument about?" Marco asked.

"Scott wanted in on the case, but Mr. L wouldn't agree, so Scott threatened to leave the firm. Mr. L told him to go, that he didn't need him. He said lawyers like him were a dime a dozen, so Scott stormed out." Joan sighed. "I felt sorry for Scott. He works hard but he's never been acknowledged."

"Did you ever talk to your boss about how he treated Scott?" I asked.

Joan glanced at me as though I'd just popped up from the North Pole. "It wasn't my place."

How frustrating for Scott. Maybe their argument had pushed Scott over the edge.

"Joan," Marco said, jerking me out of my thoughts, "I'd like to talk to the secretary who found your boss's body. I know she took time off from work. Has she returned?"

"Holly promised to come back tomorrow."

Marco put his pen and notebook in front of her. "Would you write down her contact information?"

"I'm not sure it would be wise to talk to her yet," Joan said as she wrote. "Holly's only two years out of high school. She was extremely upset about finding Mr. L's body,

357

and then she went through hours of questioning. I'd give her another week before making her relive it."

"The problem is," Marco said, "our time is running out. The DA is calling for a grand jury to convene next week to decide whether Dave Hammond will be indicted."

"Oh, dear," Joan said, biting her lower lip. "Maybe I can answer your questions. I wasn't the first one on the scene, but I entered Mr. L's office shortly after Holly did."

We ordered another round of coffee, and then Joan began.

"It was Holly's job to bring Mr. L his coffee first thing every morning. On Tuesday morning, I was collecting the faxes that had come in overnight when Holly walked past me with his mug. She knocked on his office door twice, as she always does, then opened the door and stepped inside. Then she started screaming for help. I ran to see what had happened and that's when I saw Mr. L" — Joan's chin was trembling so violently, she covered it with her hand — "lying over his desk, as though he'd put his head down to nap. But his face . . . It was horrible."

Marco let her collect herself. "What did you think had happened? Your first impression?"

"I thought he'd had a heart attack." Joan found a tissue in her purse, then wiped her eyes and blew her nose. "I'm sorry."

"What made you suspect his heart?"

"It looked like he'd collapsed. Men his age have heart attacks all the time."

"Can you picture what was on his desktop?" Marco asked.

Joan closed her eyes. "His telephone was in the upper right-hand corner. It wasn't off the hook. His computer monitor was on. His keyboard slides under the desktop. I don't remember if it was out. There was a cocktail glass near his right hand. . . . That's all I remember."

"Was it normal for him to have a glass on his desk?"

"He liked to have a glass of bourbon around four o'clock. He always kept a decanter on the credenza behind his desk."

"Was the glass full?" Marco asked.

She shook her head. "I think it was empty."

"Where was his briefcase?" Marco asked as he jotted down notes.

"On a console table under the window. That's where he kept it. I always chided him about leaving it there because he liked to have the window open a few inches, even in the winter. He couldn't stand stale air."

"Was his window open Monday when you left?"

"I'd be surprised if it wasn't," Joan said.

"Was there anything different about his office Tuesday morning?" Marco asked. "Any sign that someone else had been in that room?"

"I can't remember. Everything happened so fast. I wasn't even considering the possibility that he'd been murdered."

"Do you have an outside company clean the office?" Marco asked.

"Yes, but they clean on Friday nights," Joan replied.

"What do you know about a package that came in the mail for your boss on Monday morning?" Marco asked.

She took a sip of coffee. "I'm not trying to be difficult, but I don't think that's for me to say."

Marco leaned back and folded his arms over his chest, watching her. "What if it would help us find the murderer?"

"I'm sorry. I don't feel comfortable telling you. Perhaps you should talk to Mr. L's ex-wife."

"We have talked to her," Marco said. "She didn't mention anything about a package."

Joan sighed heavily, running her fingertip around the rim of her cup. I glanced at

360

Marco and he met my gaze briefly, giving me a look that said, *Hold on. She'll cooperate.*

"It goes against my better judgment," Joan said, "because it touches on a subject Mr. Lipinski wanted to keep private."

"I think your boss would understand," Marco assured her.

"The package was from Darla Mae. It was an artist's rendering of what their daughter would have looked like. Darla Mae sends one every year on the same date."

"I wasn't aware your boss and his ex-wife had ever had a child," Marco said.

"They didn't." Joan shifted uncomfortably.

"Was the child aborted?" Marco prompted.

Joan nodded, eyes cast down. "Please understand, Mr. Lipinski's reputation has never been the best, and that was just one more thing to tarnish it further. I realize that he often deserved the scorn he got, but he always treated his employees well and had many satisfied clients. I just wanted to see him buried with some dignity, that's all."

"Did you destroy the drawing?" Marco asked.

"I put it in the trash bin behind the building. That's what he has me do every year."

"When is the garbage picked up?" Marco asked.

"Wednesday mornings," she said. Which meant the drawing had already been taken to the landfill.

"What do you know about the gift basket the police took from the office?" Marco asked.

"There were two baskets in his office when I left on Monday," Joan said.

"I thought you told me before that there was only one basket," Marco said.

"That's wrong. I must have been in a fog. I saw the police carry out one basket, but I don't know which one. I assume they took both, though, because when I was in Mr. L's office Wednesday morning, neither one was there. I can tell you that one came last Thursday by UPS, and Mr. L brought the other one back with him after he met with Cody Verse at the hotel."

"The basket that came by UPS." I said, "Do you recall a return address or a company name on the box?"

"There wasn't a sender's name on it, but I think it came from one of those catalogs we get in the mail."

"Could it be from A Basketful of Dreams?"

"Maybe. I'm just not sure."

"Did you open the box?" Marco asked.

"Yes. I always opened Mr. L's mail. He was afraid of paper cuts." She smiled at that.

"Was there a card with the basket or anything to identify the sender?" Marco asked.

"I don't recall seeing one."

"Wouldn't your boss have asked who sent it?" I asked.

Joan shook her head. "He didn't pay any attention to things like that. If there'd been a card, I would have sent a thank-you from him."

"Did you see what was in the basket from Cody?" Marco asked.

"Yes. It had a clear wrap around it. There were various kinds of cheeses and crackers, chocolates, and a bottle of champagne. I believe that was all."

"Are you sure it was from Cody?" I asked.

"I assumed it was," she answered.

"Did you hear anything about an encounter your boss had with Lila Redmond?" I asked.

She gave me a quizzical gaze. "An encounter?"

"A sexual encounter."

"I certainly did not," Joan said tersely. She checked the time, then finished her coffee. "It's been a long day and I have to be up early tomorrow. Are we finished?"

Marco capped his pen and put away his notebook. "I think that'll do it. I appreciate your talking to us, Joan. I know it's been rough. Let's hope it gets better from here."

We said our good-byes outside the coffee shop, and then Marco and I headed toward his car.

"What are you thinking?" I asked Marco, after we were buckled in.

"That Darla Mae has spent years trying to punish Lipinski for that abortion — those drawings, her blogging. Maybe she didn't feel they were punishment enough."

"But why kill him now? She sent a drawing every year."

"Maybe something happened this year to push her over the edge."

"I suppose it's possible."

"How about you, Abby? What are you thinking?"

"That we need to talk about the bar."

Marco was about to start the engine, but stopped to give me a curious glance. "The bar?" Then his expression cleared and he turned the key. "It'll be fine, Abby. I don't need the bar to make a living."

"But you love Down the Hatch, Marco."

"No, I love *you,* Abby. Down the Hatch is just a business." Marco put the car in gear.

"Let's go see Darla Mae. Do you want to handle the abortion question? It might be easier coming from you."

"Sure." I drew a heart in the condensation on the side window. "What if you miss the bar?"

"I'm not talking about selling it today. It'll be after we get married. And by the way, we haven't selected a date for our wedding."

"Then we should set one."

"Great."

"Okay, then. As soon as we find the killer, we'll coordinate our calendars."

"Let's do it."

Somehow that lacked the romantic tone the occasion demanded.

Marco parked the car near Darla Mae's trailer, then killed the engine and sat there. "I have to sell the bar, Abby. I'm not going to jeopardize our relationship over it." Then he got out.

I jumped out and hurried around the car to walk beside him. "The thing is, I don't want to be a dream squasher."

Marco stopped. "A dream squasher?" He took my shoulders in his hands and stared down into my eyes. "Do you agree that we don't spend enough time together?"

"Yes, but —"

"Do you agree that my two jobs create the

problem?"

"Yes, Marco, but —"

"No buts." He pulled me into his arms and kissed me thoroughly, until I melted against him. Oh, that man knew how to kiss. I wished we could forget about Darla Mae and go home.

With his forehead resting against mine, Marco said, "You know how much I enjoy my PI work. It's where my real talent lies. Plus, with the bar out of the way, that frees up my day to focus on my cases. Trust me on this, Sunshine. You're not forcing me to do anything. Selling Down the Hatch is my decision. Now let's go talk to Darla Mae so we can squeeze in a little time for ourselves this evening. Okay?"

I nodded. And although Marco's reasoning seemed sound, a little voice in my head whispered, *A decision that affects two people should be decided by those people.*

As Marco had said, however, that would be after we got married. We had a killer to find first.

Darla Mae answered the door with a cigarette in her hand. She was dressed in a bright red satin robe tied at the waist, with green and pink flannel pajamas underneath, huge blue curlers in her hair, and white satin mules on her feet. Quite a study in contrasts.

"What the heck are you two doing here at this time of night?" she asked, then blew a lungful of smoke out the corner of her mouth. "Come to accuse me of something else?"

She smiled wickedly, but Marco didn't smile back, and I didn't either. "Did something happen?" she asked, glancing from Marco to me in concern.

"Your suggestion to talk to Joan was helpful," Marco said, "except that she told us some things that raised more questions."

With a frown, Darla Mae tugged her robe closer about her, shivering in the chill night air. "I don't have anything more to say except good night."

She started to close her door, but Marco stopped her. "I can ask the questions through the door, but I don't think you want the neighbors to hear." He glanced over at the next trailer, only a few arm spans away, to emphasize his point.

With an angry huff, Darla Mae moved back to let us enter. I went first, then glanced around, appalled by the size of her living space. If I had thought it looked small on the exterior, the interior was downright minuscule, crowded with books, framed photos, stuffed teddy bears, and odd pieces of furniture, including a pull-out sofa bed that was already made up for the night.

Darla Mae stubbed out her cigarette in a platter-sized ashtray overflowing with butts. She didn't ask us to sit down, which was okay since there was nowhere to sit but on her bed.

"Proceed," she said, folding her arms over her breasts.

Marco gave me a nod, so I said, "We know about your abortion, and about the artist's renderings you sent your ex-husband every year."

Darla Mae's eyes widened in shock. "Joan told you?"

"No, she merely confirmed it," I said.

"We'd like to assume you didn't tell us before because you knew you'd look suspect," Marco said, "but I've learned never to assume anything in a murder investigation."

Shaken, Darla Mae sat down on the end of the bed, her eyes filling with tears. "I swear to God I didn't kill Kenny. I only sent him the drawings to remind him of what we could've had, what we should've had — a daughter. I wanted to punish him for what I had suffered."

She wiped away her tears with her fingertips, her mascara smearing under her eyes. "That selfish SOB wouldn't let me have the baby. He was furious when he found out I was PG. He wanted my undivided attention. Wanted me to wait on him like a slave so he could concentrate on law school. He said I couldn't do that if I had a kid to raise. So he told me to do something about it or hit the bricks."

She shook a cigarette from the box nearby and lit it with trembling hands. "Losing my baby girl has haunted me every single day of my life. So I sent him a reminder every year on the day she —" Darla Mae covered her eyes with her free hand and wept.

I blinked back tears, my heart constricting in sympathy. I started toward her, intending to put my arms around her, but Marco placed a hand on my shoulder and shook his head.

Oh, right. Never a good idea to console a suspect who might turn out to be the killer.

"Can anyone verify your whereabouts Monday evening?" Marco asked.

"The doc on call," she said, sniffling, her eyes still shaded. "I told you that before."

"I spoke with him," Marco said. "He couldn't verify your alibi after five p.m."

She sniffed a few times, thinking, then looked up. "Pat was there. She'll verify it."

"Would you write down her full name and phone number?" Marco asked.

Darla Mae jumped up. "I'll do you one better. I'll let you talk to her in person. She lives one row over."

CHAPTER TWENTY-TWO

Darla Mae was right. Pat verified her alibi. And Pat's husband verified Pat's alibi. He'd phoned his wife at the nursing home during their dinner break and had spoken to both women. After talking with them, I was completely satisfied that Darla Mae could not have found enough time to jog up the highway, finagle her way into the Lip's office, drug his drink when his back was turned, and jog back without her absence being noticed.

As we drove out of the mobile home park half an hour later, I said to Marco, "I think my gut feeling about Darla Mae was right the first time. She didn't kill the Lip. So I'm for putting her at the bottom of the list."

"Mmm" was all Marco said.

"I sure wish we knew what evidence the DA has. That would make our investigation so much easier. I don't suppose you want to reconsider asking Reilly for help?"

371

"Mmm," he said again.

I should probably take that as a yes. Maybe I'd give Reilly a call tomorrow.

"I still want to find that alibi witness who phoned Bloomers," I said. "So tomorrow, while you're meeting with Dave and his lawyer, I'll call Whispering Willows and talk to the two nurses that I wasn't able to see when Jillian and I were there. One of them has to be the person who phoned me at Bloomers — or knows who did."

Marco was silent, no doubt weighing everything we'd gathered that evening. My head was certainly swimming with information.

After several more minutes of silence, I finally said, "A penny for your thoughts."

"Just thinking about making love to you."

I will never understand how a man's mind works.

Back at my apartment, which we had to ourselves until Nikki got off work, I showered, slathered myself with vanilla-scented lotion — Marco loved the scent of vanilla — and put on a sexy green negligee, then checked my reflection in the bathroom mirror. Not bad if you overlooked the freckles. Cleavage made up for it anyway.

I brushed my teeth and gargled, then

sashayed provocatively out of the bathroom and promptly tripped over Simon, who was crouched in the hallway, waiting to play Ghost Cat, his new favorite game.

"Sorry, Simon." I bent to pet him, but he ducked under my hand and stalked off toward the living room, tail swishing as if to say, *See if I ever leap out at you again, ingrate.*

I continued up the hallway toward my bedroom. The lamp on my bedside table was off. The only illumination was the moonlight streaming through the open curtains. Very romantic.

All was quiet in the bedroom, so I peered cautiously around the doorjamb, in the off chance that Marco had decided to play Ghost Fiancé and leap out at me.

First thing I saw were his clothes hanging over the back of my chair. Good.

The bedspread was turned down, too. Perfect.

Even the pillows were plumped. Excellent.

Wow. There were even two glasses of wine on the dresser. Marco had thought of everything . . . except, apparently, how tired he was. He was sound asleep.

"Marco?" I called softly. He didn't even flinch.

I slid under the covers and scooted up to him, smoothing his dark hair away from his forehead. He snorted and turned on his side. Okay, then. So much for romance.

Maybe giving up Down the Hatch was a wise move after all.

I cuddled against his warm body, put an arm around his waist, and whispered, "I love you."

He murmured something that sounded like, "Love you, too, babe."

I was going to add that I agreed with his decision about the bar, but I fell asleep, too.

My cell phone woke me up the next morning. I came out of a deep sleep and reached for it, answering groggily, "Hello?"

"Abigail?" my mom said. "I'm glad I caught you before you left for the shop."

"Mom, it's not even —" I glanced at the clock on my nightstand and gasped. Eight o'clock? Oh, no! I'd overslept.

Next to me Marco sat up straight, checked his watch on the nightstand, and muttered under his breath as he threw back the covers and raced for the bathroom, snatching up his jeans and shirt as he went.

"I wanted to remind you about dinner with the family tonight," Mom said.

"Mom, I just woke up and I'm running late. Can I get back to you later?"

"Of course, sweetheart. Marco's invited,

too, of course."

"Okay, thanks." I hung up and started for the kitchen, gasping when Simon leaped out at me. As I staggered backward, he smirked, then raced to the kitchen and meowed by his dish.

I fed him, started the coffee, popped two pieces of bread in the toaster, then ran back to the bedroom to pull on my clothes. Marco emerged just as the toast popped up and ate his while I took my turn in the bathroom. We finished our coffee, I downed my toast, we brushed our teeth together and were out the door twenty-five minutes after that phone call.

In the parking lot Marco gave me a quick kiss, then jogged toward his car in the guest parking spot. "I'll let you know how the meeting goes." He pressed his fingers to his lips and blew me a kiss, then ducked into his Prius and was gone.

Was that what married life would be like?

One thing was certain. We had to have a bigger bathroom, wherever we decided to live — yet another subject we hadn't discussed.

I got into my car and sighed glumly. There seemed to be so many details to work out before we got married, not to mention planning the wedding itself, that I was beginning to wonder if it would ever happen.

Marco pulled his car up to mine and motioned for me to roll down my window.

"What?" I asked.

"Do not call Reilly."

He'd been paying attention after all. Damn!

Fridays were busy days at Bloomers, and that morning we had customers the moment we opened our doors, when the regulars, who couldn't wait for one of Grace's scones and a cup of her secret blend of coffee, came rushing in.

Lottie was back to her usual pink-clad self. The raccoon eyes and sculpted cheeks were gone, as were the ten-pound earrings. The only remnant of her makeover was her hair, which lay in stiff, flat pieces all over her head. It seemed that the spray starch Jillian had used hadn't wanted to wash out. When Grace and I asked what had happened to her new look, Lottie would only say that scaring her dog half to death was bad enough, but when Herman, with his weak heart, nearly fainted, she decided she'd rather have a husband than be trendy.

We were surprised to see that only two orders had come in overnight for Lipinski's funeral. "That makes a grand total of —

two," Lottie said, checking our order sheet.

Grace peered over her shoulder. "Joan Campbell and staff, and Scott Hess, Esquire. How sad that not one other person ordered flowers."

"At least not from Bloomers," Lottie pointed out. "Maybe there'll be some arrangements from other florists."

"As Arthur Rubinstein said," Grace began, " 'Love life and life will love you back. Love people and they will love you back.' What a shame that Mr. Lipinski never took the time to love anyone but himself." With a regal nod, she sailed off, having illuminated us once again.

At eleven o'clock I finally managed to phone Whispering Willows and talk to the two nurses, Lauren and Kelly. Unfortunately, neither of them had any idea who had called me. All the mobile patients had been accounted for; the others were bedridden. Even more disappointing, they hadn't seen Dave visiting his mom Monday evening either.

"It was just Nadine, Kelly, and me that night," Lauren said.

"Three of you for the whole facility?"

"Budget cuts," she said with a sigh. "Luckily, we're a small facility, so we've been able to limp along with a reduced staff. Just between you and me, though, now that Attorney Lipinski is gone, things might improve."

"How?"

"He was the chairman of the Whispering Willows board."

The Lip had his tendrils in a private nursing facility, too?

"Mr. Lipinski had one goal," Lauren said, "and that was to improve the bottom line. We're hoping whoever is chosen as the new chairman will focus more on patient care."

"Good luck with that."

"Thanks. Anything else I can answer for you?"

"Just a few more questions, if you don't mind. Did any one come into the building after seven o'clock on Monday?"

"Visiting hours end at seven and then we lock the doors. Only the cleaning service is admitted afterward."

A little alarm went off in my head. "What service do you use?"

"TLC Cleaners. They're commercial cleaners."

"Would you spell that?" I asked, grabbing a pen.

"TLC. As in 'tender loving care.' "

Or as in Tansy Chapper?

"Do you want their phone number?" Lauren asked.

"I'll look it up, thanks. Do you know the cleaning crew?"

"Yes, but I couldn't tell you who came Monday without checking with the company."

"Could one of them have used a phone without being overheard?"

"I suppose a call could've been made from one of the offices while it was being cleaned."

"What time does the crew normally arrive?"

"Around eight o'clock. That's when our kitchen closes. We're very strict about keeping an immaculate kitchen."

"I'm sure you are." But eight o'clock ruled out any of the cleaning people making the call. The message had come in before seven thirty.

I thanked Lauren for her time, hung up, and stared at my notes, tapping my pen on the desktop. If it wasn't one of the staff or any of the residents, who had phoned? Who would've known that Dave was telling the truth about visiting his mom?

The curtain parted and Marco stepped into the workroom. "Hey, babe, how's it going?"

"Frustratingly." I rose to give him a kiss.

"How about your meeting?"

"I dropped by to give you the full report. Tell me why you're frustrated."

"I still can't find anyone at Whispering Willows who can back up Dave's alibi. The nurse mentioned that their cleaning company, TLC Cleaners, was there Monday evening, but they didn't arrive until after the phone call came in for me. So where is the woman who phoned Bloomers to say Dave was telling the truth? Do you think it could be Dave's mom, and she forgot?"

"I don't know her well enough to say. Maybe the woman will call again. What else did the nurse say about the TLC cleaning company?"

"Just that they usually arrive around eight o'clock. Why? Are you wondering like I am if TLC was the company Tansy owned?"

"It crossed my mind. I'll do some digging, see what I can find out." Marco pulled out a stool at the worktable and sat down. "Ready for the report?"

"You bet."

"First, the status hearing. Scott Hess appeared for Cody Verse, of course, but Cody didn't show, which was for the best, since the Chappers were in the courtroom. The attorneys told the judge they had reached an agreement, so the case will be dismissed as soon as the judge receives the written copy and signs it."

"That must have made the Chappers' day."

"It would have, except that at the next hearing the judge refused to reduce the bond, which set off Mr. Chapper. He nearly got himself ejected from the courtroom. Then Tansy fainted. It was a circus for a while."

"She *fainted?*" We were five minutes into the story and he just now mentioned that? It would have been my lead item. "Is she okay?"

"She came to right away, and Chapper quieted down after Dave reminded him that he could be jailed for his outburst. Fortunately, the judge gave the Chappers the option of using their house as collateral. Once they agreed, Andrew was free to go, but the judge made it clear that if Andrew doesn't appear for any of his court dates, he'll order a foreclosure."

"What was Mr. Chapper's reaction to that?"

"He did a lot of grumbling, but Dave kept giving him warning looks, so he behaved. Tansy was as white as a ghost, but both accepted the deal, and Andrew went home with them."

"I hope Andrew realizes how serious that is."

"Dave talked to him after the hearing. He couldn't spend too much time with the kid, though, because of our meeting with Dave's new attorney, Dimitri Ballas."

"What did you think of him?"

"I liked him. He has an excellent reputation. He'll do a good job for Dave. In fact, Ballas has already procured a copy of the coroner's final report." Marco took out his notebook and flipped to a page. "Here it is in layman's terms: Lipinski's death was caused by a mix of alcohol and amitriptyline with chlordiazepoxide, the psychotherapeutic drug commonly known as Limbitrol, in an amount more than sufficient to slow his breathing and stop his heart."

"Limbitrol? What Mr. Chapper is on?"

"I mentioned that to Ballas, but he didn't seem too excited about it. He said it's prescribed routinely for stress and depression."

"Even so, do you remember Tansy being reluctant to tell us what Mr. Chapper was taking? Might she be protecting him?"

"In all fairness, Abby, all three Chappers, Darla Mae, and even Mrs. Hammond have access to Limbitrol. I verified that with both nursing homes this morning."

"True, but if you take Mrs. Hammond out of the equation, we've already decided Darla Mae is the least likely suspect of the bunch."

"As I remember, you decided that."

And here I'd thought Marco's mind had been elsewhere during that discussion.

"Frankly, Abby, Darla Mae also has the strongest motive of any of our suspects, not to mention that she's within shouting distance of his office."

"Hess is closer. Plus, Darla Mae's co-worker Pat and Pat's husband verified her alibi."

"Only about an hour of it. Don't scowl. All I'm saying is that Darla Mae might be more enterprising than you think. I'm trying to get a copy of her phone records to see if she called Lipinski's office. Beyond that, without knowing what evidence the police have, all we can do is try to eliminate other suspects."

"We haven't even started to investigate Cody."

"He's our biggest challenge. None of his people are going to talk to us. And even if we're able to find out who his doctor is, the doc won't divulge anything."

"If I could meet with Lila in private, I'll bet I could get her to talk."

"Cody will never let you get close to her,

Abby, and that goes double if he has something to hide. Ballas told me Cody has a history of blowing his cork where Lila is concerned."

Wow. Jillian actually got it right.

"The week after he won the *America's Next Hit Single* contest," Marco said, "Cody hammered some poor guy waiting in line for an autograph because the guy tried to get a photograph of Lila. It makes me wonder if those bodyguards are for Cody's protection or to keep people away from Lila."

"Cody is sure one insecure guy."

"Insecure guys can be dangerous. And by the way, Dave explained why he's been so preoccupied. It's just what Martha thought — he was afraid he was in the early stages of Alzheimer's. But after a good checkup his doctor chalked up his forgetfulness to stress and ordered him to take a vacation and find a yoga class."

"That's terrific! What a relief. I'm sure Dave felt much better after receiving that news. Now if only we could give him some good news, too."

I sat down beside Marco and put my chin in my hand. There had to be a way to get to Lila. Too bad Jillian wasn't really her wardrobe consultant. I frowned at my reflection in the copper pot on the table. I'd pulled it out for a centerpiece I had yet to complete. I was planning a spring arrangement of bicolored tulips in bright orange and soft sherbet; hyacinths in hues of purple, pink, and mango; glamorous gloriosas in soft pink with white edges; and giant alliums . . . And there was my way around Cody!

"Marco, I can deliver flowers to Lila at the hotel. That always gets me in the door."

Marco cupped my face and gazed into my eyes. "Did you hear me mention that Cody could be dangerous? I'll handle this part of the investigation."

Before I could object, Marco leaned in and pressed his lips against mine, which made it difficult to stay focused. We kissed for a long minute, and then he straightened up and fixed me with his penetrating brown eyes. "No floral delivery to Lila. Promise?"

That kiss was a totally unfair bribe. "Fine. But are you saying Cody won't go after you?"

A flicker of a grin lifted the corners of his mouth. "I'd like to see him try."

By the steely glint in Marco's eye, I knew he'd relish the chance to mete out some punishment to Cody. But I was definitely *not* in favor of that. However, I was in favor of another of Marco's delicious kisses. His tough-guy attitude always revved my engine.

When we were halfway into our curl-your-toes kiss, Grace came through the curtain. "Sorry to interrupt, love, but Lottie is leaving for lunch, and Marco's brother is here to buy your mum's tea cart."

Marco and I glanced at each other in surprise, then jumped off the stools and followed Grace into the shop. She pointed out Rafe in the back corner beneath the towering umbrella plant, the tea cart's current spot, crouching to inspect the casters on the bottom. Lottie waited behind the cash counter with her coat on and her purse over her shoulder.

"I've got it covered, Lottie," I said, as Grace continued into the coffee-and-tea parlor to attend to customers there.

Rafe got to his feet, a blush spreading up his neck. "Hey, bro. Hot stuff. What's happening?"

"You first," Marco said, folding his arms across his chest and fixing him with a big-brother stare.

Rafe smoothed his palms down the sides of his jeans, as though they were damp. "Well, um, I was thinking of giving this — it *is* a tea cart, right? — to the Howards. Cinnamon heard her stepdad telling her mom about it after you guys took off, so I thought maybe it would smooth things over with her."

"Smooth things over?" Marco asked. "I thought you were back together."

"She's still ticked, so I thought a gift to say we're sorry for the —" Rafe glanced around to see if anyone was nearby, then whispered, "*ring mix-up* would be a good idea."

"*We're* sorry?" Marco asked, his jaw muscle throbbing.

"Okay," I said, hooking my arms through theirs, "let's take this to the back room, guys."

I signaled to Grace that I'd be right back, then led the brothers into the workroom and stood guard at the curtain in case anyone came into the shop.

"I don't have anything to be sorry about, Rafe," Marco said, obviously miffed. "*I* didn't give the ring to Cinnamon. If you want to give the cart to them, fine, but it's not from *us*. Got it?"

"I didn't give her the ring, either," Rafe shot back, locking glares with his brother. Their expressions were nearly identical. I had a feeling their tempers were, too.

"Hey," I said, stepping between them, "I think we can agree that there was a mix-up, but why do you feel like we should give

Cinnamon's parents a gift, Rafe? We didn't hurt them."

"Cinnamon says they were so upset about the way the evening fell apart that they hardly slept and are still hurt. Cinnamon's blaming us for that because of the whole ring snafu. So I thought if I took her parents an apology gift, everything would be good again between Cinnamon and me."

Impeccable logic for a twenty-one-year-old male. But not for the thirty-one-year-old. "That's crazy," Marco said. "I'm not apologizing for something that's not my fault."

"It is your fault!" Rafe retorted. "You sent me to Bindstrom's."

"I wasn't the one who put the box in the glove compartment," Marco said through clenched teeth.

Two stubborn Salvares would not a good outcome have. Or something to that effect.

"Marco," I said, "let's step back and think about this. That tea cart really needs a new home. And my mom would be thrilled to have her cart given as a gift. Wouldn't you call that a win-win situation?"

Marco pressed his lips into a hard line for a few seconds, then muttered, "Yeah."

Rafe gave his brother a smug grin, then

said to me, "How much do you want for it?"

"How fast can you get it out of here?" I asked.

"I can take it now," Rafe said. "I've got Mom's old Buick out front."

I did a quick estimate of my mother's cost for materials and labor, and said, "How about fifty dollars?" I knew I was lowballing it, but Mom always gave discounts to family, and Rafe was almost family. Plus, Mom knew he was strapped for cash.

"Sold," Rafe said. "Can I pay you tomorrow?"

Marco pulled out his money clip, peeled off seven ten-dollar bills and handed them to me. "There's seventy. Let's not insult your mom. And, Rafe, you owe me half that amount."

"Thanks, bro."

"That's really generous of you, Marco," I said. "Mom will be thrilled. So thrilled, in fact, she'll make more." I handed him twenty. "Let's not encourage her, okay?"

The bell over the door jingled and Jillian walked in, a big shopping bag in each hand. She smiled at us. "I was hoping to find an audience. I've just picked out a whole new selection of dresses and shoes for La Lila."

"Jillian, I'm in the middle of something," I said.

"Take your time. I'll get everything laid out." She went straight to the wicker settee on the other side of the umbrella plant, set her bags down, and began to unload them. "Where's Lottie? I want to see how she's doing with her new look."

I would bet heavily that Lottie was cowering in the cooler.

Marco gave me a quick peck on the cheek. "I'm due back at the bar. I'll let you know if I hear anything."

"Coward," I whispered.

Marco grinned as he backed toward the door. "Nice to see you, Jillian." He paused to fix Rafe with a warning glance, then left.

"What's his problem?" Rafe grumbled.

"It's the older-brother syndrome," I told him, wheeling the cart into the workroom to wrap the top. "I get the same kind of hassle from my brothers all the time. Hold the cart steady so I can tape the paper. Anyway, Marco cares about you, Rafe, but he expects you to think like he does. So he gets angry when you don't."

"I'm glad you understand me."

Where had he gotten that impression? "Here's a gift card and my pen. Sign."

He wrote, *From the Salvares.* I almost

390

kissed him for leaving my name off.

I taped the card onto the cart, and then we wheeled it through the shop. I held the door open so Rafe could carry it out the door to the Buick, which, fortunately, had a roomy trunk.

After we loaded it inside, he shut the lid and brushed off his hands. "Thanks, Abby. You're cool."

"Tell me the truth, Rafe. Are you really sure you want to get married?"

"Yeah, I'm sure. I'm crazy about Cinnamon. Wait till you get to know her, and then you'll understand. I'll bet you'll even be best friends."

There was something to look forward to — being Cinnamon's BFF. Move over, Nikki.

I opened the door to go back inside Bloomers, and Jillian nearly bowled me over rushing to get out. "Sorry, Abs. Emergency. Gotta run."

"What happened?"

She paused, a large bag in each hand. "My bank just called. Someone was racking up huge charges on my account, so they canceled my credit card."

"Thank goodness they're looking out for you."

"No, Abby! My card wasn't stolen. I used

it to buy these clothes!" She marched off, grumbling, "I certainly hope Lila appreciates all the work I'm doing for her."

In your dreams, Jillian.

Just after three o'clock Tara and two of her friends dashed in to announce that the plans for the contest had changed because a bad storm was approaching from the west, due to hit around six o'clock. The contest would be held in the banquet hall of Cody's hotel instead.

"Isn't that great?" Tara asked. "The acoustics will be so much better in the hall. Okay if we store our costumes in the workroom?"

"Sure."

As Tara and her buddies carried their backpacks through the curtain, my mind started working. If Cody was tied up with the contest all evening, what would Lila be doing? Watching an endless parade of contestants audition? If it were me, I know what I'd do — order champagne and chocolates from room service and watch a pay-per-view movie in the comfort of my hotel room. And if someone around my age happened to deliver flowers, I might invite her in for a glass of bubbly.

As the girls headed toward the parlor, I pulled Tara aside. "Want to make some extra money this evening?"

"Sure! What do I have to do?"

"Let me wear your costume to the audition."

CHAPTER TWENTY-THREE

Tara stared at me in astonishment. "Why do you want to wear my costume?"

"Because I need to be one of the Code Bluebirds — but just for tonight, I promise."

"No way," she said, wrinkling her nose. "That's really twisted, Aunt Abby."

"Not as twisted as it sounds. It's for an investigation."

"What kind of investigation?"

"I can't tell you, Tara, but I really need this favor. Please? For your favorite aunt?"

She pursed her lips. "If you wear my costume, what am I supposed to wear?"

"Do you have a spare?"

"No."

"Do any of the other girls?"

She got a sly glint in her eye. "Maybe."

Brat. "Come on, Tara, is there a spare costume or not?"

"Tell me about the investigation first."

I glowered at her, but she merely glowered

back. It was like looking into a mirror fourteen years ago. And I knew by Tara's expression that she wasn't about to give in.

I glanced around to be sure we couldn't be overheard. "Okay, here it is. I really need to talk to Lila Redmond, but I don't want Cody to know, so I thought if I could get into the hotel as one of your group, then I could sneak up to her room while Cody is judging the contest."

"Why don't you want Cody to know?"

"I can't tell you."

"That's too bad, because *I* know who has an extra costume."

I pulled Marco's money out of my pocket. I hadn't even had time to ring up the sale. "And I have fifty dollars." I waved the bills under her nose.

Tara was tempted. I could see it in her eyes as she gazed at the money. But then she crossed her arms over her chest. "Nope. You have to tell me *and* pay me or no deal."

I took her hand and slapped the bills onto her palm. "Fine. But if you tell one single person what I'm about to reveal, I'll have to kill you."

She stuffed the money into her jeans pocket. "Yeah, right."

"Did I say kill? I meant to say 'tell.' As in, I'll *tell* that cute neighbor of yours — what's his name, Derek? — that you have a huge crush on him."

Tara's eyes widened so far I was afraid they'd fall out of their sockets. "Okay! I swear I won't tell anyone. How did you know about Derek, anyway?"

I smiled slyly. "I can't tell you."

Marco stopped by Bloomers at four thirty, just as I was getting ready to carry the two funeral arrangements out to the van. "Hey, babe. Do you have a few minutes?"

"Of course. What's up?"

He pulled papers out of a large manila envelope and laid them on the worktable. "Take a look."

On the table were two eight-by-ten full-color glossies of Ken Lipinski lying slumped over his desk. "Holy cow, Marco. These are crime-scene photos. Where did you get them?"

"Not important."

"It was Reilly, wasn't it?"

"Don't ask, don't tell. Come on, take a long look. Tell me what you see."

I stood beside him, scanning both photos, trying not to look at Lipinski's face. Naturally, that was impossible.

In the first photo, taken from the left side of his desk looking toward the right side,

Lipinski's head was turned toward the camera, his face a mottled gray-blue, his eyes open, pupils clouded, his purple tongue swollen and protruding. He was wearing a navy pin-striped suit and a white shirt unbuttoned at the neck. His left hand rested on the desk, palm down, in a manner that suggested he might have been attempting to raise himself.

I shuddered, trying not to imagine what his last moments had been like.

"I know it's not easy," Marco said, rubbing my back.

I took a deep breath, refocused, and began pointing things out. "There's the cocktail glass Joan described. The telephone in the upper right corner. The computer monitor. The open window with a briefcase on the table below it. What's that gray smear? A bird feather?"

"Could be. Can you tell what's on the monitor?"

"Looks like a legal document." I grabbed a magnifying lens from my desk drawer and held it over the photo. "It's Andrew's lawsuit. See this? I can just make out the words *Code Blue* in the second line."

I gave Marco the lens and let him view the document. "Wait, Marco, hold the lens over this yellow item." I pointed to a small object just beyond the cocktail glass. "See it? A pack of gum, right? Can you make out the brand?"

"Not in this shot. It's the wrong angle. But take a look at this." Marco pointed out the open window on the right side of the room. "There's no screen in the window. The killer could have easily climbed in. It's a one-story building."

"Has anyone mentioned that this might have been a robbery gone bad?"

"The cops would have known that. Things would be missing, his watch, for instance."

Marco picked up the second photo, a shot taken from the front of Lipinski's desk. In it, the Lip's right hand was outstretched, as though reaching for the cocktail glass just inches beyond his fingertips. "He still has his watch. And see the Bose stereo system on the credenza behind him? That would be gone."

"That must be his bourbon decanter next to the Bose. Looks like it's half empty."

"Or half full." Marco raised an eyebrow.

I plucked the magnifying lens from his hand and focused on the pack of gum. "Juicy Fruit — Scott Hess's brand — on the Lip's desk. Maybe he left it behind."

"Or maybe Lipinski chewed it, too."

"Both lawyers in the same office chewed a

highly sweetened, fruity children's gum?"

"I don't know, Miss Glass Half Empty. Maybe."

"But do you see where it is? Just a few inches away from the cocktail glass. If you look at his hand, he seems to be reaching for the glass, but maybe he was actually pointing at the gum, trying to leave a clue as to who drugged his drink."

"You've been watching *The Simpsons* cartoons again, haven't you?"

"Make fun. But if Hess turns out to be the killer, don't think I won't remind you of this conversation."

Marco put his arm around me. "You know I like to tease you."

"I can think of better ways to do that," I said, and began to press light kisses up his neck. Yikes. But not with those crime-scene photos staring at me. I pushed them away.

The telephone rang, but before I could get to the phone, one of my assistants answered. It served to remind me that I still had work to do. "I've got to get some funeral arrangements over to the Happy Dreams Funeral Home. What do you say we continue this later?"

"It's a date." He dropped the photos back into the envelope. "Are those arrangements for Lipinski's funeral?"

I nodded. "The viewing's at seven o'clock."

"Maybe we should drop by, see who shows up. Want to meet for dinner first?"

And miss the auditions for the talent contest? No way. But what could I tell Marco?

"Never mind," Marco said. "I just remembered that Ted is coming in late. His car broke down and had to be towed. With it being Friday night, I'll have my hands full until he gets there, and I have no idea what time that'll be."

I breathed a sigh of relief. "Perfect."

Marco stared at me. "Perfect?"

Had I said that out loud? "Perfect . . . in the sense that I have other stops to make after the funeral delivery, so I'll be tied up, too. How about if we meet later, say eight thirty?"

"Sweetie," Lottie said, poking her head through the curtain, "your mom is on the phone."

I gasped. "Oh, no! Dinner! I forgot to call Mom back to tell her we couldn't make it. Now her feelings will be hurt."

"Say hi from me," Marco said, kissing me on the top of the head.

I waved at him, then sat down at my desk and picked up the handset. "Hey, Mom!

How about that! I was just getting ready to call you."

"Abigail, I'm saying this with all the love in my heart. You're a terrible liar."

"Okay. You got me. I forgot to call . . . because I was busy selling your tea cart!"

"You sold it? Oh, sweetie, that's wonderful! Tell me — who's the proud new owner?"

Could I really say that her one-of-a-kind artwork was going to the home of a loud, coarse, middle-aged male who ran a strip-tease joint and his wife, a former stripper who named everything after spices, including her daughter? "Well, Mom, what I know about the new owner is that he's an entrepreneur with an eye for beauty."

"Really?" She was eating it up.

"Oh, yeah. This man knows what form and function are all about."

"I'm speechless, Abigail. I can't wait to tell your dad. Thank you, honey. You've made my day."

"And you made fifty bucks, Mom."

I thought I heard her sob. Not such a terrible liar after all, was I?

At seven o'clock that evening, six rapper-ettes in the five-member Code Bluebird group stood in a line that wound all the way around the inside of the ginormous banquet hall of the New Chapel Inn and Suites. One of the rapperettes tugged on the sleeves of her shiny pink baseball jacket in a vain attempt to cover her wrists, which stuck out several inches beyond the cuffs.

"Aunt Abby, stop that," Tara hissed in my ear. "You'll rip the seams."

"You didn't tell me the spare costume belonged to the smallest bluebird in the group!" I hissed back.

A cheer went up, so I stepped out of line to see what was happening just as Cody sauntered onto a stage at the opposite end of the hall. Two of his burly bodyguards accompanied him — I recognized them from my run-in with them on the courthouse lawn — but Lila was nowhere to be seen. I glanced at the double doors and saw another of his guards posted there. That left one unaccounted for.

"Okay, listen up," Cody said, using the mic in his hand. "Here are the rules. You'll have five minutes to perform. A buzzer will sound at the end of five minutes, and then you'll have to get offstage so the next performers can start. No clapping between acts. No whistling, cheering —"

I didn't wait for the rest. Speaking quietly, but so that the people around me could hear, I said, "Tara, would you hold my coat?

I'm going to find the bathroom."

"Okay, Aunt Abby. Don't get lost," Tara said on cue. She poked my arm conspiratorially.

I cut through the line and headed for the double doors, tugging my pink baseball cap down to shield my eyes, making sure not to dislodge the cap and release my hair, which I'd cleverly wound into a bun on top of my head. That was a red flag I didn't want to raise.

The bodyguard gave me a questioning glance, so I said, "Gotta pee."

"Bathroom's that way." He stared at me as I passed. "I know you from somewhere."

My heart gave a lurch, but I kept moving. "Maybe at Cody's concert. I really gotta pee."

I located the restroom at the end of the hallway, where it teed at another corridor. Fearing that the guard was still watching, I headed into the women's. Two minutes later, three girls came in, giggling and talking as they applied more makeup to their already heavily made-up faces.

I washed my hands slowly, and when they started toward the door, I grabbed a paper towel and followed them out, slipping around the corner and dashing up the corridor to the lobby, where I stopped to peer around the corner. Whew. No bodyguard in sight. All I had to do was make it across the lobby to the elevators on the far wall. From there it would be a simple matter of pressing a button.

I'd phoned the hotel earlier under the pretense of having a floral delivery for Cody and was told I'd have to leave the flowers at the desk, as no one was allowed on the top floor. I didn't know Lila's room number, but how hard could it be to find her? I glanced at the reception desk, saw that the two clerks were chatting, then strolled casually toward the elevators. A minute later, the elevator opened onto the top floor. It was that simple.

I peered out, scanning the hallway for any sign of the missing guard, then stepped out and started listening at each door. There were four suites, two on either side of the hall, and at only one of them did I hear a TV playing.

I lifted my hand to knock, then paused. What if it wasn't Lila's room? What was my reason for being there? I didn't have any flowers with me.

I took a deep breath, working up my courage, then rapped softly. The door swung open and there stood the fourth guard.

"Sorry, wrong room." I turned to flee just

as a heavy hand clamped down on my shoulder.

"Hey!" I cried. "Let go!"

I managed to slip out from beneath his fingers, but then he clamped one huge paw over my head and jerked me back. In the struggle my hat came off and my hair tumbled free. His eyes widened.

"Okay, you're coming with me." He grabbed my wrist, dragged me to the elevator, and shoved me inside. He stepped in behind me and hit the LOBBY button. "I'm taking you to Security."

"What for?"

"Suspicious behavior."

I knew I wouldn't be charged with anything, but I didn't relish sitting in an office somewhere in the bowels of the hotel answering a bunch of stupid questions. When the elevator opened, I grabbed the pink cap out of his hand and fled through the lobby and out the revolving doors. I didn't check to see if he was chasing me. I just kept going until I reached my Vette, then jumped inside, locked the doors, started the engine, and tried to catch my breath as I waited for the heat to kick in. I was shivering all over, not from fear but because Tara had my coat.

Okay, Abby, that was a bust. You need a plan B.

405

My cell phone vibrated, but I had to scramble to find it in the pockets of the voluminous pink cargo pants. My niece's name was on the screen. "Tara?"

"Aunt Abby," she whispered, "are you okay? Someone said a guard was chasing you."

"Something like that. I'm in the parking lot in my car. My plan didn't work."

"It wouldn't have worked, anyway. Lila isn't here. I just got a tweet from one of the Lila-watchers that she's shopping at Windows on the Square."

And there was plan B!

"Tara, I love you. Don't lose my coat. Oh, and good luck with the audition."

Lila Redmond was in town! I couldn't believe my luck. Wait till Marco heard the news. Of course, that would be after I'd had a private conversation with her and got the lowdown on Cody.

I drove back to the town square and found a parking spot around the corner from Windows, then jumped out of the Vette, locked it, and ran. I dashed into the women's clothing shop, looked all around, even circled the clothing racks, but I didn't see Lila. Was she in a dressing room perhaps?

"Can I help you?" one of the clerks asked. I turned to reply and she gaped at me in shock. "Abby? I'm sorry. I didn't recognize you at first in your —" She made do with pointing at my outfit.

"It's a costume," I said hurriedly. "Is Lila Redmond here by any chance?"

"You just missed her."

Damn! I sighed in frustration. "Okay, Nora. Thanks, anyway."

"You might try the Daily Grind — or whatever they're calling it now. I'm pretty sure I heard her tell your cousin that she wanted to stop for coffee and dessert."

I didn't hear the last part of her sentence. My ears were buzzing too loud. "My cousin was with her?"

Nora nodded. "Jillian."

No freaking way. Either Jillian was a genius or I was hallucinating.

Three minutes later, I paused outside the door of the coffee shop to catch my breath, then stepped inside and was instantly assailed by the sweetly pungent aroma of coffee and donuts. The dimly lit café was nearly empty, but way in the back, at a small table, I spotted a head of shiny copper-colored hair that could only be Jillian's. With her was a slender figure in a black wool stocking cap, black-framed sunglasses, a long, black wool coat, and black boots. Was it really Lila?

I headed straight for their table. The barista shot me a curious look as I passed, but I merely gave a little wave and kept going. Jillian glanced up, laughing at something her companion said, and saw me. At once, she got a horrified look on her face.

"Jillian," I said, trying to catch my breath, "I've been looking for you."

"I'm sorry," my cousin said, narrowing her eyes at me, "have we met?"

Her companion took off her sunglasses to get a better look at my outfit.

I smiled in relief. It *was* Lila. Jillian had been telling the truth after all.

CHAPTER TWENTY-FOUR

"And that's how I got an interview with Lila Redmond," I reported to Marco an hour later. I was talking to him on my cell phone just outside the coffee shop. "Of course, I had to keep buying her donuts and coffee, and now I'm queasy from all the sugar and a little jittery from the caffeine, but at least I found out that Cody doesn't take Limbitrol. He uses a prescription sleeping pill at night, but he doesn't take anything for nerves because he says it blunts his reaction time."

"That's great work, Sunshine."

"That's not all. I also learned that Lila doesn't buy the whole antidepressant hype. She says when she feels down, a good workout perks her up. Their security guards get tested once a month for drugs, and so far have all been clean. Lila couldn't speak for Cody's agent, but she said his room is on another floor, and Cody doesn't care for the guy, so he sees little of him.

"Also, I asked her about the gift basket Lipinski took back with him. She said Cody had his agent purchase it here in town and sign Lila's name to it, supposedly as an apology for her snubbing the Lip. She was furious, naturally. The detectives questioned her, Cody's agent, and Cody about it, and apparently were satisfied that the contents of the basket had nothing to do with the murder.

"And guess what? Lila said the reason Cody cut Andrew out was pure egotism. He was afraid that if he acknowledged Andrew as the lyricist, people would discover that Andrew had greater talent than Cody did. And now that the new songs Cody wrote on his own have bombed, he's regretting his actions, but pride is keeping him from reconciling. Lila said when they get back to LA, she's going to dump Cody. She can't take his ego and temper tantrums anymore. Even so, she did vouch for his whereabouts on the day of the murder."

"How did you get her to open up? Donuts?"

"That was just to keep her there. No, I used a little method called girlfriend psychology, which is all about bonding. So I led her to believe you and Cody had a lot in common. Then it was just a matter of complaining about how ridiculously immature you guys behave when you're jealous, and just like that she started talking. And eating. That skinny woman burned through seven donuts and probably won't gain an ounce."

"You told her I was the jealous type?"

"I wish you could have seen Jillian's face when I showed up in a pink rapperette costume two sizes too small. She was absolutely horrified when I told Lila how we were related. She tried to pretend she didn't know me. It was a scream."

"*Am* I the jealous type?"

Men were so single-minded. "No, Marco. I only led Lila to believe that in order to bond with her. So do we move Cody to the bottom of the list?"

"I'd say that's a good call."

"Great. Now for the bad news. Jillian knows about our engagement."

"What?"

"Apparently during my struggle with the bodyguard, the chain worked its way out from under my shirt, and I didn't notice. Naturally Miss Hawk Eye spotted it."

"Whoa! Back up a minute. You didn't tell me about a struggle."

Hadn't meant to, either. Stupid sugar

411

high. "That's because I was . . . saving that story so I could tell you in person. So are you still at the bar?"

"As a matter of fact, I just got back from the funeral home. You won't be surprised to hear that only a handful of people showed up — Joan and a few others from their office. Hess made a brief appearance, but left when he saw me. But getting back to that struggle . . ."

"Don't worry. I'm fine. I'll give you the details later. But you'll be happy to hear that Jillian has promised not to say anything about our engagement for a week. If we haven't told our families by next Friday, she gets to announce it at the family dinner."

My cell phone beeped, so I held it away from my ear to look at the screen. "Marco, I need to take this call. It's from Whispering Willows. I'll be down there shortly, okay?"

I switched to the other line. "Hello?"

"Abby, this is Lauren, from Whispering Willows. I hope I'm not interrupting, but I remembered something and thought you'd want to know."

"You're not interrupting at all, Lauren. Please, go ahead."

"I told you the cleaning crew got here after eight o'clock on Monday, but I was mistaken. They were here at seven. They had to squeeze in an extra job, so they came early. I wasn't sure whether that mattered, but at least now you know."

"It might matter, Lauren. Is there any way you can find out the names of the crew that showed up Monday?"

"Certainly. I'll call their boss first thing in the morning."

"Perfect. Thanks."

I put my cell phone away and turned to find Connor McKay leaning against the bricks, smiling cunningly. "I thought you'd never stop eating those donuts."

Rats. He surely saw me with Lila. "Have you been following me again?"

"Of course not. I was following Lila Redmond."

"Then why aren't you following her now? She left five minutes ago."

"Because I want to hear more about your conversation with Lila about Cody and the Limbitrol issue. What? Didn't you see me in there? Oh, wait. I might have had my hood up."

My fingers curled into fists. "You scumbag." I started walking rapidly up the block, but Connor merely jogged alongside.

"I know. I'm a jerk — but I'm not an idiot. I didn't catch everything Lila had to say about her soon-to-be ex-boyfriend, so if you give me the full scoop on Cody, I'll give you some hot information on some of your other suspects."

I stopped. "What kind of information? And how do you know who my suspects are?"

"You're so transparent it isn't even funny. As for my info, you'll have to trust me."

"Why would I trust you after what you did to Dave?"

"I apologize for that. Believe it or not, I'm not out to hang Dave. I like the guy. I also think Darnell is on a witch hunt. That's why I've been doing my own investigation." He wiggled his eyebrows. "Do we have a deal or not?"

I studied Connor, thinking hard. Maybe I could feed him information for a story that would take the spotlight off Dave while shaming Darnell and the detectives. It was worth a try. I wasn't an idiot either. "It's a deal."

"Back to the coffee shop?"

"Back to the coffee shop." But no coffee for me. Just good ol' water.

"So what's this about an engagement?" Connor asked.

"No comment."

Half an hour later, I trotted up the block

414

and around the corner to Down the Hatch. Part of that energy was still caffeine and sugar burning off, but the rest was excitement over the information Connor had given me. I couldn't wait to tell Marco.

But Marco was still hard at work behind the bar and the place was jammed, so I decided to wait in his office, a calm, masculine space decorated in black leather, stainless steel, and gray that was the direct opposite of the burnt orange, brown, and avocado green just outside.

I sat down behind Marco's desk, in his jazzy leather chair that both rocked and swiveled, and after about five minutes of doing both, I had to stand up and take a few deep breaths. No more donuts and coffee for a while. I noticed the manila envelope containing the crime-scene photos on his desk, so I pulled them out to give them another look.

"Hey, Bright Eyes, sorry about the wait." Marco shut the door and took a seat in one of the chairs facing his desk. "I can tell by the look on your face you've got big news."

"Do I ever. After I phoned you, I ran into Connor McKay. Guess what he'd been doing? Sitting in the coffee shop, eavesdropping on my conversation with Lila. At first I was furious, but then he said he'd been doing his own investigation and uncovered some juicy info on our suspects. So I made a deal with him to trade information.

"Don't frown, Marco. Connor knows almost everything we do, and I wasn't about to say anything to hurt Dave. But he hasn't been able to get near Lila, so we made a deal. In exchange for my telling him what I learned about Cody, he told me things we didn't know about our other suspects; such as that Scott Hess was playing the slots at the Blue Chip casino at the time of Lipinski's murder. Seems he's been hiding a gambling problem. But as far as Connor knows, Hess is clean. No prescription meds."

I picked up the photo and pointed out the chewing gum. "So this pack of gum is just a fluke. But look at this." I swiveled one of the photos so he could see it, then pointed to the briefcase sitting beneath the open window. "See the gray feather on top of the briefcase? I figured it blew in the window — you know how pigeons like to roost on ledges — but now I'm not so sure because of something else Connor uncovered. Herbert Chapper was seen in the vicinity of Lipinski's office at six thirty Monday evening."

"How did McKay learn that?"

"He talked to businesses nearby and learned that the motorcycle shop half a block away has surveillance cameras. And those cameras caught Chapper heading on foot toward Lipinski's office. So I started thinking about that gray feather and how it might have gotten there."

"Chapper's parrot was green and yellow."

"Ah, but that's not his only parrot, Watson. We heard the other one, remember? But we never saw it. So my theory is that Chapper waited until Lipinski left his office, then climbed through the window and drugged his drink."

Marco studied the photo for a moment, then shook his head. "Too many holes. For one thing, how would Chapper know in advance that Lipinski would be drinking? Or how long he'd be gone? Or whether he'd be coming back?"

"Okay, it has a few holes. Let's move on to Darla Mae and her very good friend Pat, who lied to provide her with an alibi. Why? Because if it came out what Darla Mae was really doing during her dinner break, she'd lose her job, not to mention that her lover would be in hot water with his wife. Surprise! Darla Mae is having an affair with the county home's doctor on call."

Marco's jaw dropped.

"That was my reaction, too. And the reason the doc couldn't verify Darla Mae's alibi after five o'clock was that he was supposed to be seeing patients at the hospital at that time."

"How the hell did McKay get him to talk?"

"Not him. Pat and her husband, who have a little garden patch behind their trailer where they grow funny mushrooms. I have to give Connor credit. He was really on top of this. So what do you think about my Herbert-Chapper-as-killer theory now?"

"I'd like to talk to him again — unless McKay has already done that, too."

I had a feeling Marco didn't like Connor on his turf — not that I could blame him. After all, Marco was the pro. "Here's a thought. Connor mentioned that Chapper goes to the VA clinic for his group therapy session on Saturday mornings, so why don't we talk to him there instead of at home with Tansy and the birds? I don't have to work tomorrow."

"What time is his session?"

"Connor said it's from nine thirty to ten thirty. A van picks him up at nine and he's home around eleven."

There was a rap on the door, and then Gert stuck her head in. "Hey, boss, Ted just

418

phoned. He's still at Sears waiting for them to finish putting on the new tire."

"Okay, thanks. I'll be right out." Marco rubbed his jaw, thinking. "Let's do it. We'll leave tomorrow morning at nine thirty."

It was Marco's mother who woke us the next morning. Since we'd gone to bed late — making up for some of our lost evenings — we'd decided to sleep in. But at eight o'clock Marco's cell phone began to vibrate, and although vibrations are supposed to be silent, they're not when a certain feline decides to push the phone off the side table onto the floor and bat it around.

"I thought you closed the door," Marco said as he scrambled for the phone.

"I'm not sure, but I believe Simon has taught himself how to work the door handle." I threw off the covers and scooped him up. "Come on, tubby. Out you go."

"Mom! Stop! Calm down!" Marco said, bringing me to a halt. "I can't understand what you're saying. Cinnamon did what? The Howards said what?" He glanced at me, and I raised my eyebrows to ask, *What gives?*

He shrugged. "Mom, put Rafe on. He's where? Okay, look, when he gets back, have him call me." He shut his phone and flopped

419

back onto the bed, draping his arm across his eyes.

I crawled up beside him. "What happened?"

"A big blowup with Cinnamon. Rafe took the tea cart over there last night to give it to the Howards and something happened. That's all I could understand. Most of it was her ranting in Italian."

Uh-oh. I hoped my mom's artwork wasn't to blame.

An hour later, we had showered and dressed and were at the table finishing our breakfast coffee when Rafe called. Marco listened for a long time, then said, "Rafe, do not let Mom leave the house. Hide her keys. Disable her engine. Whatever it takes. I'll be there in ten minutes."

Marco hung up and glanced at me. "The wedding is off."

"Again?"

Marco took his cup to the sink and rinsed it out. "I'm going to have to go back to my apartment to calm Mom down — Rafe said she's intent on duking it out with the Howards — and I'm not sure when I'll be back. We might have to go see Herbert Chapper at home later."

"What caused Cinnamon to call off the

420

wedding this time?" I crossed my fingers and hoped that it wasn't the tea cart.

"The tea cart."

"Oh, Marco! Seriously?"

"Let's just say it got the conversation rolling. And actually it was the Howards who called off the wedding. They were out partying when Rafe took the cart over last night, so he left it for them as a surprise. They unwrapped it when they got home sometime early this morning, and that's when the storm broke. They say the tea cart symbolizes the kind of family their daughter would be marrying into."

"Weirdly creative?"

"Vulgar, crazy, rude, low-class, and uncouth."

"Wait. What? Mr. Howard owns a strip joint, lives in a garish McMansion with females named after spices, and *we're* the ones who are vulgar, low-class, and uncouth?" I shoved away from the table and took my cup to the sink, too. "I don't blame your mom for wanting to duke it out. In fact, I may join her."

"In fact, no." Marco wrapped his arms around me from behind and nibbled my neck. "We don't want to prove the Howards right. And by the way, I may have mentioned this before, but you're really hot when your temper is up."

I turned and wound my arms around his neck. "How hot would that be?"

He kissed me long enough to make me even hotter. "With any luck, I'll be back in half an hour to show you. Well, maybe more like an hour. I'll keep you posted."

I grabbed the damp dishcloth and pressed it against my forehead. "I'll be waiting."

I waited for half an hour, and when my cell phone finally buzzed, it wasn't Marco.

"Hi, Aunt Abby," Tara said dejectedly. "I just wanted to tell you we didn't make the first round. We're out of the contest."

"Oh, Tara, I'm sorry. You worked so hard."

"At least we got autographed T-shirts. That's something, right? And you'll never believe who came to the audition. Andrew Chapper."

"Oh, no! Did he cause a scene?"

"No, he played his guitar and sang. It was *awesome,* Aunt Abby. Everyone went wild, even Cody. After Andrew finished, Cody got onstage and they shook hands — and then they *hugged.* But here's the best part. Cody tweeted that he wants to work with Andrew again. Isn't that cool? Now *two* guys from New Chapel will be famous!"

Cody obviously realized he could go

farther with Andrew than without him.

I heard a beep. "Tara, I have another call. I think it's Marco. I'll talk to you later, okay?"

But it still wasn't Marco.

"Abby, this is Lauren. I'm so sorry to bother you on a Saturday, but I just talked to someone at TLC and got those names you asked for. Do you have a pen handy?"

I dashed to the kitchen to get a notepad. "Go ahead."

She listed three people; the last one was Tansy Chapper. "What can you tell me about them, Lauren?"

"Ron and Gus are the regulars. Nice older guys, hard workers. They've been cleaning here for as long as I can remember. Tansy is a sub. Very quiet and efficient, and always kind to the patients. She used to own the business but fills in now when someone is out."

"Which one of them cleans the offices?"

"Could have been any of the three, but as a rule, I've noticed the men doing the heavier work in the kitchen and rec center. Tansy would've most likely dusted and vacuumed the offices."

Was Tansy my anonymous caller?

I thanked Lauren for her help, then phoned Marco. He didn't pick up, so I left a message to get back to me ASAP. Two minutes later, the phone rang, but again, it wasn't Marco.

"Hey, Abby, Connor McKay here. I'm leaving in about thirty minutes to talk to Mrs. Chapper. I want to catch her before the hubby returns. Want to come along?"

Oh, how I wanted to talk to Tansy while Herbert was out, but not with McKay at my side. I couldn't imagine her letting a reporter into her house, especially if she was the anonymous caller. "Thanks, but I'll pass. Busy morning."

"Your loss. I'll let you know if I get any good info."

"Listen, McKay, be careful. Chapper might have decided to stay home today, and I know from experience that it doesn't take much to set him off. You don't want to be the one to do it."

"Aw. I'm really touched that you care, Abby. You know, it's not too late to back out of your engagement. You haven't made that announcement yet."

"Shut up."

I hung up and began to dry the breakfast dishes, trying to sort out what I knew. If Tansy had made the call from Whispering Willows, then I had to assume she was concerned about Dave being wrongly

424

charged. Yet there were only two ways that she could have known Dave was telling the truth. Either she saw him at Whispering Willows on Monday or she knew who the real killer was. And since I couldn't see why she'd be there on Monday and then again to clean on Tuesday, I had to go with the second choice.

If Tansy knew Herbert was guilty of murder, she must have agonized over what to do about it, especially if she took her vows as seriously as Andrew claimed. . . . *If* I believed his story. Because thinking back to that meeting in the jail, I realized some of his answers didn't add up.

"*What time did you get off work?*"

"*Five o'clock.*"

"*Where did you go after that?*"

"*Home.*"

"*You didn't stop anywhere?*"

"*No, why?*"

"*Your grandmother said you worked until eight o'clock.*"

"*Not last Monday. I got off work early.*"

"*Where was your grandfather when you got home?*"

"*In the kitchen. Grandma made an early supper that day.*"

Why had Andrew mentioned the early supper? Was that significant?

"Did your grandfather go for a walk that evening?"

"I don't know. I don't watch Herbert every minute."

"But earlier you said he was home all evening."

"I was in my bedroom recording a new song, okay? Check my computer. It logs the time and date I record. So I don't know whether he went for a walk."

"Your grandmother said he was home all evening."

"Then why are you asking me?"

"Why did you change your answer?"

"Because —" He hesitated. "I didn't want you to know I was in my room. How can I swear they were home if I say I was in my room all night?"

Something was wrong, but I couldn't figure out what.

While I waited for Marco to call, I played Ghost Cat with Simon, darting from kitchen to living room and back, letting him hide and jump out at me. The mindless game allowed my thoughts to wander, and they kept returning to the same question. Why had Tansy lied about Andrew coming home at five o'clock?

Maybe she hadn't lied. Maybe she didn't know he came home early. But why

426

wouldn't she know? I rubbed my forehead, trying to remember what else Andrew had said about that evening.

"How can I swear they were home if I say I was in my room all night?"

Andrew had used the word *they.* Shouldn't he have said *he* — as in Herbert? Shouldn't he have been concerned about providing an alibi for his grandfather? Then again, why would he be? Andrew had told us he'd leave Herbert in a minute.

Had he needed to provide his grandmother with an alibi?

I glanced at my watch. What was taking Marco so long? We had to talk to Tansy before Herbert returned, and our window would be gone in an hour.

I waited another five minutes, pacing in frustration. Finally, I grabbed my coat and car keys and headed to the parking lot. If I hurried, I might beat Connor. With a little luck and good timing, Dave could be cleared by the end of the day.

CHAPTER TWENTY-FIVE

Tansy Chapper was startled to see me. She was wearing a black cardigan over a pink-and-black floral print dress and black pumps, and had even put on lipstick, as though she might be going out for a special occasion. At the sight of me, she drew her sweater tighter around her thin body, as though to protect herself. "Yes?" she asked in her soft voice. She seemed preoccupied.

"Hi, Abby Knight again. I was here earlier this week. I wanted to follow up on our conversation with a few more questions. I hope this isn't a bad time."

"I'm sorry," she said with a regretful smile. "I can't talk to you now."

"Oh." I glanced behind her to make sure her husband wasn't lurking in the background, then whispered, "Is Mr. Chapper home?"

"No. He'll be here later."

She was shutting the door. What could I

say? "Wait, Tansy. I know you called me from Whispering Willows — and I know why."

That got her attention. She studied me for a long moment, then opened the door wide. "I think you'd better come inside."

"Please have a seat," she said, indicating the sofa. "I've just made a pot of tea. I'll get you a cup."

"Thank you." I heard a loud squawk and covered my head with my arms.

"You're safe," she said. "The birds are in their cages this morning."

While she was gone, I checked out the living room and spotted Herbert's magazines on the table beside his lounge chair, also the magazine rack with Tansy's knitting and cooking 'zines in it. I definitely had to start paying more attention. A stack of envelopes, a pen, and a roll of stamps lay on the coffee table, as though I'd caught her in the midst of paying bills.

"Here we are," she said, carrying a tray into the room. She placed it on the coffee table, sat on the love seat, and poured two cups of tea from a tall, insulated pot. "Sugar?"

"No, thank you." I accepted the cup and saucer and took a sip. Tansy did the same.

"Tea is soothing, don't you think?" She put her cup and saucer down, then began to stick stamps on the envelopes. Obviously I was going to have to start the conversation.

"I noticed you have a Basketful of Dreams catalog. Have you ever ordered from it?"

She glanced at me oddly. "Not in many years."

Okay, Abby, let's get right to it. "Why didn't you leave your name when you called my shop?"

Two spots of color appeared on her cheekbones, but she merely continued to apply stamps to the envelopes.

"You made that phone call to help Dave, didn't you?"

"Yes." She set the envelopes aside, then picked up her cup and sipped quietly.

"Then won't you please give the police a statement? The DA is convening a grand jury next week to indict Dave for Lipinski's murder."

She let out a tiny "Oh," rattling her cup as she set it into the saucer. But then she sat with her hands in her lap, her gaze far away, as though distancing herself.

I glanced at my watch. I needed to get her to talk before Connor arrived.

"I'm sure it's difficult to be disloyal to

your husband, but you can't let an innocent man pay for a crime he didn't commit. If you know who's responsible for Ken Lipinski's death —"

"Herbert isn't a murderer," she said in a fierce whisper, tears filling her eyes. She got up abruptly and left the room. I assumed she was going for a tissue, but she returned with a black leather handbag and a paper grocery sack.

"Tansy," I said gently, "your husband was caught on a surveillance camera in front of the motorcycle shop half a block from Lipinski's office on Monday evening."

She lifted her chin. "Why haven't the police come to question Herbert, then?"

"The surveillance information was just uncovered by an investigative reporter."

She began to clean out her purse, throwing away crumpled receipts and used tissues, trying to ignore me.

"Once the police get that information, Tansy, they'll find out about the lies — yours and Andrew's. You wouldn't want Andrew to be charged as an accessory to murder, would you?"

She glanced up in horror, as if she hadn't considered that point. "Of course not!" She seemed to want to say more but instead burst into tears. It was a messy, embarrassing weep, one not easily consoled with words. I finished my tea, looking out the window, waiting patiently for her to collect herself.

After a few moments, she pulled a wrinkled tissue from her pocket and pressed it against her face. "It's my fault," she said at last, her chin trembling.

"What's your fault?"

"If it wasn't for me, Andrew would be in music school. He'd already applied for the loans when Cody won the contest. But then Herbert just — fell apart. Andrew wouldn't leave after that."

"I'm sure Dave has told you that Andrew is going to get his fair share of the prize money, so he'll be able to go to school. And if you haven't heard yet, Cody is telling people he wants to work with Andrew again. It's all going to work out."

"It can't work out — don't you see?" Tansy fished another tissue from her pocket and wiped her eyes, then refilled my teacup. "Please try to understand. Herbert was a dear, sweet man, a good husband and father. But our daughter's death brought him so much pain that his flashbacks returned. At first he was able to control them with medicine, but after Cody turned his back on Andrew, Herbert snapped. Now, even on Limbitrol, he's so tortured by hallucinations that he often can't separate them from reality. He doesn't mean to hurt anyone. It's beyond his control."

She took a deep breath, then added the used tissue to the sack and went back to cleaning out her purse. "When Herbert returned from Vietnam, we promised each other that we would never let anything separate us again. As long as I'm alive, I will keep my promise. But that means that Herbert stays with me, so Andrew won't leave. He'll use the money from the settlement to care for us. It's why I have to free them."

My thoughts seemed to slow down to a crawl. "I don't understand."

She took an envelope from the top of the stack and handed it to me. "I was going to leave this on the table for Herbert to mail, but perhaps you could personally deliver it to Mr. Hammond. It would be so much nicer that way."

I blinked to see the writing on the front because my vision was oddly blurry. "What is it?"

She took her wallet out of her purse, removed the bills and credit cards and put them carefully on top of the stack of envelopes, then placed the empty wallet into the sack. "My confession."

I looked over at her in surprise, only to have the room spin. "I'm sorry, what?" I put one hand on the sofa to steady myself. Was I holding a confession of murder?

"Mr. Hammond will explain after he reads it. It will clear his name. I left letters for Herbert and Andrew on the kitchen table. Are you dizzy?"

"Maybe a little." I tried to downplay it even as a feeling of inertia was spreading rapidly through my veins, making it difficult to move. Something was wrong with me. With my tongue growing stiffer by the second, I asked, "What did you say about letters?"

Tansy set her purse aside and rose. "Here, let me help you."

As she swung my legs to the sofa and eased my head onto a pillow, I struggled through the fog filling my head to form a thought, but when I tried to voice it, my words came out thick and nearly unintelligible. "Something — in — my — tea?"

"You'll be fine," she said soothingly. "It's only temporary, although you may have a headache later." She took an amber-colored plastic pill bottle out of her pocket, poured the contents into her palm, and began to take the pills with her tea.

I blinked hard, trying to bring her, as well as my thoughts, into focus. I watched as she swallowed the last of the pills and finished her tea, sitting back with a satisfied sigh. Was she trying to kill herself? I tried to get up, but I felt sluggish and stupid, unable to make my body obey. I forced my mouth to form a word. "Why?"

"Why did I kill Mr. Lipinski?"

That wasn't my question, but it would do for openers.

"To keep Herbert from killing him. I had to protect my husband." Her voice caught. "It's my duty." She found a fresh tissue and dabbed her eyes. Then she got up, removed the magazines from the rack, and placed them carefully in the sack.

I struggled to get out another word. "How?"

"TLC cleans Mr. Lipinski's office on Friday evenings," she explained matter-of-factly. "I've been there frequently over the years. I know Mr. Lipinski's habits. He works late and always has a drink sitting on his desk. So I phoned on Monday afternoon to say one of the cleaners left her supplies and would be stopping by to collect them after five. He let me in, then went back to work, assuming I'd see myself out. It was easy to slip crushed pills in his drink. He stepped out of his office several times to use the washroom.

"My timing couldn't have been better. When I left the building, Herbert was there, in the parking lot, planning God knows what. He didn't remember any of it the next day."

She sighed tremulously as she placed her purse in the sack, too. "My poor Andrew. He suspected Herbert immediately and feared I'd be his next victim. He tried to get rid of the gun in order to protect me, and look what happened to him! So don't you see? This is the best solution. With me out of the way, Herbert will get the help he needs, and Andrew can pursue his dream."

She picked up the paper sack and swayed as she got to her feet. "It's taking effect faster than I thought. I must get to my bed now. You'll be sure to give that envelope to Mr. Hammond, won't you?"

I managed to stretch out my hand toward her. *Wait!* I wanted to cry. *You're making a huge mistake. You're not freeing Andrew. You're dooming him to a lifetime of guilt and sorrow.* But I couldn't get the words out.

Tansy placed the brown sack in the hallway just beyond the living room, where I saw a row of grocery sacks lined against the wall, some with clothing visible on top, as

436

though she'd cleaned out her closets. She was making her death as easy for them as possible.

She steadied herself against the doorjamb. "The man who came with you before, do you love him?"

With all my heart, I wanted to say. But all I could manage was a slight nod.

"Be sure to tell him." She gazed wistfully at me and then she was gone.

I heard a door shut, a lock slide home. I rolled onto my side and stretched my hand toward my purse, lying by my feet. I had to get to my phone. I had to stop her.

Someone knocked on the front door — maybe it was Connor! "Help!" I tried to call, but my voice was a mere croak. "Help!" I tried again, attempting to move my unresponsive legs.

The doorbell rang and Connor called, "Hello? Anyone home?"

I wanted to bang my fist on the coffee table, but my arm wouldn't obey. He knocked a few more times, then stopped. Would he peer in the front window and see me lying here? I tried to lift my head so I could see him, but he never appeared.

Concentrating as hard as I could, I managed to hook my fingers beneath the strap of my purse and tug it toward me. With slow, agonizing effort, I slid my hand inside and pinched my phone between my fingers and thumb, using them like a crab's claw. I finally got the phone onto the sofa beside my face, then had to pry it open. I forced my fuzzy brain to focus on the numbers until I was able to press speed dial number two. But when Marco answered, all I could do was mumble, "Tansy."

"Abby, what's wrong? Where are you?"

"Tan-sy," I said again, my head spinning from the effort. I felt like throwing up.

"Are you with Tansy?"

"Yeh."

"Hang in there, baby. I'm on my way."

I let my head loll back and the tears come.

I must have fallen into a deep sleep, because when I awoke, the house was full of cops, EMTs, the coroner, and Marco, who was sitting on the floor rubbing my hand. I pulled it out of his grasp as I struggled to sit up. "Tansy?" I asked hoarsely, relieved to sound intelligible again.

Marco took me in his arms and held me. I heard his voice in my ear. "She didn't make it."

She'd taken her life for her loved ones. The whole horrible, senseless tragedy, from Cody's selfish actions to Tansy's unselfish ones, brought back my tears. I wept hard, clinging to Marco, and it only got worse when Herbert charged into the room just as the EMTs wheeled his wife's body out of the bedroom.

"Tansy!" he cried in a panic, cradling her lifeless body in his arms. "Oh, God, no! Tansy, please don't leave me. How could you do this to us?"

Marco scooped me up, carried me out to his car, and took me to the hospital, where I was examined, tested for drug toxicity, then given the okay to go home and rest. Back at my apartment, Marco poured me a glass of ginger ale to help settle my stomach, then sat on the sofa with his arms around me, letting me know he was there.

For a while I trembled so violently that all I could do was hold on to him, letting the shock of Tansy's confession and death sink in. After a while I was able to describe what had happened in as much detail as I could remember. It still seemed unreal.

"I was so certain Herbert was the murderer," I told him. "The pieces just fit. But it was meek little Tansy. To think that the strength of her love was so powerful that she would sacrifice herself for her husband and grandson. I wish I could've stopped her."

"You did your best," he said, and kissed my forehead.

"I wanted to tell her that she was making a mistake, that killing herself would hurt Herbert and Andrew, not help them. If I could have spoken, I might have been able to talk her out of it, Marco. I might have saved her and spared her family all that sorrow."

"Listen to me, Abby. You can't blame yourself. Tansy drugged your tea because she didn't want you to stop her. She would have taken those pills no matter what you said. She wasn't thinking rationally. You can't reason with someone in such a highly emotional state. And if you had talked her out of it, she would've gone to prison. Would that have been better? Would it have made Andrew feel any less guilty? Would Herbert not be as lost?"

"No. You're right." I took a sip of ginger ale and waited for the fizz to reach my stomach. "Did you find the letter addressed to Dave? It's Tansy's confession."

"The police have it. They've already let Dave know about it."

"It's amazing, isn't it, that despite all of Herbert's problems, Tansy never stopped loving him?"

"That's what true love is."

440

"I think we have that kind of love, Marco."

"I think so, too."

I leaned back to gaze into his eyes. "I don't want to waste a moment of what we have, because we don't know what's ahead. I think we should set a wedding date."

At that, anguish washed across Marco's strong features.

"What?" I asked in alarm.

Instead of answering, Marco pulled me against him, running his hands down my back, as though he didn't want to let me go. My heart began to pound. Something had happened.

He got up from the sofa, took an envelope from his coat hanging on the back of a chair, and handed it to me. "This was waiting at my apartment."

It was a letter from the Department of the Army, addressed to Lieutenant Marco Salvare, RA 55667591.

Dear Lt. Salvare:

You are hereby notified that the current shortage of manpower mandates that we redeploy those individuals who have been previously discharged but are still committed to a six-year term. Accordingly, you will be receiving notification shortly and a set of orders as to your next assignment as an active-duty officer.

Sincerely,
Gen. I. M. Bragg, Undersecretary
Dept. of the Army

I read the letter in shocked disbelief. "An active-duty officer?" I turned to gaze at him, my eyes awash in tears. "You're being called back?"

"It appears that way."

"Do you have to go?" I whispered hoarsely.

He sat down beside me. "I took an oath, Abby. I have to fulfill my duty to my country even if it means putting our plans on hold."

My heart felt as though it were cracking into a thousand jagged pieces. "What are we going to do?"

"Let it play out, I guess."

I searched his eyes, realizing I was facing the very real possibility of losing him.

"It'll be okay, Sunshine," he said, gathering me into his arms. "Nothing can really separate us." And then he kissed me like he'd never kissed me before.

ABOUT THE AUTHOR

Kate Collins, a former teacher, lives with her husband in northwest Indiana during the mild months, then zips down to Key West, Florida, for as much of the winter as possible. She's also the author of several romance novels under various pseudonyms. Visit her at:

www.katecollinsbooks.com
facebook.com/authorkatecollins
cozychicksblog.com

The employees of Thorndike Press hope you have enjoyed this Large Print book. All our Thorndike, Wheeler, and Kennebec Large Print titles are designed for easy reading, and all our books are made to last. Other Thorndike Press Large Print books are available at your library, through selected bookstores, or directly from us.

For information about titles, please call:
(800) 223-1244

or visit our Web site at:
http://gale.cengage.com/thorndike

To share your comments, please write:
Publisher
Thorndike Press
295 Kennedy Memorial Drive
Waterville, ME 04901